MASKED SEDUCTION

AN AGE GAP, BILLIONAIRE BOSS ROMANCE

K.C. CROWNE

DESCRIPTION

She's my defiant assistant.
Forbidden. Off-limits.
Then she steps into my private sex club...
and suddenly, I'm done pretending she isn't
already mine.

At the office, Jenna's a hellraiser.
Sharp-tongued, fearless, always testing how far she can
push me.

But when she walks into my den of sin,
masked, anonymous, and utterly unafraid,
chasing a forbidden fantasy and drawing every filthy stare,
I don't just snap.
I break.

She's mine to ruin.
Mine to train.
Mine to own.

She has no idea the man taking her in the dark
is the same bastard who torments her by day.
And when the truth finally comes out...
It'll be too late for her to escape.

The Agosti crime family wants her blood spilled
for my sins.

But Abram Vasiliev?
He doesn't share.
He doesn't forgive.
And he sure as hell never loses.
Especially not her.

Readers note: This is full-length standalone, older man, billionaire, boss, bratva romance in the bestselling Silver Fox Daddies series. You'll need a cool glass of water because the HEAT level is scorching. K.C. Crowne is an Amazon Top 6 Bestseller and International Bestselling Author.

CHAPTER 1

JENNA

Mondays can fuck right off.

Standing at my desk, I suck in two steadying breaths before stepping into my boss's office, a place that feels about as welcoming as a shark tank at feeding time.

I clutch my tablet in one hand, a steaming mug of black coffee for him in the other, and prepare myself for whatever fresh brand of hell awaits me. A few weeks into this job and I'm already wondering if I'm going to last.

It's not as if he's pleasant any other day. But Mondays? They bring out an extra-special, premium-grade asshole side of him. The kind of mood that makes me wonder if he spends the weekends downing vodka shots and picking fights in alleyways just for fun, nursing hangovers come Monday morning.

Except, try as I might, I can't imagine Abram Vasiliev being anything less than impeccably controlled. Everything about the man screams meticulous precision—from the razor-sharp tailoring of his suits to the devastating cool of his expression.

So no, Abram Vasiliev isn't recovering from wild weekends. Being insufferable is just his default setting.

I learned on day one not to knock. His exact words: "If I don't want you in here, Ms. Ridley, I'll lock the door." Delivered with those icy blue eyes boring into mine, like he was challenging me to step out of line.

Taking one final breath, I push open the heavy door without knocking.

Abram is silhouetted at the window of his 32nd floor office, overlooking one of Las Vegas's several parks. The sun cuts around his tall frame, highlighting his broad shoulders, his powerful arms crossed casually over his chest. He oozes dominance.

I swallow hard, despising myself for the hot wave of arousal that runs through me. When am I going to get used to this man?

"Coffee," he says without turning around, his voice clipped, cold.

Biting back a sigh, I roll my eyes safely behind his back and stride forward. "Black," I announce, managing to thread just the barest hint of sarcasm into my tone. "Just how you like it."

As he slowly turns, my breath stalls in my lungs because, damn him, Abram Vasiliev is devastatingly handsome. Even after weeks of working for the man, the sight of him still strikes me like a physical blow.

The office lights highlight his chiseled, commanding features beneath a perfectly tailored, dark gray suit. His head is shaved, a carefully groomed salt-and-pepper beard sharpening his jawline and emphasizing those infuriatingly kissable lips.

His eyes—piercing and icy blue beneath dark, arched brows—can pin you where you stand, stripping away every defense. Just like they're doing now. His gaze slides over me, one brow rising, mastering that silent, infuriating expression somewhere between intimidating and amused.

Like a predator toying with its prey.

My pussy clenches, heat pooling low and traitorous despite my irritation. It's crazy how much my body responds to him, how every glance seems to pull at something raw and needy inside me.

I force my chin up defiantly, silently daring him to give me a reprimand, even as my pulse pounds in my throat.

He holds my stare a beat too long before his deep, velvet-smooth voice finally breaks the charged silence. "Congratulations. You finally got it right."

His words are carried on a Russian accent that somehow makes him even sexier despite what a colossal dick he can be.

My teeth grind so hard I'm surprised they don't crumble as I clamp down on the retort simmering at the tip of my tongue. I spin sharply on my heel and cross to the sleek chair opposite his desk, slipping into it and tapping open his calendar on my tablet. I focus hard, keeping my voice calm and steady, refusing to let him see how deeply he irritates and arouses me all at once.

"Conference call with Zurich at ten, lunch with investors downtown at twelve-thirty. Your lawyer is scheduled for three, and tonight's dinner reservation—"

He interrupts, his eyes narrowing slightly. "Why am I meeting with my lawyer?"

"I'm not privy to that information, Mr. Vasiliev," I reply evenly.

"You scheduled the appointment," he responds, his tone sharp.

"Because you told me to. You didn't elaborate, and I didn't think it was my place to pry."

A muscle in his jaw twitches, betraying his irritation. "A competent assistant knows every detail of every meeting. Otherwise, she's useless."

Fury boils within, swift and scorching. The insult lands like a slap, heat flaring through me until my cheeks burn. For a dangerous moment, my mouth opens, a fierce "fuck you" poised and ready. But I bite down hard, tasting copper. I need this job too badly—enough to swallow insults—at least for now.

I rise abruptly, the chair scraping loudly behind me, and stalk toward the door. I nearly slam it on my way out, managing to restrain myself at the last second. I close it firmly, the sound echoing like a small, satisfying rebellion.

Outside, I press my back to the wall, drawing a shaky breath. My heart is pounding, adrenaline surging through my veins. I'm stronger than this. Abram Vasiliev might be a powerful, intimidating, sexy-as-hell, insufferable prick, but he won't break me.

No one ever has.

With determination steeling my spine, I push away from the wall and stride down the hall toward the legal department. The heels of my shoes click against the polished marble floors, punctuating each step with stubborn defiance.

I find Mark Henley, Abram's personal lawyer, seated in his expansive, overly lavish office, fingers tapping on his laptop. When he sees me, he gives an amused smirk.

"Ms. Ridley. Did the boss send you?"

"Who else?" I say, forcing a polite smile. "He needs details about your meeting at three. Apparently, I should already know."

Henley chuckles softly. "Well, we can't have Abram disappointed, can we?"

"No," I deadpan. "Wouldn't dream of it."

He rifles through a file, quickly scanning its contents. "Ah, yes. It's regarding the acquisition of the club downtown."

"What kind of club?" I ask, careful to keep my voice neutral even as something sharp and electric stirs under my skin. Abram owns plenty of properties—some legitimate, some not—but the way Henley's eyes gleam puts me immediately on alert.

"It's, well, a sex club," he says, voice laced with dry amusement. "Though not officially. High-end. Exclusive clientele."

A flush rises beneath my skin. My brain stalls for a second, catching on the phrase like a fishhook. A sex club? That's not what I was expecting to hear. Still, I summon my training, keeping my expression calm, voice cool.

"Of course it is," I say smoothly, arching a brow. "And I'm guessing that's not exactly above board?"

Henley chuckles, but it's the kind of chuckle lawyers give right before they start dancing along the edge of legal definitions. "That depends on what you mean by 'above board,' Ms. Ridley. Is it a licensed nightclub? Yes. Does it serve alcohol legally? Also yes. Are there private areas where consenting adults can spend time together away from prying eyes? Sure. But that doesn't make it a brothel, which would be illegal under Nevada law—at least in Clark County."

I tilt my head. "So it's legal because it's not charging for sex?"

"Exactly," he says, pleased that I understand. "There's no transactional exchange of money for sexual services. No solicitation. No in-house staff providing those kinds of amenities. What the club does provide is an environment. Mood lighting. Private rooms. Security. Discretion. If consenting adults choose to engage in certain activities while on the premises, that's their business."

"And if law enforcement shows up?"

Henley shrugs. "They don't. The place is careful. Membership-only, vetted guests. Surveillance, but no recordings. The current owners aren't foolish. They don't market it publicly. No flyers, no ads. Just a space that facilitates fantasy. If anything, it's protected more by the strength of its obscurity than by any legal shield."

I nod slowly, absorbing everything he just said. It's not just shady—it's calculated. Clever.

Very Abram.

I manage a slight smirk, though beneath the surface, my mind races.

My boss is buying a sex club.

Armed with the details Abram demanded, I thank Henley and step into the hallway, heart thudding just a little harder than I'd like to admit.

A *sex club?* I knew Abram had ties to things most people wouldn't understand—shady business dealings, hush-hush partnerships, maybe even some money laundering. But this? This is different. Intimate. Personal.

My mind spins as I make my way back to Abram's office. Did he buy the place just to profit from it? Or does he actually partake? I try not to imagine him in a private room—voice low and commanding while someone is pinned beneath him, trembling and begging.

But the image won't leave. Instead, it spreads like wildfire, heat licking up my neck, curling between my thighs.

Damn it.

I take a breath. *Rein it in.*

By the time I get back to Abram's office, my jaw is tight, my face composed, and I've rehearsed my update enough times to sound coolly professional, even if my pulse hasn't quite recovered.

When I enter his office again, Abram is seated behind his desk, brow furrowed in concentration over his laptop. His attention snaps to me as I approach.

"Well?" he prompts impatiently.

I meet his gaze evenly, folding my arms over my chest. "Your meeting with Henley is about acquiring another club. It's exclusive, high-end, and skirting the boundaries of legality."

His eyebrows lift, surprise briefly flickering across his carefully controlled features only to be replaced quickly by narrowed suspicion. "Did he say anything else?"

My lips twist slightly. "He mentioned it's a sex club."

His eyes darken and something flickers in them—a sharp, brief heat that makes my pulse quicken despite myself.

"Did he now?" he murmurs, almost thoughtful. I can tell he already knew.

I tilt my head, studying him. "Would you have demanded these details if I were a man?"

His expression cools instantly, eyes sharpening. "Absolutely. My assistant should have complete knowledge of my affairs, regardless of their nature."

I let a soft, skeptical hum escape my lips, then straighten. "I've already ordered your lunch. It'll arrive promptly at noon. Anything else?"

He stares at me, unreadable, then shakes his head once. "That's all. Close the door behind you."

I turn without a word, shutting the door just a little too firmly. Back in my office at my desk, I sink into my chair, the anger and indignation slowly ebbing, replaced by reluctant curiosity.

Abram Vasiliev, Bratva kingpin and billionaire asshole extraordinaire, is about to own a sex club. The thought isn't exactly shocking—he's no stranger to power or danger—but something about it catches me off guard.

I imagine him there, dark eyes watching, that powerful, commanding presence dominating every room. Heat flushes my cheeks, and I angrily shove the thought away.

No. Absolutely not.

My desk phone buzzes loudly, pulling me sharply back to reality. Abram's lunch is here. With a weary sigh, I push aside all fantasies and head downstairs to collect the perfectly prepared meal from Abram's favorite upscale bistro. My lunch consists of a sad, and limp salad from the convenience store next door.

When I return, Abram has vanished from his office. Typical. I settle behind my desk, staring at his untouched meal, suddenly feeling foolishly hopeful he'll at least acknowledge the effort I put into making his days easier.

My phone rings incessantly, a nonstop stream of irate investors and demanding clients, all of whom expect Abram's immediate response. I soothe egos, make promises, and swallow frustration along with bites of wilted lettuce.

Abram reappears an hour later, striding through the office like a thunderstorm. He stops sharply at my desk.

"The paperwork?" he demands, voice edged with impatience.

My eyes dart toward the semi-finished stack. "Nearly done. Your clients have been calling nonstop, and I'm trying to keep them calm."

His eyes narrow to icy slits. "Ten minutes." I open my mouth to argue, but his glare silences me immediately. He leans in, voice low and dangerous. "I hired you because I believed you could handle the pressure, Jenna. Don't make me regret it."

He straightens and stalks away, leaving me trembling with suppressed rage. I channel it all into my fingers, typing furiously until the paperwork is finished.

Storming into his office, I slap the finished documents onto his desk, harder than necessary. Pages scatter. Abram glances up sharply, gaze darkening.

"That's everything," I say through clenched teeth. "If there's nothing else, I'm leaving for the day."

He regards me silently, eyes unreadable. Silence stretches between us, heavy and tense, and just when I think I might scream, he nods once. "You're free to go."

I leave quickly, grabbing my purse and laptop, my hands shaking so badly I nearly drop everything twice. Outside, the air hits my heated skin, cooling some of my temper. I'm certain I'll be fired by tomorrow, but right now, I honestly don't give a fuck.

My mind races as I walk away, replaying his unreadable expression. Was it indifference or something else? I grit my teeth, forcing myself to dismiss the thought. Abram Vasiliev's moods and motives aren't my problem.

Except they are because I need this job.

Still, there's only so much I can tolerate. I won't be his verbal punching bag forever. No matter how irresistible or powerful he is.

Determined, I quicken my steps toward home, promising myself tomorrow will be different.

Tomorrow, I'll hold my own.

Tomorrow, I'll prove Abram Vasiliev can't break me.

CHAPTER 2

ABRAM

Jenna's body could make a saint think wicked thoughts —and I'm no fucking saint.

My eyes track her ass shamelessly as she storms out of my office, fury in every click of her heels. That tight little A-line skirt hugs her curves so perfectly it's almost sinful, framing the sway of her hips in a way that makes my mouth water.

For one indulgent moment, I allow myself to imagine calling her back, locking the office door behind her. My voice would be calm yet authoritative. I'd tell her to hike that skirt up around her hips, slowly slide her panties down her thighs, and climb onto my cock, riding me until she forgets every single reason she's so damn angry.

I harden instantly, a raw surge of desire tightening in my core. I've never been a man ruled by impulse, but Jenna Ridley challenges that daily. Still, I shake the thought away with reluctant discipline.

Fucking your assistant is the oldest cliché in the book—one

of those stupid, reckless mistakes men like me aren't supposed to make.

No matter how tempting that mistake might be.

I push back from my desk and slowly stand up, rolling my shoulders as I cross to the window. Las Vegas sprawls beneath me, glittering in the afternoon sun, deceptive in its brightness.

Jenna has no real idea what it means to be involved with a man like me, though she knows enough to be wary. I'm Abram Vasiliev—head of the Vasiliev Bratva—feared and respected in equal measure.

Although she's aware of who I am, I'm not sure she fully understands what it really means, the blood that stains my hands. If she can handle that, maybe she'll last long enough to become a decent assistant. And God, I hope she does. Because the alternative—getting rid of her before I give in to temptation—is becoming less appealing every damn day.

Her fiery defiance, that blazing temper barely masked behind careful professionalism, draws me in like nothing else. Every time she walks into my office, my cock reacts instantly, shamelessly demanding what I've forbidden myself.

And each day, resisting her gets a little harder.

I chuckle under my breath, still staring out the window. Jenna Ridley. Fucking hell. The whole reason she's here is because of my meddling sisters, Anya and Tatiana. They stormed into my office three months ago like a pair of smug hurricanes in heels, sitting themselves down like they owned the place and giving me a carefully rehearsed speech.

"You need someone who can take the weight of the world off your shoulders," Anya had said with a knowing smile.

"Someone competent. Organized. Someone who won't put up with your bullshit," Tatiana added.

And then, as if they'd choreographed the whole thing, they said together: "We know just the woman."

Apparently, Jenna had done a temp stint at a boutique real estate firm where Tatiana's college friend worked. She'd filled in for an executive assistant on maternity leave and left such a strong impression that word traveled fast. Efficient, sharp-tongued, calm under pressure. A little too pretty for her own good, but my sisters didn't seem concerned about that.

I insisted I didn't need a damn assistant. I needed quiet. But they didn't give a shit about what I wanted. Their little speech wasn't about work. It was about tying me down.

They want to see me get married. Settled. Playing house like they are—soft mornings, matching mugs, fucking holiday cards. They're happy and they think I'm secretly lonely. Like I'm just waiting to be swept off my feet by the right woman and a color-coded Google calendar.

I'm not.

I like fucking too much. The real kind. Not the performative honeymoon sex newlyweds pretend they'll keep having forever. I'm talking about the kind that strips a woman down to her rawest needs and keeps her there.

Every night. Over my desk. In the shower. On the floor. Again and again.

From what I understand, wives don't like that. Not after a while, anyway. Eventually, the excuses come. The headaches. The obligation. And I don't want someone who fucks me because they think they're supposed to.

I want hunger.

Filth.

Need.

So no, marriage isn't for me.

But they got one thing right. Jenna is good. Better than I expected. She's smart. Fast. A little rough around the edges. She's emotional, impulsive, and a little too eager to talk back, but she learns quickly. She expertly manages my calendar, types quickly and accurately, and anticipates what I need before I ask for it.

She's not perfect. Yet.

And thank fuck she's not soft. She doesn't flinch when I raise my voice, doesn't blush when I look at her too long. She meets me—challenge for challenge—and half the time I don't know whether I want to bend her over the desk or see what else she's capable of under pressure.

She still needs some work, though. She hasn't been broken in yet, hasn't been taught how I like things, how I expect things.

But she will be. Because I don't accept incompetence. I don't accept excuses.

I demand excellence.

And if she's going to keep walking into my office with those curves and that mouth, she'd better learn how to be fucking flawless.

Nothing less will do.

Training her as an assistant will take time. Precision. Patience.

But there are other things. Darker things. Things I should not—*must not*—train her for.

I try to refocus, push the thoughts aside. But they slip in anyway. Uninvited. Unstoppable.

One moment I'm thinking about schedules and contracts. The next, her.

I close my eyes, jaw tight, as the image takes over. Smoke curling under a locked door. Slow. Inevitable. Her skirt sliding up, her fingers slipping beneath the hem of her blouse. That look she gives me when she's about to say something that will make my cock twitch—smug, teasing—like she's always one step ahead.

In my head, she's back in my office. That tight skirt now on the floor. The blouse, undone and slipping off her shoulders like it was made to fall just for me. She stands in front of me in black lace—bra lifting her full tits, panties hugging her hips so snugly it should be illegal.

"You're staring, Mr. Vasiliev," she says, voice low and knowing.

"Can you blame me?" I murmur, rising from the chair and circling her slowly. "You wore this on purpose."

"To distract you," she says, chin lifted. "Is it working?"

I reach out and grip her hips, firm and possessive, pulling her close. "You have no idea."

Her laugh is wicked. "Maybe I need to spell out what I'm really here for."

"Do it," I breathe, already hard. "Say what you want."

"I want your hands on me," she whispers.

I growl, mouth crashing into hers. Deep. Claiming. The kind of kiss that erases logic, torches restraint. I feel her melt into me, arching, pressing her heat against the bulge in my slacks.

"You think this is smart?" I speak against her lips. "Fucking your boss?"

She grins against my mouth. "No. But you don't hire smart girls for this."

I chuckle. "No, I hire dangerous ones."

And fuck, she is dangerous. Her body's all curves and fire, hips made to be grabbed, thighs I'd let crush the life out of me. I lift her onto the desk—sweeping everything off in one careless motion—and bury myself in her so deep she forgets her own name.

Just as she leans back, spreading her legs for me, I blink. The image shatters. She's not here. Just me and the silence of the office, a spreadsheet I've been pretending to read.

I drag a hand down my face and exhale slowly.

Dangerous, I think again. But I'm not sure I'm talking about the fantasy anymore.

I shake my head, coming back into the moment. I lean back in my chair, fingers steepled against my mouth, eyes unfocused. My mind drifts back to the conversation we'd had earlier.

"He mentioned it's a sex club."

Just like that. No hesitation, no awkwardness. Like she was reporting a fluctuation in the stock market.

And fuck me, it had taken everything I had not to react.

I'd asked the question to test her. I know what kind of club The 13th Floor is; hell, I'm the one buying it. I wanted to see if she'd flinch. See if she'd squirm.

She didn't.

I shift in my chair, jaw tight, trying—and failing—not to let the memory take hold of me.

And then she'd had the audacity to tilt her head, eyes sharp as razors, and ask, *"If I were a man, would you have asked for those details?"*

I'd kept my voice cool when I answered, telling her yes because it's true. I expect thoroughness from everyone on my payroll. But that's not what she was really asking. And we both knew it.

Because by then, the power had shifted.

And God help me, it made me want her more.

Not just to fuck. Not just to claim.

To unravel. To crack that shell. To see if she tastes just as sharp when she finally loses control.

I exhale slowly, adjusting myself under the desk.

I'm still imagining her saying all of that again—but on her knees this time, lips parted, eyes daring me to break her.

I scrub a hand over my face, trying to shake it off. But it clings to me. The memory. The heat.

And the worst part?

It wasn't flirtation. She wasn't playing a game.

She was just doing her job, which means this isn't going to go away. Not tonight. Not tomorrow. Not until I know what she looks like when she stops being so goddamn composed.

And maybe not even then.

I stare at the office door, pulse thudding behind my ears. The air smells faintly like her—sweet and warm, with a trace of something sharp underneath. Something that cuts through my control like a blade.

I should get back to work. Instead, I stay frozen, staring at the place where she stood. Where she smirked. Where she challenged me, like she doesn't know—or worse, doesn't care —who I am.

Most women in this building shrink when I speak. Most don't even look me in the eye. But Jenna Ridley? She holds her ground.

It should piss me off.

It doesn't.

It makes me hard. And it makes me curious, which is far more dangerous.

I glance down at my desk, at the spot where she'd rested her tablet. Something small catches my eye—a single strand of red hair. Long, glossy, curled at the end. She must've tucked it behind her ear when she leaned forward earlier, just before telling me all about public sex with the voice of someone reciting quarterly financials.

I reach out, fingertip brushing it before I can stop myself.

Goddamn it.

This is how it starts. The obsession. The craving. The slow undoing of everything I've built.

She's not just beautiful. She's defiant. She's clever. She doesn't flirt, doesn't posture. And somehow, that restraint makes me want her more. Makes me wonder what she'd sound like when she finally breaks—when she moans my name, desperate and ruined.

I drop the hair in the trash, disgusted with myself.

She's your assistant. You don't fuck the help and you sure as hell don't think about them after they leave the room.

Yet here I am, staring at the door like I'm waiting for her to walk through it.

CHAPTER 3

JENNA

By the time I make it home, I'm dragging. My heels are in my hand, my blouse half-untucked. My brain feels like it's been deep-fried.

My apartment is small and a little cramped, but it's mine. Mid-century meets girl on a budget. Thrift store velvet throw pillows, string lights I never took down after Christmas, and an Ikea bookshelf I put together myself that leans ever so slightly to the left. The sink's full again. The laundry basket in the corner is begging to be emptied, and there's a half-eaten donut still on a plate from... God, maybe Tuesday?

Whatever. I drop my shoes, collapse onto the couch, and sink into the cushions like the plug's been pulled on me. I grope for the remote, not even caring what I watch as long as it's something that doesn't make me think.

I pull up Netflix, scrolling for a second before settling on *Selling Sunset*. It's so aggressively stupid, it's perfect. Nothing like watching women with sculpted jaws and weaponized cleavage argue about listing prices while I debate whether I have the energy to microwave leftovers.

It's no use. I can't focus. My brain keeps crawling back to him.

Abram Vasiliev.

My boss. My tyrant. My walking HR violation of a distraction.

He works nonstop—barely eats, barely sleeps—and expects his assistant to follow suit. At his beck and call until he's finished for the day, which could mean noon or three in the morning. He'll shoot off a message at 10:47 p.m. about an investor meeting the next day and expect a response in sixty seconds. I've actually timed him. Sixty-one seconds and he's texting me a question mark.

My circadian rhythm is a mess. Coffee has replaced the blood in my veins. I've forgotten what a normal weekend looks like. And yet...

I sit up straight, realizing my body isn't tired at all. I'm *buzzing*. My legs won't stay still. My brain keeps looping little flashes of his voice, his eyes, the look he gave me when I suggested the club wasn't entirely legal. Like he wanted to devour me and fire me in the same breath.

What the hell is wrong with me?

I pick up my phone, thumb hovering over my messages. I need to talk to someone sane. Someone not brooding, bearded, and capable of killing a man with a paperweight.

Claire. My best friend. My lifeline. She always tells it straight, even when I don't want to hear it.

I open our chat and start typing.

You home?

Just walked in. What's up?

Wanna hang? Like, tonight? Now? I need wine.

GOD yes. I'll be there in an hour.

I smile for the first time all day and toss my phone onto the couch. Claire and I have been best friends since freshman orientation at Arizona State, where she rescued me from an awkward icebreaker involving a trust fall and a very sweaty guy named Chad.

We were roommates all through college and again in our first dumpy apartment post-graduation until I moved into this place, my grown-up space, complete with central air and a dishwasher that actually works.

She landed a job at a marketing firm downtown that she likes well enough but says has "too many men named Josh." Between her client meetings and my boss's erratic schedule, we barely see each other anymore. But when we do, it's still magic.

True to her word, she's knocking on the door fifty-eight minutes later. I open it to find her grinning, a bottle of rosé in one hand and a bag of cheese popcorn in the other.

"Did someone order a girls' night?" she says, breezing past me like a spring gust.

Claire's one of those women who looks like she belongs in a magazine ad—tall, lean, sleek brown ponytail, perfectly winged eyeliner she claims takes two seconds.

I've never been skinny like her. I'm more soft curves and strategic outfits. Claire's always made me feel like a walking 'before' picture, though she'd be furious if she knew that.

"Living room's a disaster," I warn, stepping over a pile of laundry.

She shrugs. "So are we."

We pop the cork and pour modest glasses. Claire kicks off her heels and sinks into the couch like she owns it. "Alright, talk to me. You're practically vibrating."

"I think I'm sexually frustrated," I mutter, sipping slowly, savoring the sweetness. "Like, dangerously."

Claire snorts. "Finally. I've been waiting weeks for this confession. Tell me everything."

I groan and bury my face in a pillow. "It's Abram. My boss."

"The Russian Bratva zaddy," she gasps. "I knew it. You're finally admitting it."

"He's not a zaddy," I mumble, though the heat in my cheeks betrays me. "He's a controlling, egotistical asshole who makes me want to throw a stapler at his face and at the same time ride him like a mechanical bull."

Claire howls with laughter, nearly spilling her wine. "Girl, I *have* to see this man."

"He's not a man, he's a tyrant."

"Alright, so he's a hot tyrant. But the job's good, right?"

"Amazing pay," I admit. "And I get full benefits. Plus, it's not boring. When he calls me into his office, I never know if

I'm walking into a scheduling emergency or a crime in progress."

Claire lifts her glass. "To hot criminals and health insurance."

We clink and drink.

Claire leans back on the couch. "So. Are you gonna show me a picture of this hot tyrant or what?"

I roll my eyes and take another drink. "Nope."

"No?"

"I'm not feeding your fantasies."

Claire grins. "Oh, so he's seriously hot."

"I'm not doing this." I stand, grabbing my phone. "Wanna go out? Catch a buzz? Make some bad decisions?"

Claire blinks, then tilts her head. "Wasn't expecting a bait-and-switch. But yes, obviously."

"How about Junebug's?" I offer. It's a dive bar on East Fremont with sticky floors and strong drinks.

She makes a face. "Mmm, tempting. But since we never get to hang out anymore, I vote we mix it up."

I hesitate. "Like how?"

She drums her fingers on her glass. "Like, let's do something we haven't done since we were fresh out of college and thought Vegas was our playground." She jumps to her feet. "Let's go dancing!"

I blink. "Like, real dancing? Music? Sweaty strangers?"

"Maybe even some making out in a dark corner."

I laugh. "Fine. Let's find a place."

I grab my laptop and set it on the coffee table. Claire plops beside me, pulling her knees up and balancing her glass on one thigh like it's a skill she's trained for. I pull up a few club sites—Velvet Room, The Underground, Haze. She scrolls with a distracted hum before stopping abruptly. Her eyes light up, her mouth curving in a way that sets off a mild alarm in my chest.

"Oh no," I say. "I know that look. That's your bad idea face."

Claire's smile spreads. "Jenna. Darling. I have the perfect idea."

I sip cautiously. "Is it legal?"

"Define legal." She angles the screen towards me.

The site is dark—literally. A deep obsidian background with red-velvet accents, moody lighting, and looping video of bodies writhing in silhouette.

The header reads: *The 13th Floor.*

Beneath it, a tagline: *Your desires. Your rules.*

There's a form for requesting access. A section called "Dress Code and Decorum" with words like *consensual voyeurism* and *performance room etiquette.* Tabs labeled "Theme Nights" and "Private Chambers." The whole thing feels like someone designed a nightclub inside a very well-funded porn studio.

My lips thin.

Claire grins. "So?"

"So?"

She nudges me. "Don't you dare act like you're not curious."

"I'm..." I trail off. "Okay, yeah, I am. But Claire, Abram is planning on buying a sex club." God, the words still feel weird to say. "What if this one is it?"

She raises a brow. "And wouldn't that be a story."

"That would be a disaster."

She holds up her glass. "Or fate."

I stare at the screen again, my pulse ticking up like I've had more wine than I actually have. The video loops back to a couple in a velvet chair, half-clothed and very into each other. My skin tingles with heat.

I think of Abram. And suddenly, I don't feel so tipsy anymore. Just alive.

I narrow my eyes at the screen, suspicious. "This isn't a brothel, right?"

Claire snorts into her wine. "No, babe. It's a club. There's sex, sure, but nobody's getting paid. No hookers, no johns, just people having fun."

I eye her sideways. "You've been?"

She hesitates for half a second too long, then nods slowly. "Yeah."

"What? When?"

She shrugs, swirling her wine like this is just casual, every day talk. "Last year. I went with Marcus."

Marcus. Her ex with the tattoos and the motorcycle and emotionally unavailable.

"What the hell, Claire? Why didn't you tell me?"

She grins, biting her lip. "Didn't know if you'd be cool with it."

I laugh. "You must think I am, since you're inviting me to go now."

She gives me that wicked grin again. "You are. You just don't know it yet."

I give her a skeptical look. "And what exactly did *you* do at the 13th Floor?"

"Oh, not much," she says casually. "Watched a couple go at it in a candlelit room. Got tied up. Had sex in a mirror-lined hallway with Marcus while a few people watched."

I choke on my wine. "*Claire!*"

"What?" She shrugs again. "It was hot. No pressure. Marcus never looked at me the same after. In a good way."

"You're ridiculous."

She nudges me with her shoulder. "And you're curious."

I have to admit I am. I mean, I've had lovers. A few one-night stands. But I've never gone looking for sex like it's an experience to chase down. Never walked into a building with the intent of getting laid. It's different. Intoxicating.

"I don't know," I murmur. "What if it's not safe?"

"It is," she says, suddenly serious. "Bouncers are every-where. No one touches you without permission. You can leave at any time. You can do nothing and just watch. It's totally your call."

I stare at the screen again, biting my lip in indecision.

Claire puts her hand on mine. "There's zero pressure, Jen. I promise. We can be wallflowers. We can flirt. Or we can just drink overpriced cocktails and mock creepy guys in velvet blazers. But you need something. Something different."

She's not wrong.

I nod slowly. "Okay."

Claire beams. "Yes!"

"What do we wear to a sex club?"

She grins. "Masks."

We stop at a boutique tucked just off Fremont Street, one of those artsy little shops where every piece feels like it belongs to a different fantasy. The walls are lined with velvet capes, leather chokers, and masks—so many masks. Feathers. Lace. Glitter. Leather. A masquerade of secrets waiting to be worn.

Claire makes a beeline for a sleek silver number, filigree swirls curling up over her brow like wings. It clings to her face in delicate lines, cool and sharp, just like her. "This one's mine," she declares, holding it up. "Total femme fatale shit."

I wander around, fingers drifting past rows of black lace and crimson velvet, until one catches my eye. It's navy blue, the same shade as the night sky just before it swallows the sun. Midnight threaded with silver. The edges flare out into tiny horns—subtle, but mischievous. It's soft to the touch but holds its shape like something made to be worn boldly.

"This," I say quietly, lifting it to my face. "This feels right."

Claire eyes it, then grins. "Mysterious."

We pay and head back to my apartment. The mood has shifted.

In the mirror, I pull on my dress—a fitted black number I've never worn before. Not clingy, exactly, but it hugs me in places that make me feel a little shy. And a little thrilled. The kind of dress that demands attention. The kind of dress I bought thinking *maybe someday*.

Apparently, someday is now.

I slip on the mask last. The horns catch the light. The navy brings out the warmth in my eyes.

Claire whistles low. "Damn, Jenna."

I turn toward the mirror again, hardly recognizing the woman staring back. Sexy. Confident. A little dangerous.

I grin.

Anything could happen tonight.

And that's exactly what I want.

CHAPTER 4

ABRAM

I stand in front of the bathroom mirror, towel slung low on my hips, the scent of shaving cream lingering sharp and clean in the air. The overhead light reflects off my bare scalp as I run the blade over the last strip of skin, smooth as marble.

Clean lines. No strays. Precision always.

I wipe the remaining foam from my jaw then stare at my reflection.

The salt-and-pepper beard suits me. It doesn't hide my age —forty-two and unapologetically carved by time. But it's also distinctive, and tonight, I need to disappear. I reach for the temporary black dye, twist the cap off, and begin working it through the coarse hair. As the grey vanishes, my face transforms into something harder, more anonymous.

Once finished, I lean back and take in my reflection. Chest solid. Abs still defined. Broad shoulders scarred and strong. Not bad for a man who spends most of his time behind a desk signing contracts.

Still, I know the clock's ticking. Too many nights spent in boardrooms and too few in the weight room and I'll end up like every other overfed, soft-palmed executive dragging himself across the Strip. I make a mental note—gym session tomorrow. Heavy weights. No excuses.

But tonight? Tonight, I have other appetites to attend to.

I tug on a crisp black dress shirt tailored to my frame. A dark navy blazer follows—structured, subtle. Italian wool. Matching trousers. No tie. Just clean lines and sharp edges.

Before I leave, I open the top drawer of my dresser.

The mask stares at me.

Black leather, smooth and angular, covering half my face with a sharp V that comes down between my brows. A vertical line of silver studs runs from the center of the forehead to the tip of the nose, catching the light like tiny weapons. The eyes are cut narrow, predatory.

I slide it on, watching as I become someone else entirely.

My mouth curves into an insidious grin.

Tonight, I'm not Abram Vasiliev, the Bratva's velvet-gloved hand.

Tonight, I'm a man with no name.

And I'm going to have some fucking fun.

My car slides smoothly up to the curb outside The 13th Floor. Neon light cascades down sleek black walls like water over polished stone. I can feel the pulse of bass vibrating through the tinted windows.

I've been a regular at this club for years, familiar enough that the staff know my preferences without needing reminders. While the papers haven't been officially signed yet, the deal's as good as done. Nothing but formalities left to iron out before I can officially call myself the owner.

Soon enough, this club won't just be my favorite haunt, it will be mine. Another jewel in the crown of Vasiliev Holdings, another indulgence I can control completely.

The building itself radiates exclusivity with minimal signage. It announces its existence with a subtle silver "13" glowing coolly above tall, black double doors. It whispers sin, luxury, and secrets.

Predictably, there's a line snaking around the corner, desperate hopefuls shifting impatiently on stilettos and expensive leather loafers, their anticipation palpable.

There will be no line to wait in for me, though.

The driver pulls discreetly around back, stopping at the private VIP entrance tucked away in shadow. The guard sees me approach, gives a respectful nod, and waves me in without a word.

The moment I step inside, darkness envelops me. Deep crimson lights scatter pools of warmth across smooth black marble floors, the scent of perfume mingling intoxicatingly with hints of leather and liquor.

A central dance floor sprawls at the heart of the club, bodies writhing in rhythm beneath chandeliers that drip like crystal tears. Plush, private alcoves line the perimeter, separated by curtains that hide nothing from wandering eyes.

As I move deeper into the club, I catch glimpses of heated intimacy: a woman pressed breathlessly against the wall, head thrown back as a stranger's hand slips beneath her skirt; another couple tangled together on a velvet sofa, oblivious to the voyeuristic crowd gathering nearby, savoring their sexy show with drinks in hand.

Here, inhibitions die at the door—this is a sanctuary for the shameless.

A hostess, professional and carefully neutral, guides me to my booth overlooking the dance floor. She brings my whiskey neat without needing instruction. I sip slowly, my gaze sweeping lazily across the sea of writhing flesh and glittering masks.

Women move like goddesses under the pulsing lights, sultry curves showcased in lingerie barely concealed by gossamer dresses and silky wraps. Men watch them like starving wolves, eyes glittering with lust and possession.

It's decadence. It's freedom. And yet tonight, strangely, none of it stirs my blood. I'm contemplating this peculiar apathy when a soft, playful voice cuts through the hum of music.

"Well, hello there, handsome."

Turning my head slightly, I see two women, young and stunningly beautiful. One's dressed in deep emerald, her body lush and perfectly sculpted beneath her dress, the neckline plunging dangerously low. Her mask is emerald satin, edged in delicate gold filigree. Her companion wears black satin—slender, angular, with the elegance of a runway model and an alluring red mouth that promises pleasure. Her mask is a sleek, glossy raven's wing, feathers shimmering beneath the club lights.

"Care for some company?" the emerald beauty purrs as she steps closer. Her fingertips tease along her friend's waist, drawing my attention to the implied offer.

"We don't bite," the raven-haired woman adds mischievously, a teasing smile tugging at her full lips. "Unless you're into that."

Under different circumstances, perhaps, I'd already have them both bent over a bed in one of the back rooms, exploring every lush curve. But tonight, something inside me resists. Neither of them moves me nearly enough.

Not the way she does.

She?

I dismiss that thought immediately.

With practiced courtesy, I lift my glass slightly, acknowledging their bold approach. "Tempting offer, ladies. But I'm not looking for company tonight."

They exchange disappointed glances, pouting slightly. Emerald shrugs gracefully, her fingertips brushing lightly across my shoulder as she turns away. "Another time, perhaps."

"Perhaps," I echo, though my tone holds no promise.

I watch them disappear into the crowd, drawing attention elsewhere. They'll find their thrills easily enough, without me.

Turning my gaze back to the main floor, I settle deeper into the shadows of my booth, sipping my whiskey slowly, savoring the burn down my throat.

I came here tonight seeking anonymity, distraction, and release. So why does it feel like I'm waiting for something or someone else entirely?

I scan the club judiciously, a habit of ownership. I might've come here to unwind, but I'm still responsible for the integrity of this place. Or I will be soon enough.

My gaze catches small details: a bouncer discreetly inter- vening with a guest who's gotten overly aggressive; a bartender swiftly pouring top-shelf bourbon for a regular; the subtle repositioning of security guards maintaining order and decorum amid the lustful chaos.

Near the bar, a couple commands an admiring audience. The woman's back arches as she grips the countertop, her masked partner moving languidly between her spread thighs, mouth teasingly out of sight beneath her skirt. Her breathless moans blend perfectly with the rhythm of the music, a decadent melody of pleasure weaving through the room.

My pulse should quicken at such sights but instead, my mind drifts stubbornly back to Jenna. Those defiant eyes, that sensual mouth, the way she boldly recited explicit details about this place without a blush or flinch.

What the fuck is wrong with me?

I down the last sip of whiskey, savoring the smooth burn, and motion sharply for another. My irritation rises. I came here to indulge, yet no woman holds my interest tonight.

Jenna's got my head twisted, an unwelcome distraction that's proving damn hard to shake.

Just as my frustration reaches its peak, I spot her.

Standing at the bar is a woman with curves made for sin, wrapped in a skintight black cocktail dress that hugs her voluptuous figure with mouthwatering perfection. Her hair is a cascade of rich auburn, tumbling in soft waves over bare shoulders.

The mask she wears is distinctive—a delicate creation of midnight velvet embroidered with intricate silver filigree, small black gems sparkling around the eyes. Her friend stands beside her in a sleek white dress, a shimmering gold mask accentuating her slender, graceful form.

My eyes linger on the redhead. Her body language tells a clear story with the nervous way she shifts her weight, fingers restlessly tracing the edge of her cocktail glass.

First-timer, I'm certain of it.

A wicked thrill of possessiveness soars within, the blood rushing straight to my cock. Finally, someone who ignites me, someone who pulls at me from across the room.

When she turns slightly, taking a hesitant sip of her drink, I freeze. My eyes narrow sharply behind my mask as I scrutinize her profile—the soft line of her jaw, the lush curve of her lips.

Impossible.

The mask might fool a casual observer, but not me. I've spent countless hours studying her face, her body, her every move, whether I want to admit it or not.

Jenna.

The woman who invades my fantasies with maddening regularity, who defies me at every turn, who's becoming an obsession I can't seem to break. And now she's here, in my club, dressed like lust incarnate, eyes wide and unsure behind that elaborate disguise.

An unexpected surge of dark, hungry anticipation fills me. My fingers tighten around my glass, knuckles whitening as I watch her. There's no escaping this now. Jenna has walked right into my territory, straight into my world.

Tonight just became infinitely more interesting.

Will she recognize me? The question churns in the back of my mind, low and hot. She shouldn't. The beard dye, the mask, the lighting—I'm practically anonymous. But women like Jenna notice details. She could surprise me.

Would I stop her if she did?

Before I can answer myself, she and her friend slide into a booth. Two men quickly slip into view, making a beeline for the two ladies. They're confident in the way jackals are confident—sharp-eyed and predatory. One of them moves toward Jenna's friend, trying too hard to be casual. The other sets his drink down beside Jenna. Even from my vantage point I can see her shoulders stiffen when he leans in and says something to her.

Neither woman is interested. I can spot it immediately in their posture, in the polite but cold smiles they offer. But the men don't move on. If anything, they double down—smirking, gesturing, edging closer.

I narrow my eyes. No single men are allowed here. Club rules. Any man inside these walls is supposed to enter with a partner. It keeps the balance, keeps the wolves from circling too freely.

I raise two fingers. Dmitri, the bouncer stationed nearest my booth, walks over with the efficiency of a man who knows I don't like repeating myself.

"The men in the booth with the two women," I say, nodding in their direction. "Do they have women with them?"

He follows my line of sight and nods once. "They each walked in with a woman but split up immediately. One's already in a private room. The other wandered off. Last I saw, she was with a couple."

Convenient. I keep my face expressionless.

"Problem?" Dmitri asks, tone carefully neutral.

"Not yet." I take a slow sip of whiskey, watching Jenna glance at the guy beside her with a look that's more warning than invitation. "If it becomes one, I'll handle it."

Dmitri nods and backs off, but I can feel the weight of his gaze, waiting for my signal.

I hate this. The idea of Jenna being approached, flirted with, hunted, while standing in *my* club under *my* protection. It sends a hot, violent streak through my blood. A fierceness I can't shake.

She doesn't belong to them.

Those curves are for me.

That smart mouth, the fire in her eyes, the way she moves—it all hits me like a loaded gun, aimed low and hard. I've tried to remain professional. I've tried not to think about what her moans would sound like or how those hips would feel in my hands.

But now she's here.

Now other men are looking at what's mine.

My fingers tighten around the glass. I don't realize how hard I'm gripping it until the edge digs into my palm.

I watch. I wait. Every second those men linger, my anger builds, heavy and silent, coiled just beneath the surface.

If they touch her—if they so much as brush her skin without invitation—I'll make them regret ever stepping foot in this place.

It's not just about sex or territory anymore.

It's about her.

And I don't know what the fuck to do with that.

CHAPTER 5

JENNA

A short time earlier...

As soon as the Uber pulls away I immediately feel like I've made a mistake.

The club is tucked into a narrow alley off an unmarked side street, a set of sleek black doors set into matte concrete, guarded by a bouncer who looks like he could bench press a sedan.

Every single person waiting to get in is stupidly attractive. Glistening skin, sculpted bodies, daring little outfits that cling to lean frames like wet silk. Even the men look like they were genetically engineered for this place—chiseled jaws, dark suits, eyes sharp and hungry behind masks.

And the women... my *god*. They're statuesque, leggy, and barely dressed. Not one of them looks like they've had to second-guess their thighs in a dressing room mirror. I tug down the hem of my tight black dress. It hugs every inch of my curves, and suddenly, I'm all too aware of every one of them.

Claire must sense it. She bumps her shoulder against mine and leans in close. "You look hot as hell," she says. "And I swear to God, if you try to tell me otherwise, I will turn us both around and walk straight back to the apartment."

I manage a weak smile. "You're not scared?"

Claire laughs. "Terrified. But that's half the fun, isn't it?"

We wait our turn in line, inching closer to the door. I watch as the bouncer turns a couple away—too drunk or maybe just not up to whatever unspoken standard this place keeps. I imagine him looking us over and deciding I'm not the right shape. That I'm not... enough.

When we reach him, however, he lifts the velvet rope without a word, his eyes flicking from Claire to me. I expect judgment. Instead, there's something closer to approval. He opens the door, and Claire shoots me a smug look.

"Told you," she murmurs as we step inside. "No one could say no to a hottie like you."

The interior is darker than I expected—low lighting, warm red tones, sleek, black accents. We step into a narrow hallway lined with doors on either side, and even though we're barely past the threshold, I can already hear the sounds of pleasure.

Moans. Deep, guttural sounds of pleasure behind the walls. Skin slapping. A woman laughing, breathless and high. The sound of someone begging, soft and urgent.

I keep walking, heart hammering in my throat. One of the doors has a panel of frosted glass, and as I glance sideways, I see the blurry silhouette of a couple tangled together. Her back arched. His hands gripping her waist. It's all suggestion—shadow and motion—but somehow it's even more provocative than seeing the real thing.

My legs feel like they've forgotten how to work. Claire's several steps ahead of me, walking with purpose, like she's done this a dozen times.

I pause just for a second and remind myself how to breathe.

What am I doing here?

Is this a terrible idea?

Claire turns when she notices I'm not beside her anymore. She grins, a gleam of mischief in her eye. "Come on, babe," she says. "We haven't even gotten to the good part yet."

I swallow hard and follow her in, each step feeling like a point of no return.

The hallway opens into a world unlike anything I've ever seen. Sultry shadows, crimson light, music with a bassline that pulses like a heartbeat. The air smells of perfume, sex, and something heady—like incense left to smolder too long. I follow Claire through the club's curved interior.

A woman reclines in a swing suspended from black iron hooks, her thighs parted, two men tangled around her like vines. One kisses her bare shoulder, slow and reverent. The other slides her panties down her legs with a grin like he's unwrapping a gift. I can't help but stare. She moans, the sound slipping beneath my skin like velvet heat.

Further down, a couple is pressed to a mirrored wall, oblivious to the audience. Her fingers rake through his hair, her dress hitched high.

Claire's talking excitedly, but her voice is just background noise. I'm too overwhelmed—in a good way. My dress feels too tight yet not tight enough. I'm nervous, but more than that, I'm buzzing. Turned on. Every inch of my body alive.

We reach the main floor, and it's stunning—sleek and polished, with black leather booths and low amber lights casting everything in soft gold. A chandelier of black crystal drips light above the dance floor, where bodies sway and grind in a hypnotic rhythm.

But it's not just dancing. A woman straddles a man's lap in one corner, his hands under her dress, her head tipped back in pleasure. No one seems to mind.

Claire's beaming. "Isn't this amazing?"

I nod, unable to speak.

"C'mon," she says, grabbing my hand. "Let's get a drink."

She leads me to the bar. On the way, a masked woman locks eyes with me. She's dancing alone, languid and sensual, like she knows exactly who she is. I feel awkward by comparison, like I'm pretending at confidence I don't quite have.

Claire turns to me. "God, I'm so ready for some fun."

"What kind of fun?" I ask.

She shrugs, grinning. "Last time I was here, I had a boyfriend. Tonight? Who knows."

I imagine her getting scooped up within minutes, leaving me behind to fumble around this adult playground on my own. I hate that the thought even crosses my mind, but I'm not like her. She's slender, fearless, magnetic. I'm curvy and cautious, and every time a man's eyes slide over me, I wonder if they're judging.

Still, my skin is humming, my thighs pressed tightly together beneath my dress. Something inside me stirs, hungry and unsure.

We settle onto the high stools at the bar. I need a drink—badly. Something to cool the heat licking at my spine. And something to shut up the voice in my head that keeps asking, *What are you really looking for tonight, Jenna?*

We order some drinks. They take the edge off just enough.

The bar is a show in itself. A few seats down, a woman with gleaming brown skin straddles her partner's lap. They kiss like they've forgotten anyone else exists. His hand disappears beneath the slit of her dress and her breath catches—soft but audible. Nothing is exposed, but the intimacy is unmistakable. Her hips lift slightly, a stutter in her rhythm, and my body responds with a sharp ache low in my belly.

At a nearby table, a woman kisses two men—alternating between them like she's trying to decide her favorite flavor. One whispers something into her ear and they all laugh. She stands, flanked by the pair, and they walk together toward a hallway draped in velvet curtains.

Claire follows my gaze and nudges me. "Want to follow them?"

"I was just... watching," I reply, cheeks warm.

I'm not just watching. I'm imagining. I'm wondering what it would be like to be that bold. That wanted.

And then I feel a prickle on the back of my neck. Like someone's watching me.

I glance up toward the floor above. There, at a sleek black booth on a mezzanine overlooking the main floor, sits a man in a tailored suit. His mask is elegant and severe, covering most of his face in glossy black, save for his mouth and a sharp jawline framed by a short, dark beard.

His eyes are locked on mine. Unflinching. Piercing.

My breath hitches. He doesn't look away.

Something about his gaze—steady, unreadable, intense—sends a flutter straight to my core. He nods once. I smile back, automatic and unsure, heart thudding.

I want to look away.

I don't.

Even from here, I can tell his body is fit. His shoulders are broad, his posture relaxed but controlled, like a man used to being in command.

Would a man like that be into someone like me? I glance around. The women here are model-thin, draped in barely-there clothes, walking with the kind of confidence I'm still working on possessing. I shift in my seat, aware of the curve of my thighs against the barstool, the swell of my chest in this tight black dress. I'm probably not his type.

But he's still watching me.

Claire leans over and grabs my hand. "Let's find a table before we get claimed."

"Claimed?"

She rolls her eyes, grinning. "You know what I mean. We don't have to settle for the first guys who hit on us."

I laugh, grateful for the distraction. For her. But as she pulls me toward the low-lit lounge seating beyond the bar, I glance back.

The man's still watching.

I wonder what it would feel like to be the one he chooses.

The bass thrums through my chest, syncing with the slight buzz in my veins. I swirl the ice in my glass, feeling the fizz and warmth of the drink bloom in my chest. Claire leans in, hair tumbling forward, eyes sparkling.

"God, I didn't think I knew what I wanted tonight, but I do now."

"Oh yeah?" I tease, raising a brow.

She laughs, a wicked sound. "Yeah. I want a hot guy to sweep me off my feet, pin me against a wall, and do absolutely *whatever* he wants to me. No names. No morning-after awkwardness. Just raw, anonymous pleasure."

"Jesus, Claire." I laugh, half scandalized, half turned on.

"What?" She shrugs, unfazed. "You come to a place like this to live out your fantasies."

I take a sip, trying to steady the strange current inside me. It's like something dormant has begun to stir. Like I've been handed a key to a room I didn't know existed in me.

Claire chats away happily, and just as she bursts into laughter, two men slide uninvited into our booth. They're both in their early thirties, one wearing a suit with rumpled lapels and beer breath, the other with greasy hair slicked back, too many buttons undone, and a necklace that looks like it came from a gas station.

How the hell did *they* get in?

"Ladies," the greasy one says, slurring a bit. "You look lonely."

"We're good," I say politely, setting my drink down. "Why don't you find your own table?"

They laugh like I'm flirting.

I glance up at the mezzanine.

He's gone. The mysterious, magnetic masked man is no longer watching me. I search for him subtly, trying not to be obvious.

Nothing. A twinge of disappointment hums in my gut.

My eyes scan the crowd. Maybe I imagined how intense his gaze felt. Maybe it was just the atmosphere.

"C'mon," the first one says, forcing me back into the uncomfortable moment. "Don't be like that. We just wanted to say hi. This one—" he nods toward me, then glances back to his friend "—has legs for days. I'm a leg man."

I press my lips together. Claire gives him a look, trying to play nice. "We were just catching up, actually."

"Even better. We'll join you." He leans in. "Double date."

I try again. "We'd prefer to sit alone. Thanks."

The greasy one doesn't move. His eyes drop to my chest, lingering there. "Don't be a bitch."

Something flares in me, and I shift my weight, square to him. "I'm *not interested*. Leave."

His face hardens. "You're lucky anybody in this place is showing interest in you," he mutters, grabbing my wrist.

I slowly look down at his hand. "You've got about two seconds to let go."

He pulls me toward him. "You need a little attention. Maybe then you wouldn't walk around acting like you're hot shit."

I yank my hand back, seething. "What the fuck is that supposed to mean?"

He laughs and gestures vaguely toward my hips.

I open my mouth to tell him off—loudly—but before I can speak, a hand slams down on his shoulder. Hard.

He startles, jerking slightly.

It's none other than the masked man who'd been staring at me.

Now he's here. And he's not screwing around.

CHAPTER 6

ABRAM

"Is this man bothering you ladies?" My voice is flat and accent neutral. No hint of the Russian bite that usually sharpens my words. I don't want to be recognized. Not yet.

Jenna turns to me, unmistakable, even behind the mask. She's even more stunning here than she is in my office. The red hair, the tight little dress hugging those damn curves. Her friend's beautiful too—tall, model-thin—but Jenna burns like a flare in the dark. She looks up at me, mouth parted slightly, her expression flickering between surprise and sultry.

The man beside her stiffens. "Who the fuck are you?"

He shrugs my hand off his shoulder and squares up to me. He's taller than I expected, but he's sloppy. His pupils are blown wide, posture unsteady. He reeks of cheap cologne and beer.

"She's with me," he says. "Back the fuck off. I've got dibs."

Jenna snaps before I have to. "Nobody has dibs on me."

There's that fire. Real heat, not just a show put on to appear brave. Her voice cuts through clean and sharp, like a woman who's had enough bullshit for one night.

I want to smile, but the prick doesn't let up. He scoffs, gesturing at Jenna like she's something on a clearance rack. "Yeah, I guess you're right. No one has dibs because no one wants them."

The blood in my veins goes molten. I breathe in through my nose, slow and steady. The club isn't for violence. It's for pleasure. But every part of me wants to break this man's wrist just for touching her.

Instead, I lift a hand and snap my fingers once. Two bouncers materialize out of the shadows. Big, silent, efficient.

"Escort him out," I say. "And his friend."

"No, man, this is bullshit."

The bouncers don't move, waiting for my final word. "Escort them out," I repeat firmly."

The mouthy one's nostrils flare. His neck flushes an ugly shade of drunk-red, and he turns to me with a sneer. "Why don't *you* escort me out, fucker?"

I tilt my head, studying him like a puzzle. He's rail-thin, all bark, and probably thinks he's tougher than he really is because no one's ever shown him otherwise. I could drop him in two seconds flat, but I've been in enough fights to know better. Even the ones you expect to be easy can go sideways. A bad fall. A cracked skull on the edge of a table. One mistake and you're knee-deep in lawsuits and blood.

Not worth it. Not for trash like him.

"Last chance," I tell him. "Walk out. While you still can."

He's past listening. He swings his fist sloppily at me—a wide, drunken arc—all shoulder and no control. I pivot, smooth as oil, his momentum working against him. A quick sidestep and his ribs are exposed. I drive my fist into his gut with brutal efficiency. A muted grunt escapes him as all the air is driven out of his lungs. He crumples forward, gasping like a fish on a dock.

No one on the main floor notices. Good. That's exactly how I like it.

I grab his shoulder and place my mouth near his ear. "You've got two choices," I murmur. "Walk out or be wheeled out."

His buddy's frozen in place but not stupid. After a few seconds, he steps in and pulls his friend upright, steadying him as the fool wheezes and gurgles, still trying to catch his breath.

"We're going," the friend mutters. "We're going."

"Smart man," I say, brushing invisible dust from my sleeve.

They stagger away under the bouncers' silent escort, the stupid one still hunched over, still wheezing. I watch until they disappear into the hallway.

Only then do I turn back to her.

She stands nearby, those wide, startled eyes fixed on me. Her lips are slightly parted, as if she's forgotten how to close them. I let my shoulders ease, just a fraction.

"You alright?" I ask, my voice low and with the American accent.

She nods once. "Yeah. I think so."

She's breathless and a little flushed. The color in her cheeks does something dangerous to me. Makes me want to see what else I can coax out of her.

Her friend moves beside her, arm sliding around her waist protectively. She looks at me like she's trying to place me.

She won't.

I offer, "Drinks. On the house. Least I can do."

The friend smiles politely. "That's kind of you, but we're okay."

Jenna doesn't agree. "Actually, I'd love a drink. Thank you."

I smile beneath the edge of my mask, just enough for her to see it in my eyes. "Coming right up."

A quick snap of my fingers and the bartender nods.

I should leave. I should walk away now, while I still have control. But I don't. I stay.

She's watching me intently, trying to read the man behind the mask. I lean in, close enough to smell her perfume—light, feminine, and subtle. "Men like that," I murmur near her ear, "don't deserve to breathe the same air as you."

She shivers once. She tries to hide it with a sip of her drink, but I catch it.

"I need to go, um, freshen myself up," the friend says. "You guys get comfortable." She hurries away before either of us can say anything.

I take a seat. Jenna eases herself into the booth next to me. The silence stretches as we get used to being close to one another. No touching. No flirting. Just presence. I've found women melt faster under stillness than under pressure.

She looks at me, eyes flicking over my mask, then to my dyed beard. "Do I get your name?"

I pause. "You don't. That's part of the fun."

I spot a slight smile below the mask before she says, "I get it. Still feels weird, though. Names are the most basic information you get from someone when you first meet them. Before, you know..."

I raise an eyebrow. "You know *what*?"

Her eyes flash. "I mean, I'm not saying I'm doing anything like that tonight. Sorry. Still just trying to figure out exactly how to handle myself here."

I chuckle. "You're doing fine."

Her curves shift as she turns slightly toward me. My cock twitches. My fingers want her waist. My mouth wants her throat. But I behave.

"Oh, am I?"

I nod. "You are. And, what's more, I like the way you carry yourself."

She huffs a small, surprised breath. "What does that mean?"

"It means," I murmur, "you walk like someone who doesn't know how beautiful she is."

She frowns and looks down, smiling shyly like she doesn't believe me. That's alright. By the end of the night, she will.

I lean back slightly. "You're not used to compliments, are you?"

She shrugs. "Not the sincere kind."

"Then let me be clear. You're stunning. More than that, you're arresting."

Her eyes flick to mine, wary now. "*Arresting*, huh? Careful. That almost sounded poetic."

"I'm not the poetic type," I reply. "But I am the kind of man who says exactly what he means. The type of man who goes after exactly what he wants."

"And what is it you want?" she asks.

I tilt my head, allowing her to feel the heat of my attention like a hand sliding over her skin. "I want to know what makes you sigh," I say finally. "What makes you curse. What makes you lose that tight grip on your composure."

Her lips part slightly. A flush creeps up her throat, delicate and pink. "I don't even know your name," she says. It's not a protest, it's armor, thin and trembling.

I smile. Slow. Dangerous. "You don't need it. Not tonight."

She raises a brow. "Oh, so now you think you can tell me what I need?"

I lean in. "More than that. I want to *show* you what you need."

She exhales shakily, a sound that betrays just how off-kilter she feels. But she doesn't move away. She doesn't shut me down. Instead, she lifts her chin and meets my gaze.

"Are you always like this?"

"Only when I see something I want."

Another beat. Then her lips twitch, the sass I love reasserting itself. "And you always get what you want?"

"Usually," I admit, eyes dropping to her mouth.

She bites her lip, trying not to smile. Like she can't quite believe this is happening. I can see the battle behind her eyes—logic versus lust, good sense versus curiosity.

And she's losing.

She turns a little more toward me. Not much, just enough so her thigh brushes mine.

And fuck, I feel it everywhere.

Her friend returns a moment later. She's cool and composed, but her eyes flick quickly between us, clocking the tension. Jenna's gaze flicks to her like she's been jolted awake. Relief blooms in her expression, but there's something else layered beneath it. Disappointment, maybe. Like she didn't want the moment to end.

"Hey," her friend says, a hint of mischief in her voice. "I just met a very hot guy who asked me to join him." She lifts a brow at Jenna. "Unless you want me to stay?"

It's not really a question. Even I can hear the undercurrent—this is her out. The moment of truth. If she says yes, the night ends here. A polite thank you and a smile, and she'll be off with her chaperone, safe and untouched.

But if she says no...

Jenna looks between us. Takes a breath. "No," she says softly. "You go have fun."

Her friend beams, eyes turning back to me with a knowing glint. She didn't meet anyone. That was for Jenna's benefit. She gives her a quick hug, whispers something in her ear, then disappears into the crowd.

Once again we're alone.

I rise from my seat and extend my hand. "Join me upstairs? My booth is private, we'll be a little more secluded."

She hesitates before placing her fingers in mine. "Yeah. Sure."

Her hand is small. Soft and warm. Mine swallows it whole.

When she stands, a slow, volcanic surge of desire pushes heat through my limbs. Her dress clings to her body in all the right places, hugging her curves like a lover's touch. Her cleavage teases just above the neckline, her hips sway as she moves, and the scent of her wraps around me like silk.

My cock stirs to life, thickening with each beat of my pulse.

She doesn't notice. Or, if she does, she pretends not to.

I smile, grateful again for the mask.

Anonymous fun—that's what this place is about. What she came here for. What I came here for.

Except she's Jenna Ridley.

My assistant. My temptation. The line I swore I'd never cross.

And here she is, stepping willingly yet unknowingly into the fire.

I lead her through the club and up the stairs to my private booth overlooking the floor. The crowd parts around us without a word. Staff and patrons know better than to interfere. I hold her hand for as long as I can, fingers brushing against the throbbing pulse in her delicate wrist.

She doesn't pull away.

When we reach the booth, I let her slip inside first. She pauses as she takes in the view—the plush velvet, the candlelight glowing low and gold. I watch her closely, watch the way her mouth parts with a soft exhale. She's nervous. Excited.

Perfect.

I slide in beside her. Not touching. Not yet.

Anticipation weighs heavily between us.

She has no idea who I am. But I know exactly who she is.

And I'm going to make damn sure she never forgets what it feels like to be wanted.

Desired.

Ruined.

Mine.

CHAPTER 7

JENNA

My body is practically humming as I follow the masked stranger toward his booth, my heart pounding wildly with each step.

This isn't me, I don't do things like this. But tonight feels different. Tonight, I'm someone else entirely, someone daring enough to take risks.

We reach the plush sofa nestled in a darkened corner overlooking the club's main floor. He gestures for me to sit first, waiting until I've eased onto the soft leather before joining me. The energy around him is magnetic. His broad shoulders fill his suit effortlessly, the expensive fabric tailored perfectly to the powerful lines of his body.

I glance at him, frustrated by the mask hiding so much of his face. The dark beard beneath gives him a dangerously appealing look, emphasizing his strong jaw and perfectly shaped lips. He feels strangely familiar, but that must be my imagination—my subconscious trying to comfort me by inventing a connection.

I study him discreetly, catching the smooth confidence in every tiny gesture—the subtle tilt of his head as he regards me, the casual way he leans back, utterly at ease despite the charged atmosphere.

A waitress materializes beside us, her posture deferential, clearly recognizing my companion. "What would you like to drink?" she asks politely, turning to me first.

"Whiskey. Neat," I say, catching the way the stranger's lips curve slightly beneath his mask, as if pleased by my choice.

It's not my usual choice, but something about the moment has given me a strange courage.

"And for you, sir?"

"The usual."

The waitress vanishes into the darkness.

"The usual?" I ask.

He inclines his head slightly, eyes twinkling beneath his mask. "I come here often enough. They know what I prefer."

"They must," I say softly, teasingly, before leaning in just a little closer, emboldened by the anonymity we share. "You must be someone important to get service like that."

He chuckles, the sound rich and deep, vibrating through me. "I tip well."

Our drinks arrive swiftly, placed gently on the polished table before us. I pick up the crystal glass and take a cautious sip, savoring the silky warmth sliding down my throat. It's smoother than anything I've tasted before, hinting at the kind of money and influence that follows this man wherever he goes.

"Good?" he asks, clearly amused by my reaction.

"Very," I admit. I take another sip, feel it loosen the nerves knotting inside me. "Expensive taste."

"I like quality," he says simply, lifting his own glass and clinking it softly against mine. The subtle note of his voice, deep and controlled, catches my attention again.

There's a faint slip in his accent, something foreign hiding beneath an American drawl. It confuses me slightly, but I push it aside.

"You're nervous," he says, leaning closer, voice dropping to a conspiratorial whisper.

I let out a small laugh. "Is it that obvious?"

"A little." His voice is velvet-soft, comforting. "Relax."

Easier said than done. My spine feels rigid, and I suddenly realize I'm perched awkwardly at the edge of the sofa, tense, as if ready to bolt at any moment. Embarrassed, I make a show of leaning back against the cushions, forcing my muscles to loosen.

"I don't usually do things like this," I admit, my voice betraying more nerves than intended.

He tilts his head, curious. "Things like what, exactly?"

I gesture vaguely at the club, at him, flushing when I realize how silly I must look. "Coming to a place like this," I say. "Meeting strange men in masks."

A low laugh escapes him, warm and indulgent. "Then why tonight?"

I hesitate, staring into my whiskey for courage. "I don't know," I finally whisper, honesty spilling out unexpectedly. "Maybe because I want to be someone else tonight. Someone brave, daring, confident."

His gaze intensifies, locking onto mine with startling directness. "I think you underestimate yourself."

I laugh softly, deflecting. "You don't even know me."

"No," he agrees. "But I know you caught my eye the moment you walked in here."

Heat floods my cheeks. I shake my head, laughing nervously again, deflecting from my insecurity. "I don't exactly fit in here. Everyone's so... perfect."

He leans in, voice low and serious. "You're wrong. Your curves, your presence—that's what drew me to you. Believe me, you fit in more than you realize."

Warmth runs through me. "Still, not knowing names..." It's a weak protest, as if I'm trying to talk myself out of what I know I want.

He shifts closer, his presence overwhelmingly masculine, intoxicating. "Seriously, relax. Anonymity makes this little adventure that much more fun."

"No names, no faces," I say, my pulse racing faster, excitement eclipsing anxiety now. "Just for tonight."

His gaze holds mine, steady and intent, as though he can read every hidden desire pulsing beneath my skin. "Exactly."

The air thickens between us, charged with possibilities. His eyes drift to my lips, lingering there as if already tasting me. My breath hitches softly, betraying my craving for his touch.

He notices. His hand slowly lifts, the rough pad of his thumb tracing softly across my lower lip, making me tremble.

His voice is husky, dangerous, when he says, "You're so beautiful, and you don't even see it, do you?"

My mouth parts but no words come, only a sharp inhale as warmth floods low in my stomach. He watches my reaction, satisfied, and cups the back of my neck gently, drawing me in.

Our lips touch softly at first, a whisper of promise before deepening, his mouth warm and firm against mine. A shiver of need races through me as he claims me with slow, demanding kisses, his tongue tracing the seam of my lips until I open them for him.

The kiss grows urgent with each breathless gasp. I lean into him, intoxicated by his taste, whiskey and something darker, tempting. His hand slides from my neck down to my waist, holding me close, fingertips pressing possessively into the curve of my hip.

When he finally pulls back, his breath uneven, he murmurs softly, "You taste even sweeter than I imagined."

My heart pounds frantically. Boldness overtakes me, fueled by whiskey and adrenaline. "And you kiss like someone who always gets what he wants."

His chuckle is low, amused. "Usually. But tonight I'm more interested in what you want."

The raw hunger in his voice sends heat cascading through me. He shifts closer, thigh pressing against mine, his fingers drawing slow, deliberate circles on my hip.

"Tell me. What do you want?"

I swallow hard, trying to summon words through my foggy brain. "I–I want to feel good. To let go for once."

His eyes darken approvingly. "Then trust me to take care of you tonight."

His words unravel the last threads of hesitation within me.

"Yes," I whisper breathlessly. "I'll trust you."

He rewards me with another searing kiss, deeper this time, possessive. It makes me feel dizzy, and I surrender to him without reservation. The way he touches me, confident but tender, ignites a need in me I never knew existed.

When he finally eases back, his voice is rough with barely restrained desire. "Shall we take this somewhere more private?"

I nod, barely capable of coherent thought. "Please."

He stands and extends his hand to me. There's confidence in the gesture, quiet but unmistakable. I slip my hand into his, and the moment our fingers touch, my pulse stumbles.

Without a word, he leads me through a hallway lined with closed doors, each one elegant and mysterious. Soft moans drift from within—fragments of someone else's pleasure—

brushing against my skin like a whisper. My breath hitches, nerves tightening and coiling with anticipation.

At the very end of the corridor, he stops. He selects a door, opening it in a way that causes my insides to flutter. He waits for me to step in first.

The room is dim. A king-sized bed sits in the center, its dark sheets crisp and expensive-looking. Everything feels opulent and private, like the world outside doesn't exist.

The door closes behind us with a quiet click. When he locks it, something inside me unlocks. He turns to face me, his gaze roaming over my body—hungry, certain, claiming.

"Are you ready?" he asks, his voice low and smooth, commanding without pressure.

I nod. "Yes."

His mouth curves, showing his approval. He steps closer, his fingers brushing over my shoulders, then drifting slowly down my arms. Goosebumps rise in their wake.

"Good," he murmurs. "Because I plan to take my time with you."

Then his lips are on mine—hot, sure, possessive. I melt into him, all my uncertainty dissolving beneath the press of his body and the promise in his kiss.

Something shifts, and I know I'm not walking out of this room the same woman who walked in.

CHAPTER 8

ABRAM

Her lips part beneath mine with a breathy sigh, sweet and soft and just a little bit unsure—like she's never kissed a stranger before.

Good. I like the idea that I'm the first.

She tastes like whiskey and warm honey, and when I tilt my head and deepen the kiss, she moans—quiet, desperate, just for me. Her body presses flush against mine, all soft curves and barely contained want.

I slide one hand up her spine, the other anchoring at the small of her back, holding her there so she can feel me, feel what she's doing to me. My cock is already hard, straining beneath my trousers, and from the way she gasps against my mouth, she feels it too.

I kiss her again. Slower. Deeper. Her hands tangle in the front of my shirt then drift upward, tentative fingers brushing the edge of my mask.

I catch her wrists gently but firmly. "Mm-mm," I murmur, voice low and amused. "The masks stay on."

"So how often do you do this?" she teases, a sly smile playing at the corners of her mouth.

I chuckle, backing her gently toward the bed. "Often enough to appreciate what's in front of me," I reply. Vague but true. She doesn't recognize my voice and I don't want her to. Not yet.

We kiss again, and this time, I let my hands explore. Her zipper is at the small of her back, and I take my time pulling it down, feeling the tremble in her shoulders as the fabric loosens around her.

The dress slips down her frame like water, pooling at her feet. Beneath it, she's wearing a dark green lace bra and matching panties—elegant and just a little daring. My gaze slowly rakes over her, unapologetic. Pale skin, red hair falling in waves down her back, green eyes that flicker with both heat and hesitation.

She's exquisite.

She bites her bottom lip. "You're staring."

I take a step closer, slide my hand to the back of her neck, and draw her against me. She gasps when her body presses against the full length of mine—against how hard I am for her.

"I'm doing more than staring," I murmur into her ear. "I'm memorizing."

She lets out a shaky laugh. "What if I don't measure up to your expectations?"

I growl softly, nipping at her jaw. "You've already ruined them, *malyshka*." I grab her hand and press it to my clothed erection. "Does that feel like disappointment?"

Shit. I spoke Russian. Did she notice?

Her breath hitches. She shakes her head.

"Didn't think so."

I kiss her again, harder this time, hungrier, hoping she missed the slip. Her arms wrap around my neck, bolder now.

I feel the shift in her, the way her fingers curl into my shirt with purpose, not hesitation. After pushing my jacket off, she slides her hands to my chest, finds the buttons, and starts undoing them, one by one, her touch light and reverent.

I let her.

When the shirt falls open, her eyes drink me in—my chest, my stomach, the dark hair trailing down. The ink on my right pec draws her attention most. She reaches out, tracing the design with gentle fingers. It's a black, intricately-drawn eagle. The ink is old, done in Russia when I was barely more than a boy.

"What does it mean?" she asks, voice husky, curious.

I glance down at her, eyes dark beneath the mask. "It means I'll never forget where I came from," I murmur. I lean in, brushing a kiss to her temple. "And that some things are earned in blood."

She doesn't press. Smart girl.

Her hands move lower, sliding over my stomach, grazing the edge of my waistband. I watch her green eyes light up with lust, lips slightly parted, as she pushes the fabric down. My slacks hit the floor, followed by my boxer briefs. When her hand curls around my length, I let out a low, guttural sound.

Fuck.

She strokes me, tentative but hungry, and for one dizzying second I feel like a beast—untamed, aching to rut. But I rein it in. She's not a quick fix. She's not a blur I'll forget by morning. I want to savor her. Every curve. Every sound. Every breath.

"Enough of that," I growl, and before she can blink, I lift her into my arms.

She gasps, arms flying around my neck, laughter spilling from her lips. Her skin is flushed—rosy and warm, her pale complexion blooming with arousal. I want to mark every inch of her.

I carry her to the couch—sleek, dark velvet—and ease her down onto it. Her hair fans out like fire. I kneel beside her and reach behind, fingers slipping beneath the clasp of her bra. I unhook it quickly, easily.

She tenses for a second, then lets it fall.

Christ.

Her breasts spill free, full and pale as porcelain, the pink tips peaked. I lean in, taking one into my mouth and sucking gently. She gasps and arches into me. I move to the other, lavishing it with my tongue before pulling it between my teeth, just enough to make her moan.

"You're perfect," I say against her skin.

Her hands cradle the back of my head as I move lower, trailing kisses down her trembling belly while her hips squirm beneath me. When I place my thumbs under the lace waistband of her panties and peel them down, she lifts her hips in offering.

And then she's bare. Completely, gloriously bare. Her perfect pink slit is glistening for me. I can't wait to taste it.

I pause, drinking her in. Then I kiss the inside of her thigh. Once, twice, higher each time.

She whimpers.

I look up at her, her eyes hazy with lust. She shivers, thighs parting.

I take my time before lowering my mouth between them, my breath warm against her slick heat. She's so wet, so ready for me. One long, slow lick, and I feel her jolt as her fingers clench the cushions, a sharp breath escaping her lips.

God, she tastes like ambrosia. Sweet, earthy, heady. I want to drown in it.

I place my arms under her thighs, holding her open, anchoring her to me as my tongue moves with unhurried precision. Every flick, every stroke, every soft suck of her clit is measured and relentless. I want to undo her.

She arches her back, unraveling while her fingers tangle in her hair. As her thighs tense and shake, I glance up to watch her. She's flushed, eyes glazed, chest heaving. Her lips are parted in a gasp, and when I press two fingers inside her, curling them just so while I suck her clit harder, she comes undone.

Her moan rips through the quiet, ragged and beautiful.

I keep my mouth on her as she rides it out, one hand cupping her breast, thumb grazing the nipple until her body shudders and stills.

Only then do I stand, licking her from my lips, savoring her taste. She lies sprawled across the couch, flushed and glowing, chest rising and falling in uneven waves. Her curls are a halo around her face, and her green eyes—my God, her eyes —are hazy and full of something close to wonder.

She's never looked more beautiful.

Never looked more mine.

She blinks slowly and asks, breathless, "What do you want now?"

I could tell her the truth: everything.

But instead I just smile and let the animal in me answer.

I grab her hips and turn her firmly, guiding her until she's on her knees, hands braced on the back of the couch. Her ass is high in the air, full and perfect, my hands spreading over her curves with reverence and hunger.

She arches her back, her hair cascading down as she looks over her shoulder at me with those wide, lust-drunk eyes.

"Please," she whispers, voice trembling. "I want to feel you."

I want to give her everything. Every inch. Every filthy promise I've ever made in the dark.

I reach for the condom in my wallet, slipping it on with practiced ease. Even now—especially now—I won't take a risk with her.

I line myself up, my hands settling back on her hips. She's still fluttering from her orgasm, and when I push in, inch by aching inch, she cries out, loud and desperate.

Fuck, she's tight. Hot. Soaked. I grit my teeth and bury myself all the way, filling her completely.

Her head drops forward with a moan and I give her a moment. My hands caress her lower back, her waist, her hips.

I begin to move, slowly at first, watching the way her body responds—arching, pushing back, welcoming me.

She feels like heaven. Sounds like it, too. Moaning, fingers clawing the cushions, her body taking everything I give her.

She's so goddamn responsive—every moan, every tremble, every time she pushes back against me like she's begging for more. I can barely hold on. The tight heat of her wrapped around me, her body slick and welcoming, is making it hard to think, to breathe.

I grab her hips, rolling mine in a slow, grinding thrust, deep and steady. She cries out, arching back into me. I do it again. And again.

"You feel that?" I growl, voice low, wrecked. "This cock was made for you."

She moans, raw and breathy. "God, yes..."

"That's it. Take it all. Every inch." I lean forward, one hand sliding up her back, gripping the nape of her neck. "You're mine tonight. Say it."

She gasps, hips rocking against me as she chokes out, "I'm yours."

I spank her lightly, but firmly enough to make her jolt and gasp. The sound echoes deliciously off the walls. Her ass is perfect, red blooming across her pale skin.

"You like that?" I murmur, rubbing the spot.

She nods frantically. "Please. Don't stop."

My control snaps. I move harder now, the slap of skin loud and rhythmic. One hand stays at her hip, grounding her. The other slides up, cupping her breast, pinching her nipple as I thrust deeper. She lets out a strangled sound—desperation and pleasure tangled together.

"You're so tight," I grit out. "So fucking good."

She's close. I feel it in the way her body clenches around me, in the soft gasps growing frantic, in the way she braces herself like she's preparing for an impending storm.

"I want you to come for me," I say, bending her over further, my mouth brushing her ear. "Come all over my cock. Let me feel it."

That's all it takes.

She shatters around me with a cry, trembling violently as I hold her still and fuck her through it. Her walls pulse around me, milking me, and I almost lose it right then and there.

But I need to see her. I pull out, gently flipping her onto her back. She's a vision—flushed and panting, hair wild against the dark fabric, breasts rising and falling, a glistening between her thighs.

"Fuck," I whisper, staring down at her. "Look at you."

I slide between her legs again, her thighs parting willingly. I thrust in with one smooth stroke, burying myself deep.

She arches with a strangled gasp, nails dragging down my back. I find her mouth, kissing her hard as I thrust, hips snapping, sweat starting to bead at the base of my neck. This angle, this closeness, drives me mad. I grip the back of her thigh, angling her just right, driving in again, harder.

"Mine," I growl against her mouth. "This sweet little pussy is mine tonight."

"Yes," she whimpers, clinging to me. "Please. Don't. Stop."

"Never," I rasp, hand braced beside her head as I fuck her with everything I have. "You're fucking perfect. You know that? Every inch of you."

Her head tips back, mouth open, legs locked around my waist. The tension coils within, tight and furious. She squeezes around me, another orgasm building fast. Our bodies move in frantic unison, every sound she makes pushing me closer.

And then it hits—her release—crashing into her like a wave, pulling me down with her. I groan into her neck, hips stuttering as I spill into the condom, teeth clenched, every muscle taut with pleasure.

We collapse together, our breaths tangled.

I stay buried in her for a beat, unwilling to break the moment. Then slowly, I slide out, rolling off the condom and tossing it into the nearby bin.

Something about it feels... off. A looseness I don't usually notice. But I don't think about it too long.

She curls into me instinctively, her leg sliding over my hips, her cheek pressed to my chest, fingers splayed softly across my ribs.

I exhale, head falling back. Fuck, she feels good like this. Warm, soft, still trembling slightly. Her hair tickles my skin. I wrap an arm around her waist, pulling her closer, kissing the top of her head.

She fits against me *too* well. Like she was built for me.

And that's dangerous.

Because I know what this was supposed to be. One night. A faceless, anonymous encounter, just like a hundred others I've had in this club. But this? Her?

She's not faceless or anonymous. And she's definitely not forgettable.

I know damn well I'm not done with her.

I shouldn't want her again.

But I do.

And I'll have her.

CHAPTER 9

JENNA

His chest rises and falls beneath me, all that solid muscle stretched out under my cheek. My fingers drift absentmindedly across the ink etched over his right pec —sharp black lines, an eagle with a crown, wings flared, claws out. It looks old-world. Regal. Dangerous.

Just like him.

I stare at it for a moment longer, trying to commit every detail to memory before lifting my head.

What the hell just happened?

I had sex. With a stranger. Masked. In a private club room. I didn't even get his name, just some evasive charm and a body that could've been sculpted by the gods.

And it was amazing.

No, amazing isn't the right word. That man *handled* me. Like he already knew every inch of me. Like he'd been starving and I was the only thing he'd ever wanted to taste. I should feel... ashamed? Nervous?

Instead, I feel like my bones have been melted into the cushions and I want him again. Right now.

A wicked part of me wants to slide my hand between his legs, take hold of him, and show him exactly what round two is supposed to look like. But then I hear it—his breathing. Slow. Even.

He's asleep.

Figures. Of course he gets to sleep like the dead after wrecking me into a state of post-orgasmic enlightenment.

I glance at his masked face. God help me, I want to see him. Just a little peek, just enough to know if he's actually as gorgeous as my brain wants to believe he is under all that leather and mystery.

But I don't move.

Because if I see him—if I *know*—then this stops being whatever it is. A wild night. A secret. Something I can hold onto, pull out of the vault when I need a little personal time and a very specific memory.

His voice. It slipped a few times. Not just a deeper timbre but a shift into Russian. One word when he was deep inside me and it made things even hotter. Now it nags at the edges of my brain.

Why does he feel so damn familiar?

Maybe it's just wishful thinking or maybe my subconscious is trying to justify sleeping with a stranger by pretending he wasn't one. But there's something there, something I can't quite place. Like I've seen him before. Heard him before. Like a dream you only half remember upon waking but it leaves fingerprints on your day.

Still, I don't lift the mask.

Instead, I slide carefully out of bed—sore in the best way, legs still shaky—and start pulling on my dress. It's wrinkled, and it smells like sex and whiskey. I slip it on, ignoring the ache between my thighs and the absurd smile threatening the corners of my mouth.

I glance at him once more before I leave. Naked. Stretched out. Beautiful.

Burn that into my memory. File it away for another day.

I close the door with a soft click and walk back to the front of the club. My heels click across the tile like a metronome keeping time for the chaos still pounding in my chest.

I don't know his name. I don't know his face. But what it felt like to be wanted like that is addictive.

The hallway feels endless. I pass door after door, each one muffling sounds that leave no question as to what's going on behind them. Moans, cries, the soft slapping of bodies meeting, gasps of breath tangled with whispered filth. One room bursts briefly into laughter—a woman's high giggle layered over a man's growl—and I can't help but wonder if I sounded like that only a few minutes ago.

I moaned in there. I gasped. I shook. I came so hard I saw stars.

Claire. *Shit.* I left her alone for way too long.

I pick up the pace, anxiety starting to nip at the back of my neck. What if she's pissed? What if she left? What if she's been cornered by some creep and she's out there throwing hands in the name of friendship?

I make it back into the main room, scanning for the tall brunette in the white dress. My eyes find her almost instantly—still at our table, drink in hand, not alone. There's a man with her. Tall and broad, dressed sharply in black with a striking silver-and-black domino mask shaped like a wolf's snarl. He leans toward her in fascination, but when Claire spots me, her whole face lights up. She's up and out of her seat before I can say a word, her drink left behind as she practically sprints toward me.

"Jenna!" she squeals, grabbing both my arms, eyes wide with anticipation. "You little ho!"

My jaw drops. "What?"

"Oh, don't play innocent with me." She leans in, speaking loudly enough to make me want to sink into the floor. "You obviously had sex."

My whole face ignites. "How would you even know that?" I hiss, tugging her toward the side so the entire club doesn't hear.

She laughs. "Your hair, babe. It's got that just-been-fucked chaos going on. Like, full blown sex aftermath. Your lipstick's gone. And your dress, it's all wrinkled and you're glowing like you just won the lottery—the prize being twelve orgasms."

I blink. "It was definitely not twelve."

Claire arches a brow. "But more than one?"

I look away, trying not to smile. "Shut up."

She's cackling now. I catch my reflection in the mirror above the bar. My red curls are in full rebellion, wild and tumbling like I've just emerged from a wind tunnel. My eyes are still a little glassy. And sure enough, my lipstick is totally gone.

I remember the moment when his hands fisted in my hair, tugging just hard enough to make me gasp as he took me from behind. No wonder it's a mess.

"Jesus," I mutter.

Claire slaps my arm playfully, grinning like a cat who just swallowed the canary. "Girl, that man rearranged your soul. I knew you were gonna have fun tonight."

I shake my head, trying not to laugh She was absolutely right.

"So," I say, giving Claire a sly look as we weave through the crowd toward the exit. "What about you? Did you have any fun while I was off being the worst friend ever?"

She shrugs, flicking her hair over her shoulder like it's no big deal. "Not really. A few tried, but no one caught my eye." She makes a face.

I blink at her. "Seriously? That wolf mask guy was all over you."

Claire snorts. "Please. He smelled like vanilla protein powder and asked me if I've ever done ayahuasca."

"What's that?"

She waves her hand dismissively. "Drugs."

I laugh. "Damn, I'm sorry. I totally ditched you."

"Babe," she says, waving me off. "This night was about you. I was just on escort duty. Mission accomplished, clearly."

I flush and nudge her with my shoulder. "Hey, don't say 'mission accomplished' like I was *that* desperate to get laid."

She smirks. "Weren't you?"

I roll my eyes, though part of me is grateful for how lightly she's handling this. Because honestly I'm still a little shaky. I'm sore in places I forgot I had muscles, my heart hasn't quite figured out how to beat normally again, and everything in me feels like it's been rewired.

"I'm ready to go," I admit. "I don't regret it. At all. But I think I hit my threshold."

Claire smiles. "Girl, your threshold got body-slammed tonight. Let's get out of here."

As we make our way toward the front, I catch myself glancing back over my shoulder, toward the hall of doors. Searching for... I don't even know. A hint of him. A shadow. A familiar stance in the crowd.

But I don't see him anywhere. Nothing but lights and strangers.

"Is it weird that I feel kinda bad for leaving him?" I ask. "As far as I know, he's still sleeping in there."

Claire arches a brow. "You mean the guy who railed you into a religious experience?"

I give her a look. "He was very... attentive."

"Oh, I'm sure!" She laughs as we step into the cool, desert night air. "But let's not pretend this was a romantic weekend getaway. It's a sex club. If he wakes up all sad and alone, maybe he should've remembered where the fuck he was before falling asleep."

I grin, but there's something bittersweet blooming in my chest. Like I left behind a piece of myself in that room.

Or maybe he took it.

The Uber ride back is quiet for about ten seconds before Claire turns on me like a lion with a gazelle.

"Okay, spill."

"Nope," I say, gazing out the window like I'm suddenly fascinated by streetlights.

"Don't you dare go all coy on me, Jenna Rose. I want details. Positions. Dialogue. How big was he?"

"Jesus," I laugh, glancing at the driver. "Claire."

She leans in. "Fine, just tell me he was hot."

"He was. He was also older," I say. "Maybe forties. But definitely unfairly hot. Big. Strong. Confident. Knew exactly what he was doing."

Claire lets out a dreamy sigh. "God, I love that for you."

By the time we pull up in front of my apartment building, the nervous buzz is gone, replaced with a warm hum in my chest, thighs, and everywhere else.

I hug her tightly before slipping out. "Thank you. Really. Tonight was more than I expected and just what I needed."

Claire winks. "You're not off the hook, by the way. I want a full debrief tomorrow."

I laugh, flipping her off as I shut the car door.

My building is dark and quiet when I step inside. Boring compared to what I just left—no scent of sex curling through the air.

It's home.

I kick off my shoes, unzip my dress, and pour myself a small glass of wine while I stand barefoot in my kitchen, trying to process what the hell just happened.

I close my eyes.

His hands flash in my mind. Large, strong, gripping my hips as he pulled me against him. The way he guided my mouth to his, fingers threaded through my hair like he needed the anchor. His voice—low and dark, speaking Russian when he got close, too far gone to pretend anymore.

A single word, whispered into the crook of my neck.

Malyshka.

I take a sip of wine, but it doesn't help. My brain won't stop connecting the dots I don't want to see.

The accent. The size. The hands. The way he moved— controlled, precise, powerful.

Malyshka.

The name he called me in mid-thrust.

I frown, set the glass down, and reach for my phone. I try to sound it out in my head then type a few clumsy phonetic guesses into Google. The last one pings Russian.

I click the translation result and stare at the word.

Baby.

My breath catches.

It means baby.

A tiny smile tugs at my lips before I can stop it. There's something unexpectedly tender about him calling me that without thinking I'd understand. Like he forgot himself for a second.

I've seen those hands before. Felt that same weight when he entered the room. The unspoken demand that makes people sit up straighter. The barely leashed danger beneath every calculated word.

No.

I shake my head, but the thought slams into me like a truck.

Did I just fuck my boss?

CHAPTER 10

ABRAM

An hour later, I'm sitting alone in the booth, the low thrum of bass vibrating through the velvet walls around me, eyes fixed on the drink I've barely touched. The glass is sweating, condensation pooling beneath it, but I don't move.

I'd been awake the whole time. I could feel the way she was looking at me—curious, hesitant—like maybe she'd been seconds away from lifting the mask and revealing my secret. I couldn't let that happen.

I'd already slipped. I'd forgotten the damn accent. Let my Russian bleed through. I remember her eyes fluttering shut, lips parted, the soft little gasp she made when I whispered *malyshka* against her skin.

Beautiful but dangerous.

Because if she hadn't been dizzy with orgasm, if she'd been thinking clearly, she might have recognized my voice. Might have put it all together.

And then what?

Then I'd be the man who fucked his assistant in a club he's about to purchase while masked, anonymous, and completely goddamn addicted to the way she tastes.

I drag a hand down my face.

Jenna Ridley.

Jesus Christ.

She's the sexiest woman I've ever had in my life—period. And that includes Paris. That includes Kiev. That includes the goddamn model in Mykonos whose name I never learned. Jenna tops all of them.

She's fire and defiance; tight, wet heat that clamped around me like her body was made for mine. That mouth, those curves, the way her hips rolled beneath my hands like she wanted me to wreck her.

Watching her get dressed was its own kind of torture. Her back arched as she leaned down to pick up her dress, that lush ass high in the air, dim light sliding over smooth, milk-white skin. Her thighs were trembling faintly, the aftermath of what we'd done.

My cock—fucking traitor—hardened again at the sight of her. She had no idea I was watching.

I almost pulled her back into the bed. Almost grabbed her by the waist, flipped her over, and taken her one more time —hard and messy, no slow buildup this time. Just possession. Just the need to feel her shatter around me again, her voice raw from moaning my name.

But she didn't want a conversation. Didn't want a reveal. She wanted to leave clean, walk out with the memory intact.

And maybe that's for the best.

Because if she'd stayed, if she'd unmasked me, if she'd looked me in the eye and said my name...

I would've been lost.

Goddamn it.

I shift in my seat, trying to adjust the tight pressure in my slacks. It's no use. She's gone, but her fucking ghost is still here—on my hands, on my tongue, in the ache still throbbing at the base of my spine.

I have to see her on Monday, sit across from her at the conference table, pass her reports, and assign her tasks. Act like I didn't spend an hour with my cock buried in her while she begged for more.

I'm fucked.

The next day...

The morning sun over the Vegas suburbs is clean and gold, the kind of morning that makes the desert look like it's been freshly painted.

I pull up to the gate of my sister Tatiana and her husband Denis's house a few minutes before ten, mimosas-in-the-making tucked in a canvas bag on the passenger seat.

The Popov house sits on a quiet, tree-lined cul-de-sac where the lawns are trimmed within an inch of their lives and the stone façades pretend not to belong to Vegas. It's tasteful, expensive, secure. Bratva money done right.

Tatiana's always been the classiest of the three of us. She could've married into any crime family in the western hemisphere and still made them look like royalty.

Denis is already waiting, swinging the door open with the easy grin he reserves for Saturday mornings and soccer matches. He's been married to my sister almost ten years, and in that time, I've come to trust him like blood.

"Mimosas?" he asks, eyeing the bag.

"As promised," I say, handing it off. "Where are the gremlins?"

"In the kitchen," he says. "Tatiana's letting them destroy her clean floor."

As soon as I step inside, the smell hits me—warm maple, butter, pancakes. I follow it to the kitchen, pausing in the doorway.

My twin nieces, Sofia and Lilia, Tatiana and Denis's girls, are parked in matching highchairs, cheeks flushed and hair sticking up in wild brown curls. One of them—I still can't tell them apart—is gleefully banging a spoon on her tray while the other laughs with food smeared all over her mouth.

My other sister Anya's son, Charles, four years old and already plotting global domination, sits at the table in a Paw Patrol T-shirt. He's got a tiny bite of syrup-drenched pancake poised in his fingers. Just as I enter, he leans over and sneaks it into Lilia's mouth like he's feeding a pet kitten.

"Uncle Abram!" he calls the second he sees me.

I crouch beside him and ruffle his curls. "You bribing your cousins for loyalty again?"

He shrugs, syrup on his chin. "They like pancakes."

I reach for a napkin and swipe it off his face. "Smart man."

The girls both babble nonsense at me, arms waving, and I make a show of inspecting them. "You two behaving?"

They giggle in unison, and I feel the same deep, anchoring warmth I feel every Saturday. These three little people are the lights of my life. Not the businesses. Not the power. This. Sticky fingers and pancakes.

Tatiana's voice floats in from the hallway, asking Denis if he remembered to put on music. He didn't. He never does.

I don't care. The soundtrack of this house is already perfect.

Denis pops the champagne cork with practiced ease, catching my eye with the kind of teasing, older-brother smirk he's perfected over the years.

"You keep showing up with booze, Abram, but still no babies. When exactly are you planning to catch up to the rest of us?"

I shake my head, leaning back in my chair. "Careful, Denis. I might start bringing cheaper champagne."

He chuckles, pouring smoothly into the waiting glasses. "I'll risk it. You really need someone to take care of you."

Tatiana laughs softly, sliding a plate of perfectly arranged fruit toward her twin girls. She glances at me warmly, eyes sparkling with gentle mischief. "For someone who claims to hate people, you're unnaturally good with children, Abram."

I shrug off the compliment, feeling an unexpected pang hitting inside. My mind drifts to Jenna before I can stop it. For a split second, I don't want to sit here pretending I'm untouchable. Pretending softness, family, and warmth hold no appeal. Jenna's face, smiling sleepily beside me, haunts the edges of my thoughts.

I push it down fast, forcing my trademark smirk back onto my lips.

"Well," I say, tipping my champagne flute toward Denis, "if you're really interested, maybe I should tell you about what happened at my new club last night?"

Tatiana throws a dish towel at me without even looking up from the eggs she's plating, her aim surprisingly accurate. "Absolutely not. Not in front of my pancakes."

Denis snorts, leans back, and shakes his head. "Come on, Abram, have some respect for the sanctity of breakfast."

Anya's husband Mikail, pouring coffee beside Denis, joins in with an easy grin. "Again with the club? At this point, you must be angling for a loyalty card."

Charles bursts into giggles, his syrup-coated fingers pointing at me gleefully. He may not understand the joke, but his laughter is infectious. Even Tatiana can't help but chuckle, rolling her eyes playfully.

"Uncle Abram, you're silly," Charles announces, slipping from his chair and scrambling into my lap without hesitation.

I catch him easily, steadying him as he nestles comfortably against my chest, tiny fingers gripping my shirt. Sofia leans forward from her highchair, holding out a sticky hand covered in mashed strawberries. I reach over, wiping it clean with the napkin Mikail passes my way. Lilia watches intently, her small, round face fascinated by the action.

"No need for loyalty cards," I say. "In a few weeks, I'll be the official owner."

Tatiana arches an elegant brow, exchanging a glance with Denis. "Seeing you with these kids? Maybe you should open a day care instead, and not a... whatever sort of business this club happens to be."

"I have my moments," I concede, gently bouncing Charles in my lap until he squeals with delight.

The door swings open and Anya sweeps into the kitchen, a stylish hurricane balancing a designer diaper bag and a large bakery box filled with pastries.

She pauses beside me, dropping a quick, affectionate kiss onto my cheek. "There's our mysterious bachelor prince," she teases, eyes twinkling. "Good morning, Abram."

"Morning, Anya."

The kitchen settles into a comfortable hum filled with familiar chaos: Tatiana plating food, Anya managing the kids with practiced ease, Denis and Mikail exchanging amused glances, the children's laughter filling every corner of the space.

Eventually, as plates are cleared and coffee refilled, Tatiana and Anya rise together, murmuring something about diaper changes and baths. They drift out of the kitchen, leaving the men alone.

The atmosphere shifts instantly, warmth replaced by an ominous tension. Denis sets his coffee cup down carefully and meets my gaze. "We have a problem. The Agostis were at Sorella last night, asking questions about protection fees. Bold, public."

The rule against talking shop at breakfast never lasts for long.

Mikail leans forward, his expression darkening. "Word on the street is that Nico is making his move. Trying to flex muscle while his father's too sick to object. He thinks it's his time."

My posture shifts. I'm no longer Uncle Abram, no longer playing nice over champagne and syrup-covered toddlers. My voice drops, hard-edged with authority.

"They think we've gone soft. We'll show them we haven't. Monday morning, eight o'clock sharp, my office. We'll discuss this further then."

Denis and Mikail nod. The understanding between us is immediate, unspoken. Family time may be sacred, but come Monday, we'll remind the Agostis precisely who runs Vegas.

Moments later, the tension breaks as Anya and Tatiana return, arms filled with freshly washed children, their laughter softening the edges of my mood. I stand up, gently lifting Charles and placing him back in his chair. Turning, I drop tender kisses onto each of my nieces' heads, inhaling their clean, powdery scent.

Charles wraps his small arms around my waist, holding on tight. "Bye, Uncle Abram. Come back soon, okay?"

"I will, buddy." I glance around at my sisters, their husbands, these children who've somehow managed to become the best part of my week. A flicker of something bittersweet curls in my chest.

This is supposed to be what I want. Family. Stability.

Again, Jenna's face flashes in my mind—soft and vulnerable beside me, a curl of fiery hair tracing her cheek.

I shut it down quickly, pulling on the familiar mask of cool detachment. "Next time, I'll bring more champagne."

Denis laughs warmly, clapping me on the shoulder as I head for the door. "See you Monday."

I step outside into the bright Nevada sunshine, breathing deeply.

Family man or Bratva kingpin.

I can't be both.

And as long as Jenna Ridley's in the picture, I'm starting to fear I might not be either.

CHAPTER 11

JENNA

The angry buzz of my phone slices through my dream, yanking me awake so harshly I nearly roll straight off the mattress. I blink groggily at the dark ceiling, disoriented and frustrated. The room is still pitch-black, shadows looming around the edges.

My alarm is set for early, but definitely not this early. Squinting against the darkness, I roll over and grab my phone, fumbling as the harsh light from the screen blinds me momentarily.

It's not the alarm. It's worse.

A text message from Abram time stamped 5:37 a.m.

Be in the office by 6:45. I need your help preparing for an important meeting.

I stare at the screen, incredulous and still half-asleep.

"Are you fucking kidding me?" My voice is a raspy croak in the quiet bedroom.

I flop back against the pillows, tossing my phone toward the far edge of my mattress in protest. For a brief, rebellious moment, I seriously consider ignoring it. Letting the text slip into oblivion and claiming I overslept when my actual alarm goes off in an hour.

It's tempting, deliciously tempting.

But I know it would never fly. Abram's built-in bullshit detector is practically military-grade—he'd spot the lie the second I stepped through the office doors. There's not enough concealer in Vegas to hide how I'd blush under his scrutiny.

Besides, as much as Abram is a certified pain in the ass, he's the best-paying pain in the ass I've ever worked for. Amazing salary, full benefits, bonuses that are practically scandalous. I can't afford to lose this job because I'm cranky from being dragged out of bed before sunrise.

Groaning in defeat, I roll out of bed, feet hitting the floor reluctantly. Goosebumps race across my thighs, exposed beneath my long, oversized sleep shirt. I shuffle toward the kitchen, yawning, already mentally calculating how little time I'll have for anything other than getting clean and dressed.

Coffee first. Always.

I punch the button on my Keurig, the comforting hiss and gurgle of water filtering through the otherwise silent apartment. The smell of French roast begins to trickle through the air, waking me enough to remember I should already be showering. *Dammit.*

As I step out of my clothes, the cool air sends another shiver racing down my spine. I glance toward the bathroom mirror, frowning slightly at my disheveled hair and sleepy expression. Turning on the shower, I let the hot water run, waiting for the bathroom to fill with steam before stepping in.

Waiting in the chilly air, my traitorous mind drifts—as it has obsessively all weekend—to Friday night.

It was amazing. More than amazing, actually. More like transformative. Heat rises to my cheeks, flooding my skin with a blush. I've relived every moment a thousand times since Friday—every touch, every sigh, every electrifying thrust.

I've had good sex before, but nothing like that. Nothing that intense or wild. Nothing so... overwhelming. That man, with his strong hands, sinful tongue, and perfect command of my body made every other man I've been with seem like amateurs fumbling in the dark.

Even now, days later, my body clenches at the memory of his mouth on me, his voice rasping that Russian word against my skin as he drove inside me, deep and mercilessly satisfying.

My stomach flips uneasily as the realization slams into me yet again. The details line up too well: tall, muscular, shaved head, meticulously groomed beard, a Russian accent slipping through when he lost control.

No. Absolutely not. It couldn't have been.

I shake my head, stepping into the hot spray, gasping softly as the heat floods over my shoulders, washing away the chill from my skin but not the uncertainty in my mind.

Abram can't possibly be the only sexy, shaven-head, bearded man in Vegas who occasionally slips into Russian during sex. The odds seem slim, but this is Vegas. Weird coincidences happen here all the time.

I scrub shampoo into my hair a bit too aggressively, as if I can physically wash away my unsettling suspicions.

Because if that masked man was Abram, I don't know what I'll do.

I freeze momentarily, the spray hitting my back as the implications crash through me again. It means my boss—the man I spend every day trying not to throttle—knows exactly how I sound when I climax. Knows how I taste. Knows exactly what kind of filthy, needy, desperate sounds I make when I'm on the edge.

Fuck.

Heat spreads lower, pooling between my thighs, and I curse myself for being so susceptible to him. Even the suspicion of it being Abram is enough to make me squirm in the shower.

Forcing the thoughts aside, I rinse quickly, wanting to get on my way ASAP. *Work*, I remind myself. Abram wanted me there early for something important. This isn't the day to be distracted by a spectacular one-night stand.

But the more I think about it, the harder it is to believe it wasn't him. I stand still, letting my thoughts get carried away.

The hot water streams down my back, soothing tired muscles but doing absolutely nothing to calm the fire still burning between my thighs. My mind drifts right back to Friday night. To that room.

To him.

I close my eyes, tipping my head back beneath the spray. In an instant, he's with me. Not a fantasy exactly, but more like a vivid memory that refuses to fade.

It feels so real.

I imagine him showing up at my apartment unannounced, uninvited, yet completely welcome. My pulse quickens, breath coming in shallow little pants as the fantasy unfolds.

He's behind me now, stepping silently into the shower. I feel the brush of his fingertips on my hips before I even see him. His big, strong hands grip me possessively, sliding smoothly over wet skin.

"You thought you could run away from me, *kotenok*?" he murmurs darkly, his voice a sensual rasp. I'd come across the word when finding a translation for the other one.

Kitten.

"I–I didn't run," I stammer, feeling heat flood through me. "I left."

He chuckles, low and dangerous, mouth against my ear. "You can't leave when I'm not done with you."

My heart thunders, knees trembling slightly. In reality, I trail my fingertips along my collarbone, slipping downward, brushing over my breasts as I picture his hands following the same path. In my mind, he cups them, pinching my nipples until I gasp.

"Tell me," he growls softly, his accent thick, almost punishing. "Did you spend all weekend thinking about how I fucked you?"

"Yes," I whisper. My hand slips lower, teasing gently between my legs, mirroring what I imagine he'd do.

His imaginary hands slip down my body, calloused palms tracing curves he's already claimed once.

"Then show me how much you missed it. Touch yourself. Let me see."

I groan softly as my fingers slide between my thighs, finding myself slick and swollen. It's been torture not doing this all weekend, denying myself this release. I rub small, firm circles over my clit, matching the intensity of the imagined pressure of his hand.

In my fantasy, he's pressed hard against me, his cock thick and heavy between us. My fingers glide against my clit, and I can hear his imagined grunt of approval.

"Just like that, Jenna. Fuck, you're so wet for me already."

Imagining hearing those words nearly pushes me over the edge. I lean against the shower wall, one hand steadying myself as my other hand works faster, aching. I picture him dropping to his knees, spreading my thighs further apart, demanding access.

The feel of his tongue is vivid, scorching, licking slow circles, his beard scratching deliciously against my legs. He eats me like he can't get enough, strong hands gripping my hips, holding me exactly where he wants me.

"Oh God," I whisper aloud, hips bucking into my hand as my body strains toward release.

In my mind, he's relentless, growling against my pussy. "You taste so fucking good, Jenna. You belong to me now. Every inch of this beautiful body is mine."

My breath catches sharply as I rub faster, tension winding impossibly tighter. My fantasy shifts suddenly, vividly. He stands, turning me around roughly, pressing the front of my body against the cool tile, his cock thick and hard, rubbing between my ass cheeks. I tremble beneath his touch.

He grips my wet hair, tugging gently but insistently. "Spread your legs wider for me."

I obey, breath hitching. He positions himself against my entrance, teasing me, sliding just the head inside before withdrawing.

"Say it," he commands, voice dark and rough. "Tell me you want me to fuck you."

"I want you," I gasp out loud, fingers frantically working myself toward climax. "Abram, please, fuck me."

With one savage thrust, he's deep inside, thick and stretching, claiming me again. My mind and body synchronize completely, and I swear I can feel him in that moment, feel him thrusting roughly, hands bruising my hips as he drives into me, again and again.

"You feel how perfect you are around me, Jenna? How tight and fucking perfect?" He snarls against my ear, accent thick and ragged. "This pussy was made for my cock."

His filthy, possessive words ignite something deep within me. My hand moves rapidly, perfectly matching the rhythm of my imagined lover.

I'm so close.

In the fantasy, he wraps one powerful hand around my throat, squeezing just enough to heighten every sensation. His voice is commanding, fierce, yet edged with raw need. "Come for me, *kotenok*. Now."

His words snap me like a rubber band stretched too far and I shatter, moaning his name, the orgasm washing over me in wave after wave of pleasure. My knees buckle, and I lean heavily against the shower wall, panting, trembling, utterly spent.

The orgasm dissolves slowly, replaced by the warm rush of reality and the pounding of water on my flushed skin. Shame creeps in just a bit, mingled with satisfaction.

I force myself upright, rinsing my body clean as I feel the delicious aftershocks of release rippling through me. I can't believe how easily, how vividly, he took over my imagination. It feels dangerous, but God help me, it feels so damn good, too.

I finish quickly, stepping out and wrapping myself in a fluffy towel. As I catch my reflection in the mirror, cheeks still flushed, I shake my head at myself.

I don't know how I'm supposed to look Abram in the eye today without blushing furiously and betraying every filthy thought I just had.

But I'm going to have to figure it out, and soon. Because after this morning, I'm not sure how much longer I can pretend Abram Vasiliev hasn't completely, irreversibly, gotten under my skin.

I slip into my professional armor—pencil skirt, silky blouse, heels—and twist my unruly red curls into submission, forcing myself back into the careful, controlled version of Jenna Ridley that Abram expects to see every morning.

But beneath the polished surface I'm still burning. Still wondering. Still remembering the way those hands felt, the way that voice sounded, thick with accent and lust.

Fuck, how am I supposed to get through today without picturing Abram naked, taking me exactly how he wanted? Without picturing myself on his desk, him pushing my skirt up, growling filthy Russian phrases into my ear?

My cheeks burn hot. I'm so screwed.

I shake my head, grabbing my travel mug of coffee and keys as I head out the door, bracing myself for whatever fresh hell Abram Vasiliev has planned for today.

As I lock the door behind me, one last shiver races down my spine, one of half excitement, half dread. Because if that masked man was Abram, it means I've seen his most intimate side, and he's seen mine.

It might already be too late to forget.

CHAPTER 12

ABRAM

S he's beneath me, legs spread, mask slightly askew as I drive into her again and again.

Her hands grip the couch, back arching as she cries out. Her thighs tremble around my hips, and her breasts sway with each deep plunge. I drag one hand up her ribcage, pin her wrists above her head, and lean down to whisper—

HONNNNK.

The blaring horn yanks me out of the fantasy as surely as a punch to the goddamn face. I swerve back into my lane with a growl, the other car speeding past, the driver flipping me off in the rearview. I don't blame him.

Get your brain out of your pants, Abram.

I grip the wheel tighter, flexing my fingers like I can shake her off. But it's no use. I've been doing this all weekend— slipping into daydreams, letting her take over. I even gave in once, late Saturday night, alone in my penthouse with the city glittering below and her scent still on my skin.

I pull into the underground lot beneath the Vasiliev Tower, thirty-two stories of glass and steel rising just off the Strip. It's one of the tallest buildings in Vegas, sleek and modern.

The valet greets me with a nod. "Morning, Mr. Vasiliev."

I toss him the keys to my black Mercedes-Maybach. "No scratches."

He chuckles nervously. "Never, sir."

The private elevator awaits, already summoned. I step in and scan my thumbprint, the doors closing behind me with a whisper. The ride is silent, save for the faint hum of the rising elevator. I try to use the silent moment to reorient, shake off the heat still prickling in my blood from the half-formed memory.

She doesn't even know it was you, I remind myself.

The elevator chimes at the top floor. I step into the office expecting silence. I told her to arrive at 6:45. It's 6:20. I was ready to make my own coffee, get started on the quarterly prep alone. But she's here.

My steps falter, just for a second.

She stands near the long meeting table, a fresh cup of black coffee in one hand and her iPad in the other. Her hair is pulled back into a sleek ponytail—tight, professional, elegant. I've never seen her wear it that way before. It shows off her cheekbones, the graceful lines of her neck, the stubborn set of her jaw.

She's wearing a tight black skirt that does nothing to hide the curve of her hips, and a silky blouse that clings to her chest in a way that's going to haunt me through every meeting today.

She's never looked sexier.

She glances up at me; calm, professional, ready. "Morning," she says, tone cool and crisp. "I've synced your calendar, printed the files for the first meeting, and arranged for Dalia to call at ten instead of eight."

I don't answer. I take the coffee from her hand a bit too fast and it sloshes, hot liquid splashing onto my fingers.

Fuck.

She lifts a brow, not quite smirking but definitely close. "I can tell you haven't had any caffeine yet."

She leans to grab a tissue from the side table. The view of her ass in that skirt is distracting. Unfair. Dangerous.

I grit my teeth.

"Thanks," I mutter, dabbing at my hand.

"Anything else you need before your first meltdown of the morning?" Another half smirk.

"Yes," I say, voice clipped. "Come into my office and shut the door behind you."

She pauses. "You do know no one else is here yet, right?"

I meet her eyes. Say nothing. She stares back before turning without a word.

We enter my office. I note a flicker of amused defiance as she pulls the door shut. I also notice the subtle eye roll she thinks I missed.

When she turns back, her face is blank. Poised. Pure assistant mode.

I almost laugh. Instead, I walk past her, still flexing my hand as I sit behind my desk. The coffee's already cooling on the surface, steam thinning.

Jenna doesn't speak. She just stands there, iPad ready, waiting.

My mind isn't on the quarterly projections. It's on how she looked beneath me. The sounds she made. The little gasp when I bit her collarbone. The moment she came apart around my cock.

I shift in my seat. She notices. Of course she does. The corners of her mouth twitch, just barely, and suddenly I can't decide what the hell I'm more annoyed about—how much I want her or how much she knows it.

I lean back and cross my arms. "Well?"

She blinks, confused. "Well what?"

"What's that smirk for?"

"There is no smirk," she replies smoothly, not even pretending to sound apologetic. "But if there were, I guess it might be because you summoned me in here like you were about to reveal state secrets, yet you're just brooding in silence."

"I don't brood."

She gives me a look.

I clench my jaw. "Update me on the Fremont property."

The mood shifts instantly. She straightens her spine, thumb gliding across the iPad with practiced precision. "There was a meeting on Friday with the tenant board. Henley confirmed a conversation between the leasing rep and a potential third-party developer. Officially, the tenant says they're not interested in selling."

"And unofficially?"

"The rep's story doesn't line up. I pulled the internal emails —they've already started exploratory pricing."

I exhale slowly. "Cowards never just say no."

She swipes again, efficient as ever. "I've flagged the corre-spondence and cross-checked it with your calendar. You'll want to review the notes before your next strategy call with legal. We may need to renegotiate the lease structure, add a non-compete clause if it's not too late."

My gaze lingers on her just a beat too long. She's sharp. Controlled. And fuck if that doesn't turn me on.

I try to focus, try to maintain my composure, be the man I'm used to being. But my gaze keeps drifting. Her mouth. Her hands. The thought of her kneeling between my thighs—

I cut the thought off and reach for the coffee. The cup's still slick from earlier and my fingers tighten too hard around it.

I'm going to lose my goddamn mind, and she's going to make sure I enjoy every second of it.

The silence lingers, thick and charged. Jenna waits patiently, her professional mask flawless, but I know what lies beneath. I know how her skin flushes pink when pleasure overtakes her, the sounds she makes when her defenses crumble beneath my touch.

But right now, her composure is impeccable. It irritates me just as much as it fascinates me.

I wonder what it would take to shatter it.

I could drop a hint, whisper something in Russian, watch her reaction. See if recognition flickers in her eyes. But I won't, not yet. Too easy. Too soon. I want to watch her figure it out slowly, watch as she unravels the delicious mystery one clue at a time.

My lips twitch at the thought. A dangerous game, but what's life without a little risk?

She clears her throat softly, shifting my attention back to the meeting and the matter at hand. It's her first Bratva meeting as my assistant. She needs to understand exactly what she's stepping into. No more shielding her from the reality of who I am.

"I want to make sure we're clear on what's about to happen today," I say carefully. "Do you know who I am?"

Jenna chuckles softly, a spark of amusement brightening her eyes. "Is that a trick question or are you having a personal crisis?"

I arch a brow. "Answer me."

"You're Abram Vasiliev," she says, her voice steady. "Leader of the Vasiliev Bratva. Billionaire, occasional pain in my ass, exceptionally particular about his coffee."

I resist the urge to smile. God, she's good. "Fair enough. But do you know what that actually means?"

Her confidence wavers slightly, a subtle tightening at the corners of her mouth. "My understanding is that Bratva means the Russian mafia. Organized crime, power, danger. That sort of thing."

Close enough. "Essentially," I confirm. "This meeting is with my lieutenants—Denis and Mikail—whom you've met briefly before. We have a delicate situation brewing. The Agosti family, our Italian counterparts on the north side, have started testing our boundaries."

She nods slowly, taking that in, processing. No flinching, no panic. Just a careful, quiet seriousness that suits her far better than I expected.

"So, it's a territory dispute?"

"More or less," I say. "The Agostis have decided to make a play while their don is sick. Nico Agosti, his son, is impatient and impulsive. And dangerous."

Jenna's brow furrows slightly, concern flickering across her face. "And you're going to discuss how to handle him."

It isn't a question, but I answer anyway. "Yes. He's been trying to interfere in businesses that belong firmly in our territory. Sending his people into establishments under our protection, trying to sow discontent. We can't let it stand."

She exhales a soft breath, and I can practically see the wheels turning behind her eyes. She's sharp, perceptive. That's part of what makes her so intriguing—both professionally and otherwise.

"I'll be taking notes?" she asks, glancing down at the iPad.

"Yes," I reply, "but mostly observing. Watching how things operate. Familiarizing yourself with the language we use, how we communicate. I need you up to speed quickly."

She nods, her expression tightening slightly. I sense a moment of hesitation building within her, something on the tip of her tongue.

"Something wrong?" I prompt.

She meets my eyes, searching carefully. "Look, I'll be honest. Everything I know about the mafia or Bratva or whatever it is comes from movies. I'm not afraid to learn, but I need to ask..."

She pauses, swallowing hard. It's rare for her confidence to slip, but the question she's about to ask seems to unsettle her, exposing a flash of vulnerability I wasn't expecting.

"Ask," I encourage, gentler this time.

She inhales deeply, visibly steeling herself. "Am I safe here, Abram? Or does working for you put me in danger?"

Something sharp twists in my chest at her words. A protectiveness rises immediately, possessive and fierce. Without thinking, I stand and move closer, closing the distance until I'm standing directly in front of her.

"You're safe," I say, my voice low, unwavering. "You have my word. No one under my protection comes to harm, not unless they cross me."

Her eyes widen slightly, but she holds my gaze, studying me intently. "And if someone tries?"

Without hesitation, I tell her, "Then I'll deal with them personally."

Her breath catches, and I can feel the tension coiling tighter between us—unspoken but undeniable. I can't resist pushing just a little further, testing those walls she's so carefully built around herself.

"I take care of what's mine," I add quietly, letting my gaze dip deliberately down her body then back up again. "Always."

CHAPTER 13

JENNA

"You're sure?"

I hate how small my voice sounds. But what's more, I hate that I've revealed a vulnerability.

Abram doesn't flinch, doesn't look away. His hands settle gently on my shoulders—warm, steady, grounding. Like everything about him, his touch feels strangely calming. Heavy with meaning.

"I'm sure," he says.

Just two simple words, but they work their way under my skin like a hot flame. His hands melt the fear right out of my muscles, making them loose and warm. Not to mention the way my stomach flips just from being this close to him. His fingers don't roam, don't linger, but still my body lights up like a struck match.

"No one will touch you," he says, his voice low, a promise.

I nod slowly. "Okay."

He lets go, stepping back. The loss of contact is more noticeable than I want to admit. I watch him cross to his desk, his expression already shifting back into that unreadable businessman coolness.

And just like that, my brain betrays me. That walk—controlled, powerful, confident—reminds me of *him*. The stranger from the other night. The one who lit my body on fire and left me gasping in the dark. I try to chase the thought away, but it's too late.

Abram's beard is streaked with gray, neatly trimmed with that rich salt-and-pepper thing going on. *He* had a beard too, but it was darker. Black. Still, the shape of the jaw, the cut of his shoulders, those *eyes*...

I shake my head. No. It can't be. I'd know. Right?

Except I don't know. Abram's a mystery wrapped in an expensive suit. I know about his sisters. Know about their children. I've seen the family photos, the vacations, the matching icy eyes in every generation. But a brother? There's never been mention of one. And if he *was* my weekend stranger, I think I'd want it to be him.

I'd want him to be the man who touched me like I was something precious. Who growled Russian into my ear while making me come so hard I saw stars. I'd want that man to be *this* man, because maybe then, this heat between us wouldn't be so confusing.

But it's all so ridiculous. Wild, wishful thinking. My imagination stirring the pot.

He glances up suddenly, as if sensing me watching him too

long. "Is there a problem?" he asks, voice sharp but not unkind.

I blink hard, my cheeks flushing instantly. "Not at all," I say, forcing a little smile that feels like it's going to crack my teeth.

He studies me a second longer than necessary. And then the moment passes.

I clear my throat, tugging my thoughts back into something resembling professionalism. "Thank you," I say softly, "for... looking after me. For keeping me safe."

Abram nods once. "It's nothing."

But it isn't nothing. I know that. I felt it. Still, I let the subject drop.

I straighten my spine. "Would you like refreshments set out for the meeting?"

He tilts his head. "What refreshments?"

"Coffee. Pastries. Water. Maybe a little something stronger, depending on how tense things get."

His brow lifts just slightly. "From where? Did you bring something in?"

"I did," I say, letting a touch of pride creep into my voice. "I took the company card and restocked the fridge, the shelves, and the liquor cabinet. They were, frankly, embarrassingly bare."

To my surprise, he nods slowly. "Have coffee and pastries on the table. Too early for anything else."

"Of course." I turn to go.

Before I can reach the door, however, his voice stops me. "Jenna."

I brace myself. Expecting a correction. A critique. One of his razor-edged, backhanded compliments.

Instead, he says, "Good work."

My breath hitches. The words sound almost out of place coming from him. But they're genuine, paired with a steady, unreadable gaze that always seems to reach further than it should.

I don't know what to say, so I just smile, a little stunned. I step into the hallway, the door clicking closed behind me, and then I stop. One hand on the wall, the other pressed flat to my chest. My heart is racing. I can feel the heat rushing up my neck.

What the hell is happening to me?

I hurry to the break room, gathering the pastries I'd purchased and stored in the fridge. When they're ready to go, I get some hot water for the French presses ready and start that process. It doesn't take long before I'm done.

The tray shakes a little in my hands as I set it down on the table in the conference room. I tell myself it's just the coffee. Just nerves. But really, it's him.

That damn smile. It looked exactly like the one I saw that night—the one that caused me to become undone, right before I begged a stranger to fuck me like I'd never begged anyone in my life. And now, here I am, laying out pastries and arranging napkins while my boss wanders around smiling like a man with nothing to hide.

I've been thinking about that night all weekend. Obsessively. I've practically memorized his taste, his smell, the shape of his lips, the way his beard scraped against my skin.

I arrange the pastries and try not to let my thoughts run wild. The smell of fresh coffee curls up from the presses I started earlier. I pour it carefully into cups, my hands trembling just enough to make the stream wobble.

Malyshka.

The Russian word hits me like a shiver. I can still hear him murmuring things into my ear in a voice I didn't understand but felt all the same. Low, deep, dangerous.

He'd slipped that night when he dropped the fake American accent. And when he did, he sounded just like Abram. But it doesn't prove anything. Not definitively, anyway.

Still, it makes my stomach twist, and not in a bad way.

If Abram isn't the man from the club, then he's the closest thing to him. My body thinks he is. Responds like he is. And honestly, I don't think I've ever been so turned on in my life.

I take a deep breath. Then another.

Focus, Jenna. Focus.

I finish setting the table. Everything looks perfect. Professional.

A moment later, Abram steps in.

"This looks good," he says. His voice is calm and cool, just like always. "The meeting will start in five."

He turns and walks out, closing the door behind him.

I don't breathe until I'm sure he's gone.

CHAPTER 14

ABRAM

The elevator dings, echoing through the private lobby of the top floor. I stand with my hands in my pockets, watching the doors glide open.

Right on time.

Denis steps out first. He's dressed in a sharp suit, an eternal half-smirk on his face. Mikail follows, slightly more relaxed, eyes scanning the space with idle amusement. I don't know if they coordinated the dark tailored suits, but they look like twins rather than brothers-in-law.

"Morning," I say, stepping forward, clasping Denis's hand first, then Mikail's. "Appreciate the punctuality."

Denis shrugs, his grip firm. "You trained us well."

Mikail chuckles. "Anya made me set three alarms. She reminded me that your mood depends on the timeliness of our arrival."

"She's not wrong," I reply, leading them toward the hallway.

They know this building, they know me. They're the only two men I trust to have my back because they're more than lieutenants—they're my family. Married to my sisters, bonded by blood and beyond.

Tatiana and Anya chose well. I've never seen either man flinch from the work. Both understand the rules. More importantly, they understand the importance of loyalty, of family.

"Kids good?" I ask as we walk.

"Charles refuses to eat anything that isn't shaped like a dinosaur and made of chicken," Mikail says.

Denis snorts. "Sofia flushed a two-hundred-dollar necklace down the toilet."

"Delightful," I reply with a chuckle.

They laugh, the sound echoing down the hallway. We reach the conference room and I push the door open.

Jenna's waiting for us, ready and professional. "Gentlemen," she says brightly. "Coffee's fresh. Please help yourselves to some pastries, fruit, and almond biscotti if you're feeling indulgent."

I feel heat coiling low in my gut.

Control yourself, Abram.

A throat clears beside me. I glance over to see Denis watching me watching her. He lifts an eyebrow, silent and smug.

I look away. Say nothing.

Mikail whistles low under his breath. "Looks like you've upgraded your hospitality, Abram."

I nod toward her. "This is my new assistant. Jenna Ridley."

Denis steps forward first, all easy charm. "Pleasure to meet you, Jenna. I'm Denis. This is Mikail."

She shakes their hands, polite and poised. There's a subtle flicker of recognition behind her eyes, and before I can speak, Denis beats me to it.

"Our wives will be thrilled to meet you."

Jenna smiles. "I've met them, actually. They recommended me for the job."

Mikail laughs. "Did they now?" There's amusement in his tone, like an inside joke she hasn't caught up to yet.

Jenna tilts her head, clearly confused. I watch the curiosity flicker in her gaze. The way her lips part slightly, like she's about to ask a question but decides to hold back.

Smart girl. Observant and beautiful.

I settle into my chair at the head of the table, motioning for them to take their seats.

"Let's get down to business," I announce.

Jenna straightens like a string's been pulled. "I'll just grab my iPad."

I shake my head. "No."

She waits a beat, expecting an explanation.

"I've decided I don't want anything written down. Not for this one. I won't need you to sit in after all."

"No need to produce evidence," Denis adds with a smirk. "Makes the Feds jobs harder."

She gives a tight nod. "Understood. Would you like me to serve the coffee before I step out?"

Mikail lifts a hand, dismissive. "We're good, thanks."

Jenna nods again, gives a polite smile to both men, and heads toward the door. I catch the faintest trace of her perfume as she passes—vanilla, with just a hint of coconut. Heat flickers low in my gut once again.

As the door clicks shut behind her, Denis lets out a low whistle. "She's stunning."

Mikail laughs. "Tatiana and Anya knew exactly what they were doing, huh?"

I raise a brow.

"Come on," Mikail continues, smirking. "You think your sisters picked her because she's got administrative experience?"

"She's got plenty of experience," I reply, smiling slightly.

That gets both of them. Denis snorts, nearly choking on his own spit.

Mikail just stares at me. "No shit?"

I don't elaborate. I simply sit back, letting the grin linger for a second before shaking my head. "Alright, I've said too much."

They laugh again, loud and full-bellied.

Once the amusement fades, I lean forward, resting my forearms on the table. "Let's get to business. Talk to me."

Denis is the first to shift gears, always quicker than Mikail. "We've got new activity in Agosti territory. Or, what used to be Agosti territory."

I tense. "Where?"

"South of Harmon. Couple of properties up for sale, warehouses mostly. Problem is, they're making plays on buildings that are already paying us for protection."

Mikail folds his arms. "And it's not a polite takeover. We're talking broken windows. Trashed interiors. Owners getting late-night visits."

"Fucking hell," I mutter.

"Got at least four business owners on record calling us this weekend," Denis says. "One of them has been paying since your father ran things. They're scared, Abram. Really scared."

"And the cops?"

Denis rolls his eyes. "Some of the people pulling this shit probably *are* the cops."

"Or paid off by the Agostis," Mikail adds.

I exhale slowly, my jaw tight. "Maybe it's time I sit down with Don Agosti. If he wants war over property lines, we'll give him a lesson in why that's a mistake."

Denis shakes his head. "It's not the don."

"You sure?" I ask.

He nods. "Don Agosti hasn't been seen in public in months. Hasn't made a statement. Hasn't been at any of the usual places. People are starting to whisper."

I narrow my eyes. "What kind of whispers?"

"Lung cancer," Denis says. "Advanced. Word is Nico's running things. Making his move early."

I sit back, my mind working fast. Nico Agosti. Arrogant little fucker with more money than sense. Spoiled and mean. Not someone I'd ever consider a true player.

But illness changes things. Succession changes things.

And the promise of power makes boys get greedy.

Mikail is already reading my mind. "We call a meeting?"

"Yes. But it needs to be done right. We invite both Nico and his father, otherwise that'll read as disrespect to the don."

"Even if the old man's on his deathbed?" Denis asks.

"Doesn't matter," I reply. "As long as he's alive, we follow the rules."

Mikail rubs his jaw. "Agreed. Show of respect will put us in a strong position."

"I'll have Jenna arrange it."

They both look at me, eyebrows raising in sync.

"You're going to have your assistant arrange a sit-down with the Agostis?" Denis asks, skeptical.

"She's very capable."

Mikail chuckles. "I suppose that's one word for it."

Denis studies me like he's trying to decode something I'm not saying. I hold his gaze until he finally drops it with a shrug.

"I'll trust your instincts," he concedes. "You've always had a good eye."

A better eye than either of them realize.

I picture Jenna again. The way she stood beside the table, the little pinch of confusion on her face when I told her she didn't need to stay, how she tilted her head like she was seconds from asking a question but too smart to interrupt.

That body.

That fucking mouth.

Yes, she's very capable.

But she's also something else. Something I haven't figured out yet.

But I will.

The meeting wraps up. Mikail stretches with a grunt, then smirks. I walk them to the elevator like I always do.

As we approach the doors, Denis lowers his voice, slipping into Russian. "I'll send the Sorella footage. You'll want to see it. It's worse than what we've heard."

"Spliced feed?" I ask.

He nods. "Amateurs. But someone cleaned up the outside cameras. Inside's intact."

"Good." I glance at Mikail. "And the Charleston?"

He sighs. "Lawyer says it's stalled. Zoning board is dragging their feet, probably waiting for a payoff."

"Then pay them," I say flatly. "And tell Oleg to lean on the board chair's brother-in-law. He runs a car lot in Henderson. Dirty financing. That's leverage."

Mikail raises his eyebrows. "Remind me to never get on your bad side."

I offer a small smile. "You're already on it."

Denis chuckles. "He's joking."

"Am I?" I ask dryly. We all laugh.

The elevator dings softly. Mikail pauses as the doors open. "You good, Abram?"

I nod once. "Always."

"Then tell your new assistant to stop bending over so much," he teases. "I nearly forgot why we were here."

I say nothing, letting the words hang as they step inside. Mikail gives me a two-fingered salute. "See you later."

The doors slide shut, sealing them off.

Restlessness rumbles beneath my skin. Like tension strung too tight across the ribs. I tell myself it's the Agosti problem. The territory lines. The shifting whispers about Don Agosti's health. There's work to be done, as always.

But that's not what's causing the tension. It's *her*.

I return to the conference room where the remnants of the meeting remain—half-empty coffee cups, half-eaten pastries, a delicate trace of citrus and berries lingering in the air.

And then there's the faintest scent of her perfume.

I sit, the leather groaning under my weight, and pick up my pen. I don't write anything, I just hold it, turning it between my fingers.

I'm a careful man. Always have been. I don't fuck employees. I don't let my mind wander in meetings. I don't imagine what my assistant would look like if she were in my bed.

Except I've done all of those things in the span of three days.

Friday night crashes into my mind like a wave I didn't see coming. Her hands on my chest, her mouth exploring mine like it belonged to her. The way she moaned underneath me.

But the real itch in my skull is whether or not she's connected the dots back to me yet.

Sometimes I can see it in her eyes, like she's replaying Friday night in her head, thinking about the word I spoke in Russian against her throat, and trying—heroically—to stay professional anyway.

Sooner or later I'm going to slip, and the whole truth will land in her lap, along with everything that comes with belonging to a man like me.

The thought settles low and heavy.

I set my pen down and lean back in the chair. My gaze drifts to the door, picturing her purposeful stride, heels tapping out a rhythm that makes every man in the corridor glance up.

I'm supposed to be running a multi-billion-dollar empire. Preparing for a potential war with the Agostis. Instead, I'm sitting in the quiet aftermath of a meeting, wondering what color panties my assistant is wearing. Wondering if she ever thinks of me the way I think of her—dark and obsessive—against her better judgment.

I close my eyes and see her face again, flushed and gasping, mouth parted, eyes begging for more.

I tell myself it doesn't matter.

But that's a lie and I know it.

CHAPTER 15

JENNA

A few minutes earlier...

I watch him from behind the glass partition. Abram stands near the elevator, tall and composed, shaking hands with his brothers-in-law. The exchange is respectful; clearly they're fond of one another. It's a side of himself he keeps buried under that polished armor of his.

As soon as the elevator doors close, it's gone. His posture changes. His face resets into the expressionless mask I'm accustomed to. When he turns, those ice-blue eyes sweep across the floor, landing on me like a spotlight.

He heads back into the conference room. Minutes tick by. The office is still technically closed; no one else has arrived yet. It's just the two of us.

I start toward my office, eager to get a jump on the day. But I barely have a chance to turn on my computer before my intercom chimes.

"My office. Now."

My stomach twists. He sounds pissed. Did I do something wrong?

I force my face into a neutral expression as I approach his office. He holds the door for me but says nothing. I walk past him, heart thudding against my ribs. No thanks for the coffee. No mention of the breakfast I arranged. Of course not. What was I expecting, a gold star?

He shuts the door behind us.

I brace myself for a reprimand, but it doesn't come.

Instead, he walks past me, circles around, and sits—not behind his desk, but on the corner of it. Close to where I'm standing. Very close. His cologne curls into my lungs—dark, musky, expensive.

My mouth goes dry.

"We need to arrange a meeting with the Agostis," he says. "It has to be handled a certain way. No mistakes."

I nod, trying to focus, but his proximity is making that nearly impossible.

"You'll reach out to Nico Agosti first," he continues, his gaze fixed on me. "But make it clear the invitation is for both him and his father. It's a sign of respect. We don't acknowledge the son without including the father."

"Got it," I manage.

He shifts slightly, leaning forward just enough to crowd my space. My breath catches.

"The location should be neutral but not impersonal. A

space that suggests we're open to diplomacy but still hold the upper hand. I'll send you a list of acceptable venues."

"Understood."

He's close enough now that I can feel the heat radiating from him. His voice. His scent. His presence. My brain is trying to keep up with what he's saying but my body's reaction isn't helping. I'm flushed. Aware of every inch of him. I fight the urge to take a step back.

He looks at me while he speaks, eyes locked on mine, and I swear something I've seen before flickers in them.

My nipples tighten under my blouse, my pussy clenching with heat as he continues. He talks about logistics—dates, attendees, optics—but I don't hear any of it. Not really. Because all I can think about is the way he touched me in the dark. The way he groaned against my neck.

I blink a couple times and look down at my tablet, hoping he can't see me blushing.

"Any questions?" he asks.

I swallow. "Just send me that list of options and I'll get started."

He gives a small nod, then gestures toward my iPad. "Pull up a map."

My fingers fumble slightly as I navigate to the city grid on my tablet. He moves around, coming to stand just behind me.

That goddamn cologne. Dark cedar, leather, a hint of spice. My body floods with heat as the memory slams into me.

I nearly moan.

"Here," he says, pointing at the tablet. "Downtown, but not central. This block is mostly commercial—clean, quiet, discreet. There's a hotel here that should suffice."

I nod dumbly.

"If they push back on that location, offer the Seville off Halden. But make it clear we'll provide security. Ours. Not theirs."

My eyes dart up to his face, needing to see him. And for a moment, I forget to pretend. I stare at his eyes. Those same ice-blue eyes that pierced through the dark in the club, searing me when my hands were bound and my body spread. They're his. On me again.

I don't blink.

Neither does he.

There's a moment suspended, hot, heavy, unbreathable. His mouth curves into a knowing smirk.

"Send me the details once they confirm," he says, turning away and slipping back into boss mode. As if nothing just passed between us.

But I'm not breathing.

"Did you know it was me?" I whisper.

He smiles, and I swear I could slap him and kiss him in the same breath.

"I did," he says simply.

I stammer, "You—you..."

He steps in front of me. I tilt my chin up in defiance. I won't let him have the last word. I won't be embarrassed. But I can't find a single sentence to say, because I have no idea whether I want to scream at him or drop to my knees.

My thoughts are like a wildfire.

He says nothing. He just leans in, eyes blazing, and kisses me.

His mouth crashes onto mine. It's not soft. It's hungry. Possessive in a way that sends a hot, electric pulse straight to my core. His lips are firm, commanding, and rough, causing my toes to curl inside my shoes.

His scent wraps around me as his body presses against mine. His hand grips my ponytail, tilting my head back, deepening the kiss. My knees go weak, but he's holding me, anchoring me against his chest.

His tongue slips past my lips, tasting, teasing, coaxing mine into the kind of dance I didn't realize I'd missed. He tastes so goddamn good. My hands fist into the front of his shirt, trying to pull him closer even as part of me whispers *this is a bad idea*.

But that whisper dies fast.

The moment his hands trail down my back, gliding over the swell of my hips like he's memorizing them again, I'm gone. Every warning bell in my head is drowned out by the river of blood rushing south, by the way he groans against my mouth like *he's* the one who can't hold back.

"I haven't stopped thinking about this," he rasps between kisses. "About you. About tasting you again."

Oh God.

Before I can reply, he lifts me like I weigh nothing, one arm under my thighs, the other braced against my spine. I gasp, clutching his shoulders as he strides to the leather couch across the room. He sets me down carefully, reverently, then peels my skirt down in one smooth motion, dragging my panties with it. Cool air hits my thighs, and I shiver.

He pauses just long enough to look at me. "Beautiful," he murmurs. "Absolutely fucking beautiful."

Then he lowers himself between my legs, eyes locked on mine the whole time. His mouth finds me with agonizing precision, his lips brushing, then his tongue pressing, circling, tasting. My head falls back with a cry. He hums against me, hands spreading my thighs wider, holding me open.

I bite down on a moan, but it's useless. He licks and sucks with the kind of experience that borders on cruel—like he knows every nerve ending by name, every flick of his tongue choreographed to undo me.

My hands grip the leather, hips lifting off the couch. "Abram—" I gasp.

He groans in response, the sound vibrating against me, and I lose it. The orgasm crashes over me hard, white heat and tension snapping all at once. I cry out shamelessly, my voice echoing off the high ceiling.

He doesn't stop until I've stilled. Only then does he lift his head, his lips slick and glistening, his mouth curved into the same wicked smile that started this.

"You taste even better than I remember," he says, voice low and thick with desire. "And I could listen to you come like that forever."

He leans in and kisses me again, and I taste myself on his tongue. It only makes me hungrier.

My breath is still coming in shallow gasps when he stands and pulls me gently to my feet. My legs are still shaking from the aftershocks of his mouth. His arm slips around my waist to steady me, and for a second, I lean into him, practically melting.

Then his hands are on me again, deft and needy, peeling away what little clothing remains. My blouse comes off first, then my bra, his mouth trailing kisses down my neck, across the swell of my breasts, teeth scraping just enough to make me whimper. He tongues a nipple and I gasp, arching into him, needing more.

I reach for him, cupping him through the fine wool of his slacks, and he lets out a low groan that goes straight to my core.

I kiss him, hard and hungry, feeling him twitch beneath my palm. "It's funny," I whisper against his lips. "Even if you hadn't told me, I had my suspicions. Your eyes, the way you touch me."

He chuckles, his mouth grazing my jaw. "Touch you?" he murmurs. "I haven't even *begun* to touch you yet."

The words send a jolt of heat through me so intense I nearly moan again. Instead, I take his hand and guide him backward, toward his desk chair.

"Sit," I command.

He does, eyes smoldering. I drop to my knees between his legs, my hands sliding beneath his crisp white shirt to feel the solid muscle of his torso. Then I press my lips to the bulge straining against his slacks, kissing him through the fabric, slow and teasing.

He grits his teeth, his hand finding the back of my head. "Jenna..."

I undo his belt with steady fingers, lower his zipper, and pull him free. God, he's rock hard, his long, thick cock stiff and glistening just for me.

I kiss the tip, then look up at him, lips parted, flushed and breathless. "What do you want?"

His eyes burn into mine as he smiles mischievously.

"You."

CHAPTER 16

JENNA

"Yeah, just like that."

The words slip out of Abram as I take him in my mouth slowly, savoring the way he groans, low and guttural.

The taste of him is clean and intoxicating, tinged with something masculine and salty. He's hot and heavy on my tongue, and the way his hand gently pulls my ponytail makes my stomach tighten with pleasure.

I glance up. His head is tilted back against the chair, mouth parted, throat exposed, vulnerable in the sexiest way. His suit jacket hangs open along with his white shirt, and that expression on his face—eyes dark, jaw tight—drives me to near madness.

Abram brings out something in me I never knew existed.

Something hungry. Something wicked.

One hand rests on his thigh, the other at the base of his cock, my mouth working him in long, deep strokes. When I swirl my tongue just beneath the crown, I feel his whole body tense, his breath stuttering. He's close and I want it. I want to taste him, to feel him erupt against my tongue.

Suddenly, his hand tightens in my hair, and he pulls me gently off him.

"Fuck," he mutters, standing and drawing me to my feet. His eyes are wild, his mouth dangerous. "I'd love to watch you drink every last drop, *kotenok*. But I'm not done with you yet. Not even close."

Before I can catch my breath, he pulls me to my feet and turns me around, pressing me down against the desk. His hand rests on my lower back, pinning me there. My pulse spikes. I love it. The roughness. The way he takes control.

I've never experienced anything like this before, never let anyone take me in this way. Not because I didn't want it but because no one's ever deserved it.

But Abram?

He doesn't ask. He claims.

I hear the crinkle of foil, the soft *snap* as he slips on the condom, and then—

He thrusts inside me in one smooth, deep motion.

I cry out, gripping the edge of the desk. The stretch is so intense, so perfect, I can hardly breathe. He fills me completely, like we were made for each other.

He takes me from behind, his touch sure and commanding. My palms press against the cool surface of his desk as his body moves with mine, steady, relentless.

The sensation is maddening—each thrust tightening the coil inside me until I'm breathless, aching, filled with heat and the quiet knowledge that I'm completely his in this moment.

He presses deeper into me, slow and sure. His hands are firm on my hips, guiding me, anchoring me. He leans in, his mouth brushing the shell of my ear, his voice low and rough as gravel.

"Fuck, Jenna," he murmurs, every word curling down my spine like smoke. "You feel even better than I remember."

I shudder. The memory of that night has already been burned into me, but hearing him speak it aloud—like he's been thinking about it too—sets something wild and loose inside me.

"You were made for this," he says, his breath hot, his pace steady and relentless. "For me. The way you move, the way you squeeze around me... you have no idea what you do to me."

A moan escapes before I can stop it, high and broken.

He groans, thrusting deeper. "That's it. Let me hear you. I've been thinking about this from the second I saw you walk into my office."

My head dips forward, hair falling into my face, and I bite my lip to keep from whimpering too loud. But he notices. Of course he does.

"No," he growls. "Don't hold back on me. You wanted this and now you've got it. You've got me."

"Abram." His name leaves my lips on a shaky breath, hot need pooling low in my belly.

"Say it again," he commands, voice like thunder against the storm of my thoughts.

"Abram," I gasp, desperate now.

He grunts his approval, fingers tightening on my hips, and then his mouth is at my neck, teeth grazing skin as he says, "You're mine, Jenna. Say it."

God help me I do.

"I'm yours."

I grip the edge of the desk, heart pounding. I'm so close, trembling with the effort to stay on my feet, with the weight of how much I want this.

And somehow, he knows. He leans in, his chest brushing my back, his breath hot against my ear. "Not yet," he murmurs. "You don't get to finish until I say so."

A sharp little sound of half frustration, half bliss escapes me. Part of me wants to push back. But another part, a stronger one, thrills at being undone by him. "Yes," I whisper.

His hand stills on my hip. "Yes what?"

My breath catches. The air thickens. "Yes... sir."

He groans, satisfied, and picks up the pace again, faster this time. My body's on fire while my mind unravels. But still, I hold back, right on the edge, held there by sheer will and the sound of his voice.

"Ask me," he says.

I try to form the words, but they catch in my throat, tangled in pleasure. Finally, breathless and desperate, I manage, "Please, can I come?"

There's a heartbeat's worth of a pause before I hear, "Now."

The orgasm crashes over me like a wave, shattering me in the best way. I cry out, raw and open, the sound echoing in the office like a secret that can't be taken back. He holds me through it, steadying me, his hands sure and strong, even as I tremble beneath them.

When I finally find air again, he pulls me gently to my feet, turning me around to face him. His expression is different. There's still hunger, but there's something softer, too. He brushes a thumb across my cheek, leans down, and kisses me slowly, like he's tasting me for the first time all over again.

It's a perfect contrast. The man who just wrecked me now holding me like I'm something precious.

And I let him.

My hands curl against his chest as his mouth lingers on mine, and I swear I could live in this moment forever. The way he balances force and tenderness, roughness and care. It's everything I didn't know I wanted.

And maybe everything I'm a little scared I might need.

He lifts me onto the edge of the desk, his hands firm under my thighs as he steps between them. My heart's racing—I can hear it in my ears, feel it in my fingertips. I gasp when he enters me again. It's deep and slow, like he's savoring every inch of me, and my legs instinctively wrap around him.

His eyes are locked on mine, and for a second, the whole room feels suspended. I feel full, claimed. My fingers dig into his shoulders, broad and strong beneath his shirt, and I hold on as he moves. Each thrust is deliberate, patient but powerful, like he wants to make sure I remember every second of this.

His muscles flex beneath my hands, every motion sending heat curling through my belly. I look at the unmistakable tattoo on his chest. The one I'd memorized that night.

A grin tugs at my lips.

He notices my smile and raises an eyebrow, still moving inside me. "What?"

I shake my head. "Just wondering how long you planned to keep it a secret."

He chuckles, a deep, husky sound that vibrates straight through me. "Not long, apparently."

His mouth finds my neck, then my shoulder, and I arch into him, needing more. Needing *him*. The heat is building again—my body humming, core tightening. I glance down to see the way we fit together, and when I glance up again, I see the way he's watching me, his face intent with focus.

"Tell me," I whisper, breathless. "Tell me what you want."

He leans in, brushing his lips against my ear. "I want to see you fall apart for me. I want to feel you shake around me. I want to take you right to the edge and keep you there. Again."

And just like that I'm close, so close it's almost unbearable.

My hands find his jaw and I kiss him, hard and open, moaning against his mouth as we move faster. His rhythm grows erratic, breath ragged. I can feel him holding back, the tension in his body like a wire about to snap.

"Together," I whisper. "Please. I want to feel it with you."

He pulls back just enough to look at me, grip tightening on my hips. He doesn't need to say a word.

The final thrusts are almost too much. My name on his lips, his body trembling with mine. I cry out into the crook of his neck as pleasure crashes through us like a wave.

We slow together, our bodies slick with heat and sweat. He doesn't pull out right away. Instead, he holds me, his hand stroking along my back, grounding me. My head drops to his shoulder.

"I can't believe..." I start to say, but trail off, lost in the joy of the afterglow.

He presses a kiss to my temple. "Believe it."

At that, I melt a little bit more.

CHAPTER 17

ABRAM

"What are you staring at?" she asks.

I'm seated on the couch, one arm draped over the back, shirt still unbuttoned, chest heaving faintly. I lean back, letting my gaze travel.

She's slipping her blouse back over her shoulders. The way the fabric glides over her skin, the way her hair sticks slightly to the back of her neck, still damp with sweat... it's all I can do not to pull her back to me again.

I grin. "You're too smart to ask a question like that."

That earns me a flicker of a smile. But I spot subtle tension in her shoulders, just beneath the surface. She turns, shirt unbuttoned, bra and no panties, and I beckon her over with a curl of my fingers. She hesitates before crossing the room and sinking into the space beside me. Her body fits against mine like it's always belonged there. She's warm and soft. I rest my palm on her thigh and lean in, letting my breath ghost over the shell of her ear.

"I'm glad the secret's out," I say.

She tenses slightly but nods.

"I could barely keep my hands to myself. Now I don't have to."

That should make her smile. Maybe throw one of her cheeky comments back at me.

But she doesn't. She's quiet.

Too quiet.

Her fingers toy with the edge of her shirt, her eyes fixed somewhere across the room. I can practically hear her thoughts clicking into place like dominoes. I know that look —she's overthinking, analyzing, retreating.

I draw her closer, kissing her cheek, her jaw. "You don't have to feel awkward."

She blushes, almost imperceptibly, and nods again. But still, she doesn't speak. That's not like Jenna.

"Alright," I say softly, letting my hand settle at the small of her back. "What's wrong?"

She shakes her head.

"Jenna."

Still nothing.

I tip her chin up with my fingers and her eyes meet mine, wide and uncertain. "Tell me."

I don't say it like a demand. Not quite. But my voice is firm, coaxing. At that moment, I can feel her slipping into a shell.

I won't let her. Not after this.

Her lips part like she's about to answer, but then she stops herself. I wait, giving her space. The silence stretches. She's quiet for a few more beats, fingers tracing the seam of my shirt. Then, she exhales softly and looks up at me.

"At the club," she says, her voice low, "I didn't know who you were."

I stay quiet, letting her talk.

She swallows. "And because of that, something in me let go. I wasn't thinking about how I looked. I wasn't over-analyzing every part of my body. I just felt..." She pauses, searching for the word, "Free."

I am genuinely surprised. "You?" I ask. "Self-conscious?"

Her brow furrows slightly. "I can be." She lifts a shoulder, half shrug, half shield. "But that night, it was like my brain switched off. I wasn't thinking about my hips or my stomach or if I looked stupid in that dress. I was just... me. And you made me feel wanted. Desired."

I don't speak for a second. I just watch her. She's beautiful—fiercely so—and the idea that she doesn't see it, or doubts the effect she has, rattles me more than I expected.

"I had no idea," I finally say. "You always seem so sure of yourself."

"Professionally I am," she replies. "It's the personal part I struggle with sometimes."

I brush my thumb along her cheek. "Jenna, you're the sexiest woman I've ever seen. And I mean that." I lean in, eyes locked on hers. "Your curves? That's exactly what drew me in at the club. I didn't know it was you when I saw you at the bar. I was already planning to approach you before you even turned around."

Her eyes soften. "Seriously?"

"Seriously."

She smiles, slow and a little bashful, then leans back, a small smirk forming on her lips. "Well. I should probably be irritated with you for tricking me."

"Trick is a strong word," I reply, amused. "I didn't exactly know it was you either. Not at first."

She narrows her eyes. "But you didn't stop it when you did realize."

"No," I admit, unapologetic. "I didn't."

She tilts her head, mock stern. "Should I be mad?"

"Are you?"

She hesitates, that slight pause her answer. "Probably not," she admits, her smirk fading. "But I don't want to be that woman. The one who fucks her boss."

I raise an eyebrow. "Are you willing to be *a* woman who fucks her boss?"

Her laugh escapes before she can stop it, caught somewhere between exasperation and arousal. I lean in close, brushing her lips with mine.

"Because I have to warn you," I whisper against her mouth, "twice isn't going to be enough."

She breathes me in like she already knows it and laughs. "Well. I guess I *am* that woman now."

"And what kind is that?"

"The kind who sleeps with her boss and doesn't regret a damn second of it."

I let my gaze roam over her slowly. "Good."

The smirk returns. "Apparently not good enough to keep her panties."

I beat her to them, snatching them up from where she left them on the arm of the couch. "You won't be needing these."

She lifts an eyebrow. "Oh, really?"

I open the drawer on the end table beside me and slip them inside, shutting it with a satisfying little click. "I want to think about you without them the rest of the day."

"Naughty," she says, voice playful, curious.

"What do your plans look like this week?" I ask. "I want to take you out to dinner. Some place nice."

"That's a little backwards, isn't it?" she teases, her breath brushing my neck. "Dinner *after* you've had me screaming in your office?"

I chuckle. "I like doing things out of order."

"I've noticed."

Her mouth is so close. I tilt her chin and press a kiss to her lips—soft at first, but she meets me with more. Hunger flares instantly. My hand slips beneath her blouse, finding the smooth skin along her hips. She sighs, melting into my touch. The other hand traces up, fingers sliding under her bra to cup her breast. She gasps into my mouth, her body pressing against mine, wanting more. I can feel her heat, the ache, the need in her breathless little moans. I could take her again so easily

She bites my lip lightly. "We're really about to do this again?"

"Apparently so."

As I brush my thumb over her nipple she arches into me. And then—

Knock-knock.

We both freeze.

It's sharp. Purposeful. Not like a staff member's knock.

Her eyes widen. "No one should be here. The phone didn't ring. There hasn't been a call to let anyone up. Staff's not in yet."

I pull back from her slowly and move toward the desk, opening the top drawer. My Glock is in there—always. Just in case. I lift it out and tuck it against my back.

"Go to the far wall."

She nods then moves, watching me with wide eyes.

I cross to the door and unlock it. I open it fast.

And curse.

Standing there, poised like a goddamn storm in stilettos, is a nightmare from my past.

"Hello, Abram."

CHAPTER 18

JENNA

I slap a hand over my mouth to keep from yelping.

Shit. Shit. Shit.

I scramble, snatching up my skirt and my heels—grateful I'd already put my bra and blouse back on. I duck behind the couch out of view of the door, wriggling back into my clothes with shaky fingers. I smooth my blouse, slide my heels back on, and practically crawl to the mirror beside the bookcase.

My reflection stares back at me—flushed cheeks, swollen lips, pupils far too wide. I look like a woman who just got thoroughly, unapologetically railed. I dab at my mouth, swipe under my eyes. My hair's a mess. I fix my ponytail with trembling fingers.

I strain to hear the conversation taking place near the door.

"Well. That's quite the welcome. Is that a gun tucked into your waistband or are you just thrilled to see me?" The woman's voice is velvet-lined steel. Unmistakably Russian. Like a Bond villainess.

Abram replies, his voice colder than I've ever heard it. "Daria. You don't show up unannounced. You know that."

I exhale and gather myself, then step forward.

She's still in the doorway, leaning slightly into his space with a smirk that says she believes she's superior to most. Her beauty is otherworldly—long legs in sleek black trousers, blood-red lips, raven hair pinned back in a neat bun.

Her nails are like claws. Her blouse is silk, open at the collar. Her eyes—icy blue, but colder than Abram's—fix on me like a hawk spotting a mouse.

She narrows them. "Who are you?"

Before I can answer, Abram steps between us, his tone sharp. "Show a little respect."

I straighten my shoulders and smooth my skirt although it isn't wrinkled. "Jenna Ridley," I say, offering my hand. "I'm Abram's assistant."

Daria's gaze drops to my hand before taking a slow, calculated trip over my body. Her lip curls. She doesn't take my hand. Instead, she tilts her head and lets out a low, mocking hum. "His assistant," she says, as if the word tastes sour in her mouth. "Is that what we're calling it now?"

My cheeks burn, but my smile is even. There's no way she knows. Still, something about her tone makes my stomach twist.

She looks back to Abram. "You've been busy. Locked doors and flushed cheeks... I wonder what your sisters would say."

I stand my ground. I won't let her see me squirm. But behind my calm façade, I'm screaming.

Abram's voice sharpens like a knife. "Mind your own business. And again, show my assistant some respect."

Daria chuckles, low and sinister, the sound curling through the air like cigar smoke. Her eyes flick back to me, narrowing slightly, like she's taking a measurement.

She knows. And it's obvious.

I can't tell if she's amused, jealous, furious or all three wrapped up in her tight little sneer. A corner of her mouth twitches.

And then I get my answer. Not to what she's feeling but to who she is.

Abram crosses his arms over his chest and says flatly, "Jenna, this is Daria Vasilieva. My ex-wife."

My stomach drops. Ex-wife?

I blink, trying not to show how hard the revelation lands. Of course he had a life before me, I know that. He's older. Powerful. Gorgeous. Of course there's a past. But an ex-wife? The kind of woman who shows up unannounced, acting like she owns the place?

I have no right to feel anything. He's not mine. So far, we've only slept together.

"Charmed," Daria says in a tone that suggests the opposite.

She turns to Abram again, all syrup and bite. "If your assistant's done gawking, maybe she can get us some drinks? Or is that a service she doesn't provide?"

My jaw tenses. Oh, she's good. Polished. Deliberately insulting. I open my mouth to reply, but Abram beats me to it.

"Keep up the attitude and you won't be here long enough to enjoy a drink," he says, in the kind of tone that makes grown men shut up and listen. "Let's not waste Jenna's time."

Daria's posture shifts. It's subtle, but I catch it in the way her shoulders droop, the shift in her hips, the softening of her expression. Like a snake coiling into a silk ribbon, suddenly, she's all charm.

"Oh, Abram," she purrs, brushing an invisible speck off her blouse. "Always so dramatic."

The change is so instant it makes my teeth clench. I want to roll my eyes but don't. Professional. Polite. I've got no claim here. There's no reason for me to be angry.

Except I am.

Not necessarily because of her, but because he hasn't said a damn thing to make her leave yet.

And because some part of me is already wondering what else I don't know about him, about his past.

"Jenna," Abram says, switching back to reality. "Would you mind bringing each of us an Irish coffee?"

I nod, keeping my composure. "Of course."

I don't look at Daria as I turn, though I can feel her eyes on me, tracking, assessing. Like she's trying to decide if I'm a bug to squash or a threat to neutralize.

In the kitchenette, I pour two fingers of whiskey into mugs before adding some leftover coffee from the earlier meeting. Beverages in hand, I return to the Abram's office, pausing near the door before entering. I listen.

Daria isn't saying much. She stays quiet, and I soon realize she's waiting for me to leave. I square my shoulders and walk back in, offering the drinks with a pleasant smile that feels too tight.

"Here you are," I say, extending hers first. But just as she takes it, she jerks slightly, a splash of coffee landing on her blouse. It's barely the size of a quarter, but she gasps like I doused her in lighter fluid.

"Oh my God!" she snaps, leaping up. "Are you serious? You can't even serve a drink without screwing it up."

I blink, stunned. "I didn't, you grabbed it too quickly—"

She cuts me off with a sharp gesture, examining the tiny spot like it's acid. "I just bought this," she hisses. "You'd better hope this comes out. Get me some club soda and a cloth. Now."

She doesn't say please. She doesn't even look at me when she barks the order.

But Abram does. He steps in between us, his tone final. "That's enough."

She opens her mouth, ready to argue, but he doesn't let her.

"Jenna," he says, turning to me. "You're fine. Go. I'll handle this."

Without another word, he gently guides me to the door with a hand at my back—and shuts it in my face.

Just like that.

Dismissed.

I stand beside the door for a beat, breath caught halfway between my lungs and my throat. My fingers curl into fists. Not because of her. Because of him. The way he sent me out of his office like a servant being excused.

I remind myself that I am his assistant. But that doesn't quiet the anger rising within. I stare at the closed door, fists clenched at my sides. I want to press my ear to it to hear what they're saying. I want to know if he's still in control or if she's digging her claws back in.

But I don't need to get any closer because the yelling starts quickly.

And whatever quiet Abram had managed to preserve is now gone.

CHAPTER 19

ABRAM

I clench my jaw so tightly that pain shoots down my neck. Every muscle is rigid, fighting the instinctive urge to physically throw Daria from my office. Instead, I walk silently to the wet bar, grab a fresh cloth and the bottle of club soda.

"Here." I thrust them toward her abruptly. "Clean yourself up."

She snatches the towel from my hand. Without another word, she douses the cloth then slams the bottle hard onto my desk. She scrubs violently at the tiny coffee stain, each aggressive stroke turning the quarter-sized spot into a blotchy mess three times larger.

"You're making it worse," I say coldly.

Her eyes flash with contempt. "You'd love that, wouldn't you? Watching me ruin something else?"

"I don't have time for your theatrics, Daria," I snap. "Get to the fucking point. Why are you here?"

Her gaze narrows, mouth curving into an ugly smile. "What's wrong, Abram? Worried your precious secretary might overhear us?"

The venom in her voice makes my blood boil. "She's none of your goddamn business."

"Oh, please." She rolls her eyes dramatically. "Do you really think I don't believe you're sleeping with her?" She scoffs, tossing her hair over her shoulder with practiced indifference. "Are you getting desperate? I mean, big girls aren't exactly your style."

My temper snaps, words spilling out before I can stop them. "You don't know what the hell you're talking about. Jenna's more woman than you could ever hope to be."

Fuck.

The second I see the triumphant gleam in Daria's eyes, I realize my mistake. She tricked me, baited me into defending Jenna, admitting something that was none of her business.

"Oh, Abram," she purrs, voice silky with satisfaction. "Always so predictable. Always playing protector. You've made yourself an easy target."

"I won't discuss Jenna with you," I say, my voice ice-cold. "Not another word."

She shrugs, glancing down as she continues to ruin her blouse. "Fine. But it's sweet, really, how much you care. A man like you could have anyone, but I suppose you've grown desperate since our divorce."

I refuse to rise to the jab, remaining silent though anger simmers just beneath my skin, barely contained.

"I came here," she continues, voice turning serious, "because I wanted to tell you myself. I didn't want you to hear it from someone else."

"Tell me what? We have nothing left to say to each other."

She tosses the cloth onto the bar, turning fully to face me. Her lips curve into a cruel smile. "I'm seeing Nico Agosti."

Every nerve in my body goes on high alert, tension radiating throughout my chest. Nico fucking Agosti—my most persistent rival. The son of the don who's determined to reclaim territory his family lost decades ago.

"Agosti," I say, my voice carefully neutral. "Interesting choice. You really think he gives a shit about you?"

Her eyes flash. "He's a perfect gentleman, and he knows exactly how to treat a woman."

I chuckle humorlessly. "Daria, please. You really haven't considered that maybe, just maybe, Nico's using you to get to me?"

Her expression hardens, fury radiating off of her in waves. "God, you are unbelievable. It's always about you, isn't it? Nico didn't even know my last name when we met."

I laugh outright. "You honestly believe that? The man's been trying to infiltrate my territory for years. He knows exactly who you are."

She visibly flinches, masking her doubt with anger. "You're pathetic, Abram. Jealousy doesn't suit you."

I lean forward, my gaze hardening. "I don't give a damn who you fuck. But if you think Agosti isn't playing you, you're a fool. Just keep my name out of your mouth."

"Don't tell me what to do," she spits, her voice rising. "You lost that right when you walked out!"

My temper flares. "*You're* the one who walked out, Daria. The only regret I have is saying 'I do' to a snake like you in the first place."

She lunges forward, one manicured finger pointing accusingly. "You loved me. You'd have given anything to keep me!"

"I was blind," I growl, standing straight, towering over her. "But thankfully, I got my sight back. Now get out of my office before I throw you out."

She scoffs, folding her arms defiantly. "Make me."

I snatch up the phone on my desk, stabbing the numbers to the security line. "Send two men up to my office immediately. I need them to escort Ms. Vasilieva off the property."

She screams, her voice shrill enough to shatter glass. "I don't go by that fucking name anymore!"

"Then change it legally," I reply, calmly replacing the receiver. "I don't want to be associated with you."

She stares at me, chest heaving, eyes filled with pure venom. She hurls her coffee mug at me with impressive force, aiming for my head. I see it coming just in time and catch it reflexively, coffee sloshing out and soaking into my shirt sleeve. It burns a bit, but I ignore the pain.

"You fucking—" My teeth grind together so hard my jaw throbs, vision narrowing to a pinpoint.

Before I can take another step toward her, the door swings open. Jenna stands there with two broad-shouldered security guards behind her. Her eyes dart from my soaked sleeve to Daria's defiant stance.

Daria instantly straightens and smooths her hair, her stature switching back to calm, polished, and infuriatingly poised. "No need for dramatics, boys. I'm leaving."

She moves toward the door with exaggerated grace, pausing just long enough to lean close to Jenna, eyes filled with cruelty. Her voice is low but loud enough for everyone to hear.

"Enjoy being his chubby little whore while it lasts."

Jenna pales, shock flickering across her face, quickly replaced by fury. My fists clench so tightly my knuckles crack audibly.

"Get the fuck out, Daria," I snarl.

She smirks, sweeping from the room without another word, security following closely. Jenna steps aside stiffly, avoiding my eyes.

The elevator doors click shut, silence slamming down like a hammer.

I stand there, heart pounding, ears ringing. Jenna's still in the doorway, arms wrapped tightly around herself, her expression unreadable. My stomach twists, guilt pooling low and hot. I hate that she had to hear any of that, especially Daria's venomous words. I can handle Daria's cruelty. But Jenna shouldn't have to.

"Jenna—" I start softly, taking a step forward.

She lifts her chin, eyes bright with unshed tears. "I'm fine."

"You're not." I move closer, gently gripping her shoulders. "She had no right to say that."

She shakes her head, stepping out of my grasp, her gaze dropping to the floor. "It's nothing I haven't heard before."

"Not from me," I say firmly. "You're stunning and she knows it. She's lashing out because she's jealous."

Jenna's expression softens slightly, though pain still flickers behind her eyes. "I don't want your pity, Abram."

"It's not pity. It's honesty."

She hesitantly meets my gaze, searching. "You didn't tell me you had an ex-wife."

"Because she doesn't matter," I state firmly. "Not anymore."

"Clearly, she thinks she does," Jenna replies. "Or she wouldn't have come here."

I sigh heavily, running a hand over my face. "She's poison. I made a mistake marrying her. She's manipulative, selfish, and thrives on drama."

"Then why did you?" Jenna asks softly. "Marry her, I mean."

It's a fair question, one I've asked myself a thousand times. "Because at one point, I believed she was someone else. I fell for an illusion."

She nods slowly, absorbing my words. Her guard seems to lower slightly, vulnerability softening the set of her shoulders. "She mentioned Nico Agosti. Should I be worried?"

My jaw tightens again. "Yes. Not about Daria but about Agosti. He's dangerous. He'll use anyone to get to me, even her."

She swallows hard, a shadow of fear crossing her features. "What does all of that mean?"

"It means," I say, reaching out to gently touch her cheek, "you need to be careful. Stay close, do exactly as I say, and trust me."

She searches my eyes, then nods. "I trust you."

The relief that floods me is intense and unexpected. "Good. Because I won't let him or Daria hurt you."

She gives me a faint smile. "If you didn't scare the hell out of me, I'd say you're trying to be romantic."

I chuckle softly. "Maybe I am. In my own fucked-up way."

She lets out a small laugh, genuine this time. The sound makes something inside me loosen just a bit.

"I'm sorry you had to deal with Daria's shit," I tell her sincerely. "I promise it won't happen again."

She nods, looking down briefly before meeting my eyes again. "Thank you."

We stand there for a long, quiet moment. I sigh, glancing down at my coffee-soaked sleeve. "Guess I need a new shirt," I mutter.

Jenna smiles softly, amusement returning to her eyes. "I might know where to find one."

I smile back, feeling the warmth return. "Good. I'll need it before the next meeting."

She turns toward the door then pauses, looking back at me. "Abram?"

"Yes?"

"She doesn't get to me. Not really."

I nod slowly, relieved. "Good."

"I mean it." Her voice steadies, quiet strength shining through. "What she thinks doesn't matter."

"Damn right," I agree.

She smiles again before turning and walking out the door, leaving me alone.

I drop heavily into my chair, exhaling deeply. My hands still shake slightly with adrenaline, rage still simmering beneath my skin. Daria's reappearance is trouble enough. But now she's aligned with Nico Agosti?

That's a dangerous game, even for her.

The question is, what is Agosti's endgame? And how far is he willing to go to get it?

More importantly, how do I keep Jenna from being caught in the crossfire?

My mind flickers back to Daria's venomous parting shot. She has no idea who Jenna is. No idea of the strength, the fire beneath Jenna's calm exterior.

Daria underestimates her. And that might just be to our advantage.

I lean back and stare at the ceiling, formulating plans and contingencies. One thing is clear—Agosti is making his move.

The rules have changed, and I have to be ready.

CHAPTER 20

JENNA

I'm still a little pissed as I open the closet door, reaching for Abram's private stash of fresh shirts.

I told Abram what she said didn't bother me, but I wasn't being entirely truthful. Her words cling to my mind like cobwebs, each insult a sticky strand of irritation. Chubby whore. Seriously? How the hell did Abram ever marry someone like her?

I take a moment to let the anger flow out of me. With a frustrated sigh, I push aside a couple of empty hangers. Where the hell are the shirts?

Shit.

There are no shirts. Just a mocking empty space. I knew he'd kept some here, yet there aren't any now. *Great.* I shut the door with more force than necessary and head back to Abram's office. He glances up from his desk, eyebrows raised in curiosity at my expression.

"Problem?"

"Your secret stash of shirts is empty," I say. "Either your dry cleaning hasn't arrived yet or there's a shirt thief on the loose."

He leans back in his chair, the corner of his mouth ticking upward. He winces, remembering something. "I sent them in for dry cleaning but forgot to pick them up. My fault, not yours."

I huff out a breath. "What are you going to do? You can't exactly lead meetings smelling like a distillery."

He rubs a hand over his jaw, amusement forming in his eyes. "You're right. I'll have to work from home."

I pause, caught off-guard. "From home?"

"Yes. It's quiet. Secure. And I have plenty of shirts there," he adds with a wink, then leans forward, hands clasped loosely. "You'll come with me."

I stare at him, unsure I've heard correctly. "To your apartment?"

"Yes."

Heat flickers through my veins, my pulse quickening. "Is that appropriate?"

He chuckles, a deep, rich sound that only makes my cheeks burn hotter. "Considering what we just did on my desk, Jenna, I think appropriate is a bit irrelevant now."

"Fair," I say, a reluctant smile slipping through. "But—"

"There's plenty of room," he assures me, interrupting.

"You'll have your own office space if you want it. We can coordinate from there."

Being in Abram's apartment, his private space... the thought sends a wicked thrill straight down my spine. I bite my lip, trying to appear unaffected.

"Look, if you're not comfortable with it," he says, watching me closely, "you can take the rest of the day off. No pressure."

I straighten immediately, shaking my head. "No, that's fine. I'll go with you."

He smiles, genuine and pleased. "Good. I'm glad."

My irritation at Daria begins to fade, replaced with anticipation. There's something else too, something softer. Being wanted by Abram like this, seeing him genuinely pleased at the thought of me being close, feels good. Really good.

He stands, grabbing his keys from the desk. "You can ride with me. Easier than dealing with valet today."

"Sure."

I follow him down to the private elevator and into the basement garage. When we reach his parking space, the car parked there makes my jaw drop. A sleek, powerful black Mercedes-Maybach, waiting for us.

"Wow," I breathe.

He smirks, opening the passenger door for me. "Get in."

I slide onto buttery soft leather seats, inhaling deeply. Everything smells like him—leather and something deliciously masculine. He slides into the driver's seat, taking control with practiced ease. He grips the steering wheel and starts the engine, the car humming quietly to life.

We glide through Vegas traffic, the city shimmering in the morning sunlight. It's weird being with him in his car, outside of the office. No work interruptions, no ringing phones or unexpected visitors. Just us.

Abram glances sideways at me, eyes glittering. "You're staring."

I flush, turning to face forward again. "You look good behind the wheel."

He chuckles. "Glad you think so."

I bite back a smile. "Don't let it go to your head."

"Too late," he says, grinning, his hand slipping from the wheel and moving gently onto my thigh. My heartbeat accelerates immediately.

"What do you think you're doing?" I ask, my voice hitching despite my effort to sound calm.

"Keeping you close," he says, palm sliding slightly higher. "That's why I wanted you with me today. So I could show you exactly just how close I'd like you to be."

My breath hitches again, and I part my thighs instinctively, heart hammering in anticipation. His hand moves higher, fingertips tracing teasing patterns over my legs. Even through the fabric, the heat from his touch radiates into my skin, pooling heat low in my belly.

His eyes stay on the road, completely calm and composed, but his hand grows bolder, slipping beneath my skirt. I gasp softly, gripping the leather seat as pleasure spirals through me. He smiles, eyes still straight ahead, completely in control as he strokes and teases, slipping deeper, caressing exactly where I need him most.

"Abram," I whisper, head dropping back against the headrest. My hips rock instinctively into his hand, body humming with desperate need.

"Relax," he murmurs. "Let me take care of you."

His fingers swirl gently before firmly pressing in exactly the right spot, working me expertly, steadily. His fingertip drags up along my lips, spreading me just enough to tease my clit perfectly.

Pleasure coils tight and hot, breath coming faster as I spiral closer to the edge. I barely recognize the city streets sliding by, aware only of his hand, his touch, the skillful way he plays my body.

"I'm..." I choke out, arching helplessly.

"I know," he says, voice like silk. "Let go, Jenna. Now."

I shatter at his command, biting back a cry as I come around his fingers. He continues to gently stroke my pussy, easing me down slowly, my breath ragged and shallow. By the time I open my eyes again, we're pulling up to an exclusive building. His building.

My limbs are jelly as he parks the car in a private underground garage. He finally turns, regarding me with quiet satisfaction, and withdraws his hand. My body aches deliciously, craving more already.

"Ready to get to work?" he asks, a wicked gleam in his eye.

"Why do I get the feeling you're not talking about spread-sheets," I say breathlessly.

He grins, getting out then coming around to open my door. "Maybe. Maybe not."

I take his hand, legs still trembling slightly. I never thought Abram Vasiliev could make me this reckless, but I like it. God help me, I like it way too much.

As the elevator doors close behind us, heat pulses through me again. If Abram wants to keep me close today, I'm not going to argue. Not even a little bit.

When the doors slide open, Abram leads me inside with a confident stride. Immediately, the lobby steals my breath. Sleek marble floors gleam beneath towering windows, lush, green plants artfully placed like subtle sculptures. Everything whispers elegance and power. Luxury practically drips from the walls.

The attendant at the front desk glances up and nods respectfully, eyes flicking quickly to me before returning to Abram. His presence clearly commands respect here, but I don't miss the curiosity in her gaze. She's probably wondering what the hell I'm doing here, and frankly, I'm wondering the same.

Abram doesn't pause, guiding me straight to a gleaming glass elevator marked with his private access. The doors part silently, and we step in, soaring smoothly upward, Vegas unfolding beneath us in a glittering panorama. It's breathtaking, majestic, and completely forgotten the instant Abram's mouth finds mine again.

His kiss is fierce, hungry. His hands grip my waist posses-sively, and I melt into his chest. My heart pounds against his as he backs me firmly against the glass. A faint rush of vertigo hits me as the city stretches out beneath us, but Abram's mouth quickly distracts me from it.

"You drive me fucking insane," he growls against my lips, one hand sliding roughly over my thigh.

"I could say the same about you," I manage, fingers buried in his shirt, desperate for the heat of his skin.

His tongue plunges deep into my mouth, demanding and irresistible. I moan against him, my legs trembling as the elevator continues its ascent, our bodies pressed impossibly close. His dominance ignites every nerve ending, his rough-ness exactly what I crave.

The elevator halts smoothly, doors gliding open directly into Abram's penthouse. He pulls away just enough to lead me inside, and my breath catches all over again.

His home is nothing short of spectacular. Floor-to-ceiling windows frame an astonishing view of the city, sunlight cascading over modern furniture, tasteful artwork, and plush rugs. It's open, spacious, and beautifully masculine. It suits him perfectly.

"This place is incredible," I say, gaze sweeping across the luxurious space.

His eyes are locked on me. "Glad you like it. But right now, I have other priorities."

His tone sends a thrill cascading down my spine. "Such as?"

"Strip."

My heart skips a beat. "Really?"

He leans against the marble kitchen island, crossing his powerful arms, eyes dark and intense. "Consider it your work uniform while you're here."

Heat floods my cheeks, excitement spiking through my blood. I reach for my blouse, but he stops me immediately.

"No. Slowly." His voice is husky, commanding. "Show me."

My pulse quickens as I comply, fingers trembling slightly with nervous anticipation. I leisurely undo the buttons, letting my blouse slip over my shoulders. Abram's eyes darken further, his chest rising and falling at a slightly quicker pace with each measured breath.

I drop my skirt next, sliding it slowly down my hips. His gaze traces every inch of exposed skin, stoking a fire deep in my belly. Down to nothing but my bra, I pause, waiting for his next command.

"Turn around," he says.

A thrill dances through me, and I obey without hesitation. I can feel his eyes on me, hot and possessive. It's intoxicating.

He's behind me in an instant, spinning me around and scooping me into his arms effortlessly, his powerful muscles flexing around me. I wrap my legs around his waist, gasping slightly when he sets me down atop the cool marble of the kitchen bar. He kneels between my thighs, eyes blazing.

"I can't wait to taste you again," he says, mouth descending, warm breath brushing sensitive skin.

His tongue glides over me, soft and sure. My head falls back and I gasp, my fingers holding him in place, needing the contact, the connection, the closeness of him.

He takes his time, like this is exactly where he wants to be. He kisses around my lips, his tongue darting out teasingly before spreading me open.

Each stroke of his tongue over my clit feels like heaven, like he's speaking a language only my body understands. My thighs tremble around him, the heat building slowly, achingly, deliciously.

The sight of him between my legs, face buried in me with such single-minded devotion, is almost too much. It's beautiful. It's overwhelming.

My heart squeezes in my chest because it's not just erotic, it's tender.

It's real.

He groans, the vibration sending another jolt of pleasure through me. I bite my lip, breath catching, hips tilting into the rhythm he's building. He knows exactly what he's doing to me. Every swirl and flick of his tongue, every pause is intentional. He slips a finger inside, curling into my warm wetness.

The pleasure crests even higher, stealing my breath, my thoughts, everything. And still, he doesn't rush. He stays patient and focused, anchoring me even as I start to come undone.

"Oh, God, Abram—" I choke out, hips bucking against his mouth.

"Come for me," he commands, his voice deep and rough, vibrating deliciously against my pussy.

I cry out sharply as overwhelming pleasure tears through me. My vision blurs, shattering into brilliant sparks. As the orgasm begins to fade, he stands, capturing my mouth in a searing kiss. I'm dizzy with need, utterly lost to him.

He lifts me again and carries me down the hall to his bedroom. Inside, it's all dark wood, silken sheets, and subtle masculinity. He lowers me onto the massive bed before stripping off his clothes, revealing that powerful body that haunts my fantasies.

He climbs onto the bed, guiding me to my hands and knees. "Damn, I can't get enough of you."

I gasp as he enters me from behind, hands gripping my hips, claiming me deeply, his thick cock stretching me in the way only he can. Right away, his rhythm is strong, commanding. Over and over he thrusts into me.

The sound of our breathing and bodies meeting fills the room, mingled with his growled praises and dirty whispers.

"You're perfect, Jenna. Every fucking inch of you," he groans, thrusting deep, his cock hitting just the right spot deep inside my pussy.

"Yes," I whimper, clutching the sheets. "God, Abram, yes—"

He leans forward, lips brushing my ear. "You're mine, Jenna. Say it."

"I'm yours," I gasp, pleasure swelling.

He flips me onto my back in one swift move, never breaking contact. His eyes blaze into mine as he positions himself above me, muscles rippling as he plunges deep once more. I catch the sight of him vanishing into me, and I wrap my legs tightly around him, digging my nails into his broad shoulders, needing him closer, deeper still.

"You feel like heaven," he murmurs, pressing kisses along my neck. "You're everything I want. Everything I fucking need."

I arch against him, hips rising desperately, meeting every thrust, igniting flames that consume me completely. "Don't stop," I plead. "Please."

He thrusts harder, deeper, driving us both toward the edge. Our moans blend, spiraling higher, until we shatter together in an explosive climax. I cling to him, trembling, my body utterly spent and satisfied beneath him.

Slowly, gently, he pulls me close, pressing soft kisses to my temple, my cheek, my lips. The aftercare is tender, affectionate... almost just as perfect as the intense passion we just shared. My heart squeezes dangerously in my chest.

"You're incredible," I whisper, tracing my fingers gently along his powerful chest, feeling the steady beat of his heart beneath my palm.

He kisses my forehead, holding me closer. "So are you."

Lying in his arms, warm and utterly content, a sudden nervous flutter takes root in my chest. Because as much as I've tried to deny it, I can't. This is more than lust, more than physical pleasure. My heart's in this too, and I'm starting to fall.

Oh God.

I glance up at Abram's face—strong, powerful, possessive—and realize just how much danger I'm in.

But even knowing the risk, I still find myself holding him tighter, breathing him in deeply.

Because despite all my fears, falling for Abram feels too good to fight it.

CHAPTER 21

ABRAM

Sunlight spills across Jenna's bare skin, highlighting every gorgeous curve, every delicious inch. I prop myself up on an elbow, admiring the beauty sprawled beside me. Her fiery hair cascades over the pillow, a wild tangle I long to wrap around my fist again. As her chest rises and falls gently, I trace the soft, inviting swell of her hip with hungry eyes.

God, she's perfect.

Every single part of her, those thick thighs I love gripping as she rides me, the generous hips that fit perfectly beneath my palms, her perfect, pink nipples that taste as sweet as candy. Every mouthwatering curve brings me to my knees, again and again.

She catches me looking and arches a teasing eyebrow. "Shouldn't we be getting back to work?" she asks playfully, lips curling into a smirk.

I chuckle. "I'd say we're already putting in a full day's work," I reply, my eyes drifting slowly down her flushed body, making my point crystal clear. "In a matter of speaking."

A blush blooms across her pale skin before something shifts subtly in her expression, a shadow passing behind those luminous green eyes. Before I can ask, she suddenly sits up, grabbing a blanket to cover herself.

"Jenna?"

She offers a quick, forced smile. "Just need some water. I'll be right back."

She disappears into the bathroom before I can say another word. I hear the sound of water pouring into a glass. A convenient excuse, but I recognize it for what it is—a reason to put space between us. A reason to hide whatever sudden insecurity just flared to life inside her.

Anger rises like a hot wave in my chest. I know exactly who planted that insecurity: Daria with her venomous tongue. The bitch.

When Jenna returns, she's still wrapped in the blanket, eyes downcast. I sit up, gesturing gently. "Come here, *krasivaya moya*," I say. "Tell me what's wrong."

She hesitates, her embarrassment evident, but she finally walks over to the bed, sinking down beside me. She twists the blanket nervously in her hands, refusing to meet my gaze.

A moment passes. Finally, she speaks. "I hate admitting this," she begins quietly, "but that comment your ex-wife made really got under my skin. Not the whore part—I know who I am—it's just..." she trails off, swallowing hard. "I know I said it didn't bother me, but it did."

Something twists painfully inside my chest at her confession. Sympathy battles fiercely with fury, but I push away any thought of Daria and focus solely on Jenna. I reach out, tipping up her chin gently until she meets my gaze.

"Listen to me," I say. "You are, without question, the sexiest goddamn woman I've ever laid eyes on. Do you hear me?"

Her eyes widen slightly, but I don't let her look away. I brush a thumb over her cheekbone.

"Your curves are fucking addictive. The way you feel beneath my hands, the way you look... it does things to me I didn't even know were possible. Every inch of you drives me insane."

Her lips part, her breath quickening. I move my hand, pulling down the blanket, revealing those full, beautiful breasts and thick, delicious thighs. I press soft, open-mouthed kisses to her collarbone, her shoulder, whispering as I go.

"Do you have any idea how gorgeous you are, Jenna? How perfectly you fit against me? The thought of touching you, tasting you, being inside you... it consumes me. Constantly."

She gasps as I spread her thighs, fingers tracing the inner side of them slowly, deliberately. Her hips shift, instinctively seeking more.

"You're beautiful," I speak against her throat, tasting her pulse. "You're stunning. And you're mine."

My fingers slide over her slick heat, and she arches with a broken moan. I tease her slowly, gently, bringing her to the edge again and again. Each stroke, each whispered compliment sends shivers racing through her.

"You're perfection. Every single goddamn inch."

"Abram," she pants softly, nails digging into my shoulders as I circle her sensitive spot, edging her closer and closer to release. "Please."

"You don't have to beg," I whisper, sliding my fingers deep, watching her unravel beneath my touch. "I'll give you everything you need."

I pull my hand away, shifting my body until I'm settled above her, positioned at her entrance. My heart thunders fiercely in my chest as I gaze down into her beautiful face.

"Look at me," I command gently. "You're the sexiest, most incredible woman on this earth, and I'm going to prove it to you."

She nods breathlessly, locking eyes with me. I plunge deep, savoring her gasp, the exquisite sensation of being buried to the hilt inside her warmth.

We move together seamlessly, her legs wrapping around my hips, holding me close. Our bodies surge, rhythmic and intense, passion rising hot and fierce. I kiss her mouth, her face, her throat.

"You feel like heaven," I tell her, my voice husky. "Everything about you is perfect. You're all I want. All I need."

She moans, clutching me tighter. "Yes. God, please don't stop."

"I couldn't if I tried," I promise her, driving deeper, pushing us both to the edge. "Come for me, baby. Come knowing exactly how much you turn me on."

She shatters beneath me, arching beautifully. Her orgasm drags me under, fierce and powerful, and I finish deep inside her with a ragged growl, pulse hammering against hers.

We collapse together, bodies tangled, breathing harsh. I cradle her close, gently smoothing damp curls away from her face. Tenderness washes over me, stronger than I'm prepared for. My heart thuds painfully, an unfamiliar tightness blooming in my chest.

I study her quietly as she catches her breath, eyes closed, utterly stunning in the aftermath of pleasure. I trace gentle fingers along her curves, marveling silently. There's something more between us now than pure lust. Something deep and fierce, something dangerous.

I never intended to fall for her. But in this moment, tangled together in my bed, I'm forced to confront the truth.

I've never felt this way about anyone before. And it scares the living hell out of me.

She opens her eyes slowly, her emerald gaze searching mine, soft and vulnerable. "Abram?" Her voice is hesitant, almost shy.

"Hmm?" I murmur, unable to tear my eyes away from her.

She bites her lip softly. "Did you mean all that? Everything you said?"

I nod slowly, brushing my thumb gently along her jaw. "Every single word. You are incredible. Inside and out."

Her smile lights up the room. She snuggles closer, resting her head against my chest. I hold her tight, heart pounding.

I don't know exactly what this means, but I do know I don't want to let her go. Whatever happens next, whatever chaos may come, I want her at my side.

I tighten my arms around her, pressing a soft kiss to her temple.

Maybe I am falling for her. Maybe it's reckless, maybe it's dangerous. But with Jenna warm and safe in my arms, it feels right.

So damn right.

CHAPTER 22

JENNA

One month later...

The office is alive with activity.

It's barely past eight when I step into Abram's office and he already looks delicious. Charcoal grey slacks, white shirt rolled up at the sleeves, top button undone, grey vest snug over his chest like it was custom-stitched for his body.

He looks up from whatever document he's destroying with that predator stare of his.. His mouth curves into something I've learned to translate as, *good—you're here. I need you.*But he doesn't say anything.

I shoot him a smirk. "Good morning to you too, boss man."

He grunts, then motions for me to sit.

"Two things from legal," I say, clicking open my tablet. "One, our Nevada liquor license renewals for our food and drink properties are squared away through next year. And two, your signature's needed on the zoning variance for the downtown property. I emailed it over, but the city's asking for a hard copy."

Abram nods, already scribbling something down. "Have Julian handle the courier. I don't want to babysit city paperwork."

"Done. Also, FYI. Your little side venture in Prague? We got confirmation that the shell company's now fully operational. Even the tax nerds were impressed."

His smirk returns. "Tell them I'm touched."

I cross my legs and lean back in the leather chair. "Don't tempt me, Vasiliev. I'm trying to be professional this morning."

"Trying," he murmurs, eyes flicking down my body before snapping back to mine. "Keyword."

A beat of silence, thick and charged, passes between us. Then he straightens, his mood shifting. "Did you nail down that meeting with Nico yet?"

I exhale, tapping to my notes. "I've tried every number I've got. Twice a week, for the past three weeks. They keep telling me Don Agosti is too ill for a formal meeting."

Abram's brow tightens. "I smell bullshit."

"Yep. And now two of your guys have reported issues at the Blue Anchor."

His hand clenches where it rests on the desk. "They're testing us."

I don't answer, letting the silence speak for itself. Because I believe they are testing him. I'm not exactly a Bratva expert, but it's not a stretch to imagine the Agostis are sniffing around for an opening.

Abram leans back in his chair, staring at the skyline. "You've been trying to reach Nico for three goddamn weeks. He's dodging me. Either because he's up to something, or he's too stupid to see how important it is that we meet."

"Want me to try again?"

His jaw flexes. "No. I'll handle it."

I don't press. Not when he's like this—calm on the surface but starting to crack underneath.

I close my tablet, acting more casual than I feel. Something tells me this Agosti situation is only getting started. And it's not going to have a pretty ending.

Abram exhales heavily then pushes back from the desk. He circles around like a lion in a cage, stopping in front of me.

"Come here."

I stand, almost as if gravity itself pulls me to him. He wraps his arms around my waist, firm and sure, pulling me flush against his rock-solid chest. My palms settle lightly there, the scent of him wrapping around me like silk.

"You," he murmurs, brushing his nose against mine, "are too brave for your own good."

I grin up at him. "Funny. I was just about to say the same to you."

He huffs something close to a laugh, and I rise on my toes to kiss him—slow and warm—teasing just enough to make him tighten his grip on my hips.

"So tell me," I whisper, lips still brushing his, "what would you like your too-brave assistant to do?"

He leans back just enough to meet my eyes, a flicker of something sharp in his expression. "It's time I make a call to Don Agosti myself."

I blink. "Wait, you're bypassing Nico and going straight to the don?"

Abram nods, his jaw tight. "Nico is the one showing disrespect. And I don't believe for a second that Don Agosti's too sick to meet. My sources say he's still taking visitors."

I shift slightly in his arms. "You sure you want to poke that bear? Didn't you say that old school men like him care about hierarchy? Protocol?"

He brushes his knuckles down my cheek. "If the messages aren't reaching him, that *is* the breach in protocol."

The heat in his voice gives me goosebumps. He kisses me again, slower this time, hands slipping down to cup my ass with zero shame. It's the kind of kiss that says he's not thinking about organized crime anymore.

"Enough business talk," he says, lips trailing toward my jaw. "I've been imagining bending you over this desk since you walked in."

It's tempting. Very tempting. But one of us has to stay on task.

"Oh really?" I chuckle, sliding a palm between us and patting his chest twice. "Hate to break it to you, boss, but you've got a meeting with Mikail and Denis in an hour."

He groans.

"Which means," I add, stepping out of his arms with a little sway in my hips, "you've got exactly fifty-eight minutes to review their proposal before you start winging it in front of your two most important lieutenants."

"You're no fun."

I flash a grin over my shoulder. "Oh, I'm a lot of fun. Just not the kind you can squeeze into an hour."

With a sassy wink, I head for the door—hips swaying, grin wicked, leaving him to his meeting and his frustration.

"We could accomplish a hell of a lot in an hour, ya know," Abram calls after me, tone laced with a smoky promise.

I pause at his door, glancing back over my shoulder with a teasing smirk. "And yet, think of all the ways I can reward your patience tonight." My voice drops into a playful purr. "Trust me—it'll be worth the wait."

His eyes darken in that way I've come to crave, and he closes the distance in two long strides, taking my face gently in his hands. "Are you sure you want to wait?"

God, the way he kisses me—possessive yet tender—melts every last ounce of my resistance. My fingers thread through his shirt, tempted to tug him back toward that damned irresistible desk. I pull away just enough to catch my breath, my lips tingling with the ghost of his kiss.

"Barely," I whisper honestly, feeling the heat rising within. "But yeah. I'm sure."

Abram chuckles, giving my ass a playful slap as I finally turn away.

I whirl back around, mouth dropping open in mock outrage. "You're going to pay for that!"

He leans casually against the wall, those ice-blue eyes gleaming with mischief. "And you're going to love every minute of it. I'm well aware how much you enjoy a little spanking, Jenna."

A blush heats my cheeks. Damn him. He's right. "Behave," I scold, closing his office door firmly behind me but not before I catch the smug grin spreading across his face.

God, he's trouble.

Smiling to myself, I cross to my office, my pulse still pleasantly buzzing. I groan at the clutter before me. Papers are scattered everywhere; I've let it get completely out of hand.

I sit down and start sorting, stacking papers into tidy piles, trashing useless printouts and sticky notes. As I file and organize, my mind drifts inevitably to Abram. That little slap echoes in my memory, stoking a fantasy that slips in uninvited:

Abram bends me over his desk, his hands firm on my hips, pressing himself against me, while whispering dirty promises that send heat shooting through my entire body. His hand slides slowly up my thigh, teasing my skirt higher until...

I catch myself, cheeks heating again as I smile like an idiot. I'm hopeless around that man.

Determined to regain focus, I move onto the drawers, pulling them open and sorting out pens, paperclips, and random office supplies. Satisfied, I tug open the third drawer, and stop cold.

A box of tampons stares back at me.

I frown, confused, and pick it up slowly. When was the last time I...?

Oh.

A flicker of unease ripples through me. My period. When exactly did I have it last? I rack my brain, trying to remember.

I glance at my desk calendar, then open my phone and swipe through my cycle-tracking app. My heart jumps unpleasantly. According to the app, I'm overdue. A full week overdue, to be precise.

This doesn't happen; I'm never late.

I stare at my phone, trying not to panic. It could just be stress. I have been busy—working long hours, sleeping with my sexy-as-hell boss in between. Stress can definitely delay periods.

My phone buzzes suddenly, causing me to nearly drop it. Claire's name pops up on my screen. I open the text.

Remember—happy hour at five o'clock! Don't stand me up!

I reply immediately, fingers trembling slightly.

Wouldn't dream of it. See you there.

My heart pounds hard against my ribs. Happy hour with Claire is usually my favorite way to decompress, but today it feels daunting. If anyone can see right through my carefully constructed wall of composure, it's Claire. I haven't even told her I'm seeing him. How am I supposed to casually mention I might be pregnant with Abram's baby?

Oh, God. Could I actually be pregnant?

A million thoughts spin through my head. We've been careful, but not every time. My stomach tightens with an odd combination of nerves and excitement.

I exhale slowly, forcing myself to calm down. Jumping to conclusions won't help anything.

I give the box of tampons one last glance, then close the drawer slowly, willing my heart rate to return to normal. Pregnant or not, panicking won't change anything. I'll buy a test on the way home, take it in the privacy of my apartment, and go from there.

Until then, I have work to do.

I busy myself again, tidying my desk with renewed determination. But no matter how hard I try, my thoughts keep drifting back to the possibility that there might be a tiny life already growing inside me.

Abram's child.

The idea simultaneously thrills and terrifies me. Abram's world isn't exactly white picket fences and suburban bliss. Could I bring a child into it? Could I handle it? How would Abram react?

My pulse quickens and I press my hands to my face, breathing in and out slowly. I'm getting ahead of myself again. I don't even know if I'm pregnant, and already I'm spiraling.

Pull it together, Jenna. One step at a time.

With a deep breath, I glance at the clock. It's nearly noon. Drinks with Claire is just a few hours away, and I need to look like I haven't just had my entire world potentially flipped upside down.

I head to the restroom, taking a few moments to freshen up. I stare at myself in the mirror. I appear calm and collected on the surface, but beneath that facade, my nerves are uncertain and jittery.

"No matter what, you've got this," I say to my reflection.

My voice sounds unconvincing. I splash cool water on my face, dab away any stray mascara smudges, and smooth my hair, trying to look and feel normal.

When I return to my desk, my phone vibrates again.

Abram.

I swallow hard as I open the text.

Have a good rest of the day. I'll be counting the minutes until tonight.

Warmth floods me despite the anxiety humming beneath my skin. I reply quickly.

Counting them myself. Behave while I'm gone.

His reply is swift.

No promises.

I laugh softly, shaking my head. Even through the haze of worry, Abram still manages to make me smile.

Maybe that's a sign.

Whatever happens, we'll figure it out.

CHAPTER 23

JENNA

I'm already perched on a barstool when Claire walks in, and I've got butterflies in places I didn't know could flutter.

The plan was to have a drink or two, catch up, maybe gush a little about Abram, then head off to Abram's for our date.

But now... I'm not exactly in the mood for merlot. And if I am pregnant, I can't be drinking anyway.

Claire spots me instantly and beams, practically skipping over in her heels. "Well, well, well," she grins, pulling me into a tight hug. "If it isn't the personal assistant badass. What the hell have you been up to?"

I laugh, the sound more nervous than I'd like it to be. "Oh, you know. Work. Life. Debauchery."

Claire narrows her eyes. "Debauchery, huh? You do look suspiciously well-laid."

I arch a brow. "Suspiciously?"

"Yes. Suspiciously." She slides into the seat beside me, tossing her purse onto the bar with a dramatic flourish. "So spill. Who is he? And don't try to distract me—I will stab a bitch for answers."

"Jesus, Claire." I laugh genuinely this time, trying to play it cool, but there's no hiding the flush in my cheeks. "Okay, fine."

She leans in. "So?"

I smile. "He's intense. Rich. Smart. Hot as hell." I pause, fiddling with the edge of my napkin. "We've been seeing each other. Well, kind of seeing each other, for a little while now. He was actually the guy that night at the club... the one I hooked up with."

Claire blinks. "Wait. Wait. *Wait*. Is this the boss? *Your* boss?" she says a little too loudly.

I wince. "Yes."

"Holy hell, Jenna." She grabs my arm. "You've been thirsting over this man since you started there, and now you're just casually telling me you're seeing him?"

"It's complicated," I reply. "But then again, it isn't. I didn't plan for it. It just happened."

Claire stares at me like she needs a second drink just to process what I said. "You're dating your hot mob boss and you didn't lead with that?"

"Claire—"

"No. No. I need to lie down. Or scream. Or get every single detail. Preferably all three."

I glance at the bartender. "Can I get a club soda with lime, please?"

"Club soda?" She studies me like she's trying to read the fine print. "And you're not drinking wine tonight because...?"

I hesitate just a beat too long. Her eyes sharpen. "I..."

"Okay, now I'm officially concerned."

I sigh, shoulders slumping as the bartender sets my drink in front of me. "I might be pregnant."

Her eyes widen. She doesn't say anything for a beat, just watches me. When she does speak, it's a curse. "Well, shit."

"Yeah."

She rests a hand on mine, steady and warm. "How late are you?"

"A week. Maybe more. I didn't even notice until I found a box of tampons in my desk drawer today and realized I haven't needed them."

Claire nods slowly. "Okay. So, are you big-time freaking out, or just a little bit freaking out?"

"Both," I admit. "It's not just the maybe-being-pregnant part. It's what it would mean. A baby. With Abram. A child born into all this danger and secrecy... honestly, I don't even know what he does half the time. I don't want to raise a kid in that kind of world."

Claire squeezes my hand. "That's valid. But you're not alone. And no matter what happens, you'll handle it. You always do."

I smile weakly. "You're a good friend."

She shrugs. "It's my job. Besides, you're the one who got knocked up by a hot mobster. I can live vicariously through you for the drama."

I huff a laugh, finally exhaling. "So what now?"

Claire tosses back her hair like a woman with a mission. "Now, we get you a test. Let's go."

"Wait, *right* now?" I squeak.

"Yes. Before your hot mob boyfriend wines and dines you. Let's rip the Band-Aid off."

I slide off the stool, nerves buzzing. "God, what would I do without you?"

"You'd be peeing in fear. Come on."

We walk out of the bar, no drinks, no food. Just two women with a pharmacy in their future.

The fluorescent lighting in the drugstore makes everything feel just a little more dramatic. Or maybe it's just me, staring at a shelf of pregnancy tests like I'm trying to crack a code. Why are there so many options? I just need a simple yes or no answer.

Claire, bless her, senses the spiral. She steps in like a shopping ninja and grabs two boxes off the shelf without even blinking. "Done. Let's go. You can have your existential crisis in peace."

Ten minutes later, we're back at her apartment—all Claire —boho meets hipster chic. Mismatched throw pillows, string lights over the windows. She sets the record player to spin some mellow indie track before getting me a glass of water.

She thrusts it into my hand like I'm a prizefighter about to enter the ring. "Knock 'em dead."

I laugh, mostly to keep from falling apart, and head off to the bathroom, test in hand.

The mirror catches my reflection—pale-faced, wide eyes, mouth set in a line that's trying too hard not to tremble. I follow the instructions, do my business, and then I wait the longest two minutes of my life. My heart pounds in my throat the entire time. When I finally look...

Two lines.

Positive.

I sit on the side of the tub for a second, staring at the little window like maybe if I squint hard enough it'll change its mind.

Nope. Still pregnant.

I walk out, feeling like a puppeteer is moving my limbs for me. Claire's perched on the arm of her velvet green couch, half-eaten chocolate bar in hand.

Her face falls instantly when she looks up. "Holy shit."

I nod slowly.

"What are you gonna do?"

I collapse onto the couch beside her, the test still clutched in my hand. "I have to tell him."

Claire doesn't say a word. She just waits with a quiet stillness. Finally, she says, "You need to think about what you want to do. Like, *really* think about it."

I frown, a little thrown. The statement hangs in the air. I haven't even thought about the alternative. Not really. The idea of not keeping it doesn't feel like an option at all. This tiny, sesame-seed-sized life is already tethered to me, to my heart.

"I want to keep it," I say softly, voice cracking just a little. "I mean, this was never part of the plan. I was supposed to wait until I was more established, but that's out the window now. I'll figure it out."

Claire smiles. "Okay. Then that's what you do. But maybe you should sit on telling him for a few days, see a doctor first."

I shake my head. "Claire, my period's never been late. Not once. This test is positive. I'm pregnant. And maybe it sounds weird, but I can actually feel that I'm pregnant."

She studies me. "You don't seem upset."

I look down at the test in my hand, the ghost of a smile tugging at my lips. "I'm not. Not really. Scared, yeah. But upset? No. I've always wanted kids. Just didn't expect it to happen so soon."

Claire leans her head on my shoulder. "So you're telling him?"

"I have to. If he's not on board, I'll walk. From the job. From him."

Because this isn't a maybe anymore. It's real. And I've never felt more sure.

Claire watches me with the gentle best friend concern that always makes me feel like I'm ten years old and have just scraped my knee.

"Listen," she says, "I'll cancel my date with Tyler tonight. We'll order Thai, binge something stupid on Netflix, and pretend your uterus isn't secretly running your entire life right now."

I smile, touched by her offer. "That sounds super tempting. But I've got a date with Abram. At his place."

Her brows shoot up. "Oh? At *his* place?"

I nod, cheeks flushing. "Yeah. It's kind of become our thing lately—he likes to cook."

Claire lets out a low whistle. "The terrifying, sexy Russian mob boss cooks?"

I shrug nonchalantly, but my shy smile gives me away. "He's good at it, too. Like, really good. He says it's stress relief."

"That's so hot I don't even know what to do with myself," she says, flopping dramatically back onto the couch.

I laugh before getting serious again. "It is. But honestly, I don't know what we are exactly."

Claire sits back up. "Girl. You're sleeping with him. You're going to his place for dinner. And you're pregnant with his baby. If that's not dating, I don't know what is."

"Exactly," I mutter, rubbing my temples. "And that's the

problem. I'm pregnant with his baby, yet I'm not even sure if I'm his girlfriend."

Claire's lips twitch into a mischievous grin. "Alright. I have an idea. A fabulous, shallow, gloriously girly idea."

"Oh God."

She ignores me, grabbing her keys. "There's this cute-as-hell little boutique around the corner from here. Right next to a hair salon. You're going to get a killer dress and a blowout, and you're going to walk into Abram's place making him determined to end this situationship you've got going and make it official."

I start to shake my head, but she doesn't let me speak.

"He won't know what hit him. Maybe that will make it crystal clear what he's about to lose if he doesn't get his head out of his ass."

I hesitate, chewing the inside of my cheek before nodding. "Alright. Let's do it."

The boutique is small but packed with charm—exposed brick, minimal lighting, racks of vintage silky dresses and daring little numbers that would have terrified me a year ago. Claire pulls one out with a dramatic flourish.

"This."

It's a deep emerald green, the kind of green that makes my eyes pop and my skin look like I spent the weekend in Capri. The neckline plunges low, with delicate straps that crisscross at the back.

A few minutes later, I've got it on, stepping out of the dressing room. The bodice hugs my curves like a second skin, the hem hitting mid-thigh with just enough flare to flirt with modesty.

I stare at myself in the mirror, feeling a flicker of real confidence pulse through me.

Claire beams. "You're going to kill him."

I purchase the dress. Next, we move on to the salon. The stylist knows what she's doing, giving me a soft, voluminous blowout with just enough wave to make me look like I wasn't even trying. Add a little dewy makeup, a dab of highlighter on my cheekbones, and I look downright hot.

Claire grins as I step out of the chair. "If he doesn't propose on the spot, I'm breaking his kneecaps."

I laugh, heart fluttering for a different reason entirely.

With perfect timing, my phone buzzes in my purse. It's a text from Abram.

Where should I have the car pick you up?

I type out Claire's address, then grin at my reflection in the salon mirror.

CHAPTER 24

JENNA

The car pulls up to Abram's building, sleek and silent. I smooth my dress, exhale deeply, and step out into the crisp Vegas evening.

Part of me is glad he suggested a night in. Between the boutique, the salon, and the positive test, my nerves are strung tighter than piano wire. Being in public tonight would've been too much.

But up in his penthouse, just the two of us and a little candlelight, that I can handle.

The elevator doors close behind me with a soft chime before ascending to the top floor. The glass walls reveal an amazing, glittering view of the Strip, the city slowly slipping into its nighttime splendor. It's sunset, and everything's bathed in a honeyed gold—buildings edged in light, sky streaked with rose and violet.

When the elevator glides to a stop, the doors open into Abram's penthouse like magic.

He's at the dining table, dressed in a pale grey button-up and tailored black slacks, sleeves rolled to the elbows, collar open just enough to tease. He's preparing the place settings, a soft, domestic moment that sets every nerve in my body on fire.

The scent of something delicious floats in from the kitchen, garlic, herbs, and butter. Light jazz hums low in the background, candles flickering golden across the glass table.

It's too much. Too perfect.

He looks up and smiles when he sees me. My breath catches.

"*Bozhe moy*," he says, crossing the room. "You look unbelievable."

"Thanks," I manage, feeling like a teenager on prom night. "You look pretty amazing yourself."

His arms wrap around me, one hand skimming down my back to rest just above the swell of my hips. He kisses me, slow and warm, with just enough pressure to make me melt into him. I soak in his presence, trying to keep my brain from shouting "I'm pregnant!" at full volume.

He pulls back and brushes a knuckle down my cheek. "Wine?"

I hesitate, then shake my head. "My stomach's been a little weird today. Probably stress."

His brows twitch into a slight frown, the wheels starting to turn. But he doesn't press. He just gives me a nod and steps back toward the table.

"You hungry?" he asks.

"Starving," I reply, easing out of my heels. "Smells amazing."

He grins, a flash of pride in his eyes. "Osso buco. My mother's recipe."

I smile. "Are you trying to seduce me with veal shank, Mr. Vasiliev?"

"Is it working?"

Oh, it's working. Everything he does works.

"I'll have to taste it first."

I grin, but I'm shaking beneath my brave exterior. Because this might become more than a dinner. It might be the last night of us, before things change forever.

I perch at the kitchen bar, resting my chin on my palm as I watch him move around the stovetop like he was born to cook. I've seen him cook before, but there's something different about tonight. I'm no longer evaluating him as just a cook; I'm now looking at him as a potential dad.

The thought is so intense I push it out of my head as quickly as I can.

"Am I dreaming?" I ask. "You're really pulling off domestic god tonight."

He gives me a sideways glance, smirking as he drizzles sauce with precision. "You haven't even tasted it yet."

"Doesn't matter. Watching you do all of this in slacks and a dress shirt is already worth the trip."

He chuckles, something in his face softening as he spoons risotto onto plates. "You ever cook?"

"Does Trader Joe's orange chicken in a wok count?"

He snorts, then smirks. "Not even a little."

"Well, then no."

"I could teach you," he says, glancing at me again, more curious than flirty now. "If you ever wanted to learn."

I tilt my head. "You'd be patient with me?"

"Depends on how cute you look screwing up."

"Oh, well, in that case, I'll burn everything." I give him a wink.

He grins and slides the plates onto the bar, pouring each of us a glass of sparkling water before gesturing toward the table near the floor-to-ceiling windows.

The view is breathtaking—the glamorous lights of Vegas stretches out below us as far as the eye can see, glittering and alive. We sit across from one another, and when we clink our glasses, his eyes linger on mine.

"To beautiful nights," he says.

"To beautiful nights," I echo.

God help me, I think I'm falling in love with this man.

The food is incredible. I keep taking slow bites just to stretch out the experience, but even then, my plate empties faster than I'd like.

"You weren't lying," I murmur between bites. "Your mother deserves a Michelin star."

He smiles, his eyes settling on something behind me. I turn and see a small pile of toys tucked neatly in the corner of the hallway—colorful blocks, a plush dinosaur, a tiny pink handbag.

"What are those?" I ask.

"Oh," he says, pouring more sparkling water. "For my nieces, Emma and Lilia. I'm planning on surprising them with a few more things the next time I see them."

He smiles, bright and genuine. Seeing him light up like that, as if all the carefully arranged pieces of him just cracked slightly open, does something to me.

"You sound like a great uncle," I say softly.

"Well, they're great kids," he replies, setting the bottle down. "Smart, wild. Denis says they get their wild side from me. He's probably right."

"And your nephew?" I ask, recalling framed photos on his desk.

"Charles. Mikail's boy. That one's got a steel-trap brain. He's going to outsmart us all by the time he's ten."

He sounds proud. More than proud, attached. My heart stretches a little wider, wondering if he wants a family of his own someday.

"Do you spend a lot of time with them?" I ask.

"I like being able to visit. Spoil them, play the fun uncle, then come home and have my own space. My life is too full for much more than that."

My fork pauses mid-air. I look at him, but he's unaware of the quiet way my heart's sinking.

His life is too full. No room for more.

I can't help but wonder if that includes me.

I look away.

Abram's words keep echoing in my head... *then come home and have my own space.*

That isn't very promising for the whole "Hey, surprise, I'm carrying your child" conversation I'm supposed to work up the courage for tonight.

I can feel Abram watching me.

"You okay?" he asks, quiet and careful. He knows something's up.

"Yeah. Why?"

"You're not a great liar," he says with a little smirk. "You're staring off into space."

I force a chuckle. "Guess I'm just tired. Long week."

He gives me a look that says he doesn't buy it, but he lets it go. He gets up and starts clearing the plates, moving with that infuriating sex appeal, even when doing something as ordinary as rinsing dishes. Seeing him like this, in a domestic and homey setting, makes my chest ache.

He returns a minute later, carrying two dessert plates and a cocky grin. "Olive oil chocolate mousse," he says as he sets one in front of me. "With blood orange and Maldon Sea Salt flakes."

My eyes widen. "This looks amazing."

"Desserts are my thing," he says with a shrug, like it's no big deal. As if this man isn't already too good to be true.

I take a bite and holy hell—it's divine. Deep, dark chocolate. Silky texture. The citrus hits next, bright and sharp, followed by the crunch of sea salt like a little surprise party on my tongue. I moan before I can stop myself. And then I devour the whole damn thing like I haven't eaten in a week.

When I finally come up for air, I notice his plate's only half-touched. He's watching me, amused and a little turned on.

I groan. "That was not cute. I just blacked out and inhaled that like a woman possessed."

He leans in, reaches across the table, and wraps his hand around mine. His touch is warm and grounding, and it sends a little flutter through me. "Don't apologize," he says. "I love seeing you enjoying what I make. Never be embarrassed about that."

I try to look away but he holds my gaze.

"Don't ever feel like you have to shrink yourself," he says. "Not your appetite. Not your laugh. Not your body. Not one damn thing."

My breath catches.

"I want you satisfied. Always."

Something stirs deep inside me—a mixture of lust, longing, and once again, something dangerously close to love. For a brief moment, any fear I had fades away.

Abram clears the table while I savor the last bit of that wicked mousse still lingering on my tongue. A moment later, he returns with a drink in hand. It's citrusy and herbal, served in a rocks glass with a fat slice of orange.

"Ginger, lemon, chamomile," he says, handing it to me. "Helps with digestion. And stress."

I give him a soft smile. "What doesn't this man do?"

He chuckles.

We settle onto his sleek charcoal couch. The lights are low, the city glowing beyond the glass like it's putting on a show just for us. I sit close. I want to be near him, but my body feels split—half desperate to melt into his arms, half aching for the quiet safety of being alone.

I thought maybe I'd be able to tell him tonight. Rip the bandage off, like Claire said to. But now, curled up next to him on his sofa, with the weight of it all pressing on my chest, I know I can't. Not yet.

He glances at me, eyes dark. "I wanted to tear that dress off you the second I saw you walk through the door," he says. "Still do. But I can tell that's not where your head is tonight."

I swallow, guilt thick in my throat. "I'm sorry. I'm just stressed. My friend Claire, you remember her, from the club? She's dealing with some stuff. I guess it's weighing on me too."

It's not the worst lie I've ever told, but it's still a lie. And judging by the quiet in his expression, he knows it. But he doesn't call me out. Doesn't press.

Instead, he runs a knuckle gently down my cheek. "You want a bath and a good night's sleep? You can have your own bed if you'd prefer."

Part of me wants to say yes. To stay. To let him hold me and pretend, just for a few hours, that the world isn't tilting under my feet.

But I decline.

"Thank you. Really. That sounds amazing, but I think I need to go home tonight. I'm afraid I'm not very good company right now."

He nods once. No judgment. Just quiet understanding that somehow makes him even harder to walk away from.

"I'll call the driver," he says softly, reaching for his phone.

I glance down at my glass. "You're not mad?"

"Of course not," he says. "You don't owe me anything, Jenna."

That about undoes me. Because the truth is, I might owe him everything, and he doesn't even know it.

He finishes his drink in one smooth gulp. I sip mine, just to have something to do with my hands. It helps. A little.

The car arrives too quickly. Or maybe not quickly enough.

He walks me to the elevator, his hand settling low on my back, fingers spread wide over my hips like he can't quite let go yet. At the doors, he turns me toward him.

"You look beautiful tonight," he says. "Just wanted to tell you that again."

My breath catches. He leans in, kissing me slow and deep, like he's trying to memorize the taste of me. For a heartbeat, I nearly cave. I could stay. Let him undress me, carry me to bed, make love to me in that all-consuming way that makes everything else—my fears, the pregnancy, all the unknowns —fade away as he tells me I'm his...

The elevator dings.

"Jenna," he says, voice low, fingers brushing my cheek. "You sure?"

I nod, even as everything in me aches to stay. "Yeah. I just, I need some air."

"Okay." He presses one last kiss to my forehead. "I'll be here."

I step in, heart pounding, my eyes glued to him until the doors slide shut.

Once I'm alone, falling back down to earth, I nearly collapse.

I have no idea what I'm going to do.

CHAPTER 25

ABRAM

She's gone.

Her scent lingers, vanilla, warm and sweet. It makes my hands clench and my breath catch. I want her back. In my arms, in my bed. I want her laughing and looking at me like I hung the goddamn stars.

It almost scares me how much I want her.

But whatever she needed tonight, it wasn't me. Or, at least, not the version of me I'm used to offering.

I pour myself a whiskey—neat, two fingers—and head for the glass wall overlooking the Strip. My kingdom. Glittering, dangerous, drunk on its own power. For the first time in a long time, I don't feel like the man who owns it. I feel like a man who just let something priceless walk out his door.

She's hiding something. I know it as sure as I'm breathing, but I won't push.

She'll tell me when she's ready.

Or she won't.

Either way, I won't chase her. Not tonight.

I take my drink and head upstairs to the second-floor office. It's minimal—a long, modern desk, two guest chairs that no one ever sits in, and a massive oil painting of St. Petersburg in the snow I've stared at more nights than I can count. I keep the recessed lights dim, just enough to work by. The city glows below me, a living, breathing thing.

I hit the speakerphone. "Call Mikhail."

The line clicks before Mikhail's voice comes through, low and throaty. "Boss."

"You get anything out of Agosti yet?"

"Not a damn thing. Nico's stonewalling. Still saying the don's too sick for visitors. Same bullshit as always."

I slowly sip my whiskey. "Same story I'm hearing. You believe it?"

"No." A pause. "You want me to escalate?"

I swirl the amber liquid in my hand, eyes on the skyline. "No. But I want a meeting. Tomorrow morning."

"With Nico?"

"No. With Don Agosti."

Silence. Then a soft whistle. "You planning to knock on the front door?"

"In broad daylight. We go in clean. No threats. No games. Just a visit."

"Smart," he says. "So if anyone starts shit, it's on them."

"Exactly."

Another pause. "You want Denis to join us?"

"Yeah. Nine a.m. Tell him to meet us at the office. And bring a couple heavies but nothing flashy."

"Consider it done."

"Good. I want this handled before it turns into something we can't walk back from."

"Understood." He hangs up without fanfare. That's why I keep him close. He doesn't waste my time.

I set the glass down and stare out the window, deep in thought.

This city never sleeps. Neither do the men who want to take it from me. But they don't understand the difference between wanting power and being bred for it. I didn't claw my way up from the dark just to lose ground to some pampered princeling shithead like Nico Agosti.

Still, something's shifting. I can feel it. Like a storm pressing in behind the neon.

Jenna's in the path of it now. Whether she knows it or not.

God help me, I'll burn down half this town before I let it touch her. But that will only work if I know what I'm protecting her from.

I glance out into the night, the city alive with sin and secrets, wondering just how long she can keep hers from me.

And what it'll cost us both when it comes out.

~

Sleep evades me.

I toss and turn all night, entangled in dreams of Jenna in my bed, Jenna laughing in my arms, Jenna walking away... looking back just once before disappearing into the shadows.

It's unsettling. Not the dreams, I've had worse, but how much they affect me.

I've had one-night stands, flings, women I saw a handful of times, women I've dated on and off. Hell, I've been married.

But Jenna? This is something else entirely. I *miss* her. I feel like she took a part of me with her last night, and now I'm walking around without it.

If I feel this way already, if she means this much, then she's a liability. A weakness someone could use against me.

If my enemies were to find out...

She could be in danger. No. I will never allow it. She'll be protected. I'll make damn sure of it.

By the time the sun rises over the city, I'm already in the car. I skip the valet, taking the long way around to the private parking entrance under the building. The office isn't open yet, but I told Mikhail and Denis to meet me there early. We need to be ready before paying the Agostis a visit.

However,, something feels off. The tight coil at the base of my neck, the one that starts to wind when shit's about to go sideways, is tugging hard. It's the kind of edge I've learned to trust. It's saved my life more than once.

I pull into the private garage and kill the engine. My hand goes straight to the glove box, retrieving my Glock. I tuck it into the waistband at my back, covering it with my suit jacket.

It's probably nothing. But probably has no place in my world.

I get out, slow and steady, eyes scanning the shadowed corners of the garage. It's too quiet. The familiar air smells of concrete and car exhaust. But the tension in my gut doesn't ease.

No guards. No entourage. I don't keep a detail around me constantly—not because I can't, but because I don't like the message it sends. Makes a man look weak. Afraid.

I'm not afraid nor am I weak.

I'm cautious, smart.

And it appears I'm alone.

I'm halfway to the private elevator when I hear it.

Engines. Low. Controlled. Three of them.

I turn just as they appear—three black SUVs rolling in like goddamn storm clouds, driving just a little too fast, parking just a little too close.

My jaw tightens. Nico Agosti doesn't believe in subtlety. Or respect.

I don't reach for my gun. I won't give Nico the satisfaction. He wouldn't dare try anything. Not here. Not with his father still clinging to power and the Bratva watching every move.

My senses are sharp; I notice every detail in my periphery.

The first SUV door opens. Then the second. Then the third. One by one, six bodyguards step out—jacked, suited, all wearing an unmistakable air of overcompensation. Expensive watches. The obvious outline of a weapon under each of their jackets. Dark sunglasses.

Then Nico emerges.

He's in his early thirties, handsome in a way that probably works on club girls and Instagram models. His hair is slicked back, and he wears a charcoal pinstripe suit with shiny loafers and a watch that screams *new* money. His smirk is all teeth and ego, and he walks like he owns the goddamn world.

His cockiness will be his undoing.

"Morning," I say dryly. "Was bringing the cavalry really necessary?"

He spreads his arms, cocky and defensive, like a teenager trying to act tough when he's been caught with his daddy's car. "You wanted a meeting," he says. "Let's meet."

I don't move. "How the fuck did you get into my private garage?"

He grins, teeth glinting. "I can get into wherever I need to go. You should keep that in mind."

I let out a low chuckle as I reach into my pocket. Three of his men tense immediately, hands flying to their weapons. One of them takes half a step forward.

"Jumpy fuckers, aren't they?" I say, amused, pulling out my keys and jingling them in the air. "Relax. I've got plans this morning. So let's keep this little soap opera moving."

Nico's face flushes, rage climbing into his cheeks like he's about to explode. "You disrespectful prick."

I grin wider. *God, it's too easy.*

I'm in his face before any of them can blink. My pistol presses under Nico's chin, steel to skin. The little bastard freezes like a rat caught mid-scamper.

"Disrespectful?" I say, voice calm and lethal. "Let me explain something to you, Agosti. You don't get to show up in my garage with a goddamn entourage, threaten me with your goons, and call *me* disrespectful."

His bodyguards shift uncomfortably, weapons drawn, but they don't make a move.

They know who and what I am.

I lean in. "Does your father know you pulled this little stunt? That you just accosted the head of the Bratva in his own territory?"

His face pales. He doesn't answer.

I press the muzzle a little harder. "That's what I thought. I don't give a fuck how sick he is, Nico. He's still the don. *Not you.* You might be playing dress-up in his shoes, but they don't fit. And if he dies while you're pulling this kind of shit..." I smile coldly "...I'll explain to the Commission why there's suddenly a power vacuum on the north side."

He swallows hard.

"Now," I continue, pulling the gun away but keeping it in my hand, "you're going to deliver a message for me. You tell Don Agosti I'll be at his home tomorrow morning. Ten o'clock. We'll sit down like the civilized men we pretend to be and discuss the little boundary issues we've been having."

Nico nods once, eyes still locked on my pistol.

"And if your men so much as breathe in my direction again," I add, "I'll kill you first, just to make a point."

I step away, placing the gun at my back as I pivot toward my car. I don't look over my shoulder. They won't follow.

Just before I slide into the driver's seat, I turn to give him one last look. "Be at the meeting tomorrow, Nico." My voice is calm, but the warning beneath it cuts like glass. "You won't want to miss it."

I get in, shut the door, and drive away.

This city is mine.

And I'm done asking nicely.

CHAPTER 26

JENNA

It's a quiet Saturday morning, but there's a buzz beneath my skin that won't quiet. Even the gentle spring sunshine filtering through the window of the small waiting room can't soothe the fluttering in my chest. I stare down at my lap, counting the seconds as they tick by.

My hand keeps slipping to my stomach like it might tell me something to make this feel real.

Claire sits beside me, flipping through a celebrity magazine. Her leg bounces impatiently, jiggling the entire row of plastic chairs attached to ours. When I shoot her a glance, she shrugs, an apologetic smile quirking at her lips.

"I feel like I'm waiting for my own results," she whispers, closing the magazine and setting it on the side table. "This is torture."

"Imagine how I feel," I mutter.

She snorts a laugh, earning us a glare from an older woman across the room. We duck our heads simultaneously, and I bite my lip to stop from laughing again. I don't know how Claire managed it, but she got me into her OB/GYN's office on a Saturday, last minute.

I owe her something spectacular for this—designer shoes, some fancy chocolate, my firstborn child. Well, maybe not that last one.

The thought hits me like a gentle wave. *Firstborn child.* My hand settles again on my stomach, protectively. Could it be real?

The door opens, and a nurse with a clipboard smiles kindly as she calls, "Jenna Ridley?"

Claire squeezes my hand tightly. "You've got this."

I manage a shaky smile. "Yeah. Totally got it."

I sit on the edge of the exam table, feeling like a kid as my legs swing above the tiled floor. The walls are painted a soothing shade of pale lavender, posters about prenatal vitamins and pregnancy health lining every available surface. My stomach flips again as I wait.

Finally, the door opens, and the doctor walks in. She's warm and professional, with kind eyes behind black-rimmed glasses. "Hi, Jenna," she says, extending a hand. "I'm Dr. Martinez."

"Nice to meet you," I say, returning the handshake, my palm embarrassingly sweaty.

She doesn't seem to mind. "So, you're here to confirm a pregnancy?"

"Yep." My voice sounds higher than usual. "I took a home test, but I need, like you said, confirmation."

She smiles gently. "That's a good idea. Always helps to be certain. We'll just need a quick urine sample, and we can confirm for sure."

She hands me a plastic cup, and I duck into the attached restroom, heart pounding as I fill it, seal it, and place it behind the little metal door as instructed.

Back on the table, I wait for what feels like an eternity, though it's probably only a few minutes. When the door opens again, Dr. Martinez has a gentle expression on her face, like someone delivering good news.

"Well, Jenna, you are definitely pregnant," she says, handing me the results as though I might want proof.

For a second, the whole world slows. I stare down at the paper, at the bold word "positive." The letters swim slightly, blurring together as reality fully hits. Then, the strangest thing happens. I smile. A big, stupid, unexpected smile. My eyes sting a little.

"Are you okay?" Dr. Martinez asks softly.

"I am," I whisper, astonished at my own reaction. "I really am."

I'm pregnant. Abram's baby is growing inside me. She goes over some instructions, giving me a list of vitamins to take and foods to avoid, then tells me to schedule my next appointment where we'll do the first ultrasound.

As I stand to leave, I feel a bit unsteady, but for the first time in days, it's not fear making my knees weak. It's joy—clear, bright, unmistakable joy.

Claire jumps up the moment she sees my face. "Well? Tell me!"

"It's official." My voice shakes, but I'm smiling so hard it hurts. "I'm pregnant."

Claire shrieks so loudly that everyone around us jumps. She throws her arms around me, nearly knocking me down. "Oh my God! Jenna, you're going to be a mom!"

"Shh!" I laugh. "Not so loud!"

"I can't believe it!" she says, hugging me tighter. "This is huge! How do you feel?"

"Good." The word comes out quickly. "Really good. Is that weird?"

Claire pulls back, smiling tenderly. "Not at all. Come on— we have to celebrate."

I arch a brow at her. "Celebrate?"

She winks mischievously. "Crumbl. Right now."

I laugh, feeling giddy. "Definitely Crumbl."

We sit on the curb outside the bakery, an open box of cookies balanced between us. The scent of freshly baked sugar and butter wraps around me. I take a giant bite of a chocolate-chip monstrosity, my eyes nearly rolling back in my head. Pregnancy hormones or not, Crumbl never misses.

"So," Claire says, nudging my shoulder with hers, "now what?"

I swallow, glancing at her thoughtfully. "I'm going to tell Abram tonight. We have a dinner date, so now's the perfect time."

Claire's eyes widen a fraction, but she nods, supportive as always. "Are you nervous?"

I sigh, picking at the edge of the cookie. "A little. He's so intense. His world is intense. I can't even imagine how he'll react."

She squeezes my hand reassuringly. "He cares about you, Jenna. That much is obvious."

"I know, but..." I trail off, uncertainty creeping back in. "A baby? That's huge. I'm afraid it might be too much. Abram leads a dangerous life, Claire. Is it even fair to bring a kid into it?"

She pauses, the concern in her eyes softening. "Maybe it's exactly what he needs to settle him down. You never know. Either way, you're going to be an amazing mom, with or without him."

Her words comfort me more than she could possibly realize. "Thank you," I whisper, leaning my head against her shoulder. "For everything."

"Always," she whispers back.

For a while, we eat quietly, savoring the cookies, letting reality sink in. I picture Abram, his strength, his dominance, but also the way he can be so gentle when he holds me. The man he is beneath the power and control, the man I see glimpses of when he's cooking dinner, the way his face lights up when he talks about his nieces and nephew.

"Do you think he'll be happy?" I ask quietly.

Claire doesn't hesitate. "I think he'll be over the moon. Even if it takes him a minute to admit it."

I nod slowly, pressing a hand to my stomach again. "Yeah. I think so too."

She leans back, polishing off another cookie. "Besides, you're glowing, Jenna. You're totally in love with him. Everyone can see it."

"I don't know if it's love," I say, but as the words come out, I know they're a lie. "Okay, maybe I do. God, Claire. I'm totally screwed, aren't I?"

"Hopelessly," she agrees, laughing softly. "But it looks good on you."

I exhale deeply, my decision firming up in my chest. Tonight is the night I tell Abram. No matter how he reacts, no matter what this means for my future, I won't face it alone. Claire's words echo gently in my ears, reminding me I'm strong enough to handle anything.

"We should go shopping," she says suddenly, eyes sparkling. "Get you dolled up before tonight. Give him another little taste of what his everyday life could be like."

I laugh, warm anticipation filling me. "He's already seen me naked, Claire."

"Not like this," she says confidently. "This is special. Trust me."

I smile softly, feeling hopeful. "Okay, you win."

As we gather our things and head toward the boutique Claire's already gushing about, my heart pounds wildly. But this time, it's excitement, not fear. Because tonight, my whole life is going to change.

And I'm ready for it.

CHAPTER 27

ABRAM

"You pulled a gun on Nico?" Denis asks, like he's not sure whether to be impressed or pissed.

It's late, the last streaks of gold slipping beneath the skyline as I sit in my work office, locked in yet another conference call with Denis and Mikail.

I lean back in my chair as I roll the crystal tumbler in my hand, watching the ice melting slowly. "I didn't shoot him."

"That's not the point," Mikail snaps. "You shoved a pistol under his chin in your own damn parking garage."

"He brought six men. Into *my* space. Unannounced. You think I'm going to let that slide?" My voice is low, sharp. "He needs to know I'm not some bureaucrat he can posture in front of. His daddy's still breathing, and until he's not, Nico is nothing."

There's a long pause. I hear Denis exhale sharply through his nose.

"So," Mikail says finally, "the meeting's pushed to tomorrow then."

"Ten a.m., Agosti family home," I confirm. "No more games. No more chasing. They want to talk, we talk. If they don't," I drain my whiskey, "then they'll see what happens when they play footsie on my turf."

"Keep me with you from here on out," Denis says, tone clipped. "I don't like this."

"Agreed," Mikail adds. "From now on, you're not walking around alone. We've let it slide too long."

"I'm going out with Jenna tonight." I glance at the time, heart racing at the thought of her probably slipping into something that'll make me lose my self-control. "After that, we'll talk guards. Starting tomorrow."

They don't like it, their disapproval evident in their silence. But they don't argue, either. I'm still the boss.

I end the call and set the phone down, letting the quiet settle over the room. I pour one more drink, just a small one. The kind meant for contemplation.

If I'd pulled the trigger today, things would be simpler. Nico's body in a grave. Don Agosti too frail to retaliate. It would create a few waves, some noise. But no war.

No honor, either.

That matters. At least to me.

I finish the whiskey and stand, smoothing my jacket. I've got a woman to see. One who's starting to matter more than I ever expected.

And if Nico or anyone else lays a finger on her, there won't be any hesitation next time.

I lock the office and step into the elevator, eager to see my girl.

The valet pulls up with my car. I thank him with a nod and a gracious tip, then slip into the driver's seat. Normally, I'd park it myself, underground, tucked in the garage beneath my building. But after yesterday's little stunt, I'm not taking any chances. New security measures are already in the works, but until the system's rebuilt from the ground up, the place is compromised.

I merge onto the Strip and head toward Jenna's place. Traffic is light, the city still stretching its limbs after the heat of the day. It gives me time to think—too much time.

Last night, she was... off. Not cold, not angry. Just somewhere far away. Wrapped up in something I wasn't allowed to touch.

She said she was worried about Claire, but I know she was lying. I could see it in her eyes. I didn't push, and that restraint is still eating at me. I hate being kept at arm's length. But I've done the same to her—hell, worse.

What the hell are we, anyway?

She's more than a distraction. More than a beautiful woman I can't get enough of. She's clever, grounded, real. She walked into my world without flinching, and she's made herself at home in it—despite the danger, despite the challenges.

She came with me to my family brunch last weekend. She sat beside my sister and won over my nieces with lopsided pancakes. She laughed with Mikail and Denis. Everyone loved her.

So why have I kept her a secret?

Because it's safer. Because if anyone ever found out...

My hand tightens on the steering wheel.

I picture Nico again. Only this time, it's not me he's confronting in the garage. It's her.

I see the flash of a gun in his hand, the way he smirks because he knows he's holding something precious to me hostage. That image, the possibility sets fire ablaze beneath my skin. I'd kill him. No hesitation. No warning.

I inhale slowly, forcing myself to focus. Jenna's safety has always come first, which is why our relationship status is vague. Undefined. Why I don't call her mine outside of the bedroom.

But maybe I've been going about it all wrong.

Maybe what she needs isn't space but the truth.

Tonight, I'll ask her to stay over. If she says yes, I'll tell her. Tell her what she means to me. Tell her I want her close, that I'll always keep her safe, even if the world is burning down around us.

I pull up to her building and kill the engine, eyes sweeping over the place. It's a fine apartment, location. But fine isn't good enough. Not for Jenna. Not anymore.

She deserves better and I'm going to give it to her.

One step at a time.

I sit outside her building for another moment, hands on the wheel, eyes unfocused as thoughts of Jenna invade every inch of my mind. I want her. Not just for tonight, not just in my bed. I want to wake up beside her every single morning, watch the sunlight slide over her curves, kiss her awake, and savor the sleepy smile on her lips.

Am I insane to think this way?

We've only known each other a short time, been sleeping together barely six weeks. Any rational man would tell me to slow the fuck down.

But rational flew out the window the minute Jenna Ridley walked into my office.

What I feel for her doesn't compare in the slightest to what I felt—or thought I felt—for Daria. With Daria, it was infatuation, physical attraction, a surface-level hunger. Jenna's different. She's sunk so much deeper. She's lodged somewhere I didn't even know existed, carving a place inside my heart and refusing to budge.

I climb out of the car and walk up the stairs to her apartment, tension humming beneath my skin. Her door opens a second after I knock, the sight of her hitting me like a shot of whiskey, potent and intoxicating.

"Hi," she says softly, giving me a smile that could bring a lesser man to his knees.

My breath catches. She's stunning, dressed in a dark green dress that clings to her curves like it was tailored just for her. The neckline dips just low enough to tease, revealing a tantalizing hint of cleavage I want to taste.

It hugs her full hips and her gorgeous, round ass, accentuating every inch of her deliciously feminine shape. The silk skims over her thighs, smooth and inviting, ending just above her knees. Black heels make her legs look endless, and her red hair is loose, cascading over her shoulders in soft waves, framing a face I want to spend a lifetime memorizing. My cock pulses to life, and it takes all the restraint I have not to ravage her on the spot.

"God, you're beautiful," I say, stepping closer and sliding an arm around her waist. When I glance into her apartment, I notice her friend is there, watching the whole thing eagerly.

Jenna appears nervous, her anxiety puzzling me, and I wonder if she's still uneasy from last night. But when I lean in, brushing my lips softly over hers, the uncertainty melts from her gaze like mist burned away by sunrise. She sighs against my mouth, causing warmth to flood through me.

I pull back, cupping her cheek. "Ready?"

"Almost," she says, smiling. "Let me grab my purse."

She turns back to get it, but her friend is there, holding it out, grinning like she's been waiting all day for this moment.

"You must be Abram," she says, eyes sparkling as she passes Jenna the purse.

I extend my hand. "That would be me. A pleasure to meet you."

She grins. "Well, we've already met once. Sort of."

"We have?" I give her another look. There's something

familiar about her. Then it hits me. She's the friend from the club. I smirk, not saying another word about it.

She shakes my hand, a mischievous smile lighting her face. "Anyway, I'm Claire. It's great to finally meet you officially. Especially after everything Jenna's told me."

I raise an eyebrow and glance at Jenna, whose cheeks are beautifully blushing. "Is that right?"

Jenna shrugs, her lips twitching into a teasing smirk. "Don't get a big head. Before all this, I mostly griped about my hard-ass boss. It's only recently I've been saying nice things."

I chuckle, shaking my head. "Then I'll have to make sure tonight makes you completely forget about the asshole I used to be."

Claire laughs, clearly pleased. "Oh, I like him already. Have fun, you two."

Jenna steps forward and loops her arm through mine. "We intend to."

I look over my shoulder, giving Claire a smirk. "Don't wait up."

She smiles, waving us off. Jenna laughs softly as we head downstairs. The scent of her perfume curls around me, making it nearly impossible to focus. I open the door for her and guide her toward the car, my palm against the small of her back. "You look incredible tonight."

Her eyes glitter. "And where exactly are we headed?"

I shake my head. "That's a secret," I respond playfully.

She pauses, one eyebrow raised in challenge, lips curving into a mischievous smile. "You're not taking me back to The 13th Floor, are you?"

I surprise myself with my laughter, though the wicked spark in her eyes suggests she's not just teasing—she's actually interested. "Do you want to go back there?"

She shrugs, nonchalant, but the blush that blooms across her cheeks tells me everything I need to know. "Maybe. Not tonight, though. But I wouldn't say no to another visit sometime."

I lean in, brushing my lips over hers, savoring her taste. "I'll keep that in mind. Tonight, it's just dinner and then back to my place."

She pulls me closer, her voice dipping into a sultry whisper that nearly has me taking her against the car right then. "Sounds perfect."

I manage to hold back, opening the passenger door. Jenna slides gracefully into the seat, her dress riding up just enough to show a flash of her creamy thighs. I clench my jaw, swallowing hard. It takes everything in me not to change my mind about dinner entirely.

Closing her door, I walk around to the driver's side and climb in, starting the engine.

I glance at her as we pull away from the curb. "Everything alright?"

She gives me a quick smile, a little too bright. "Of course. Why?"

"You seemed nervous when you answered the door."

She looks down, her fingers toying with her purse. "Just thinking about things. Nothing to worry about."

Still, I sense there's more, something she isn't sharing. Tonight, I plan on finding out exactly what's going on behind those beautiful green eyes.

"Jenna," I say quietly, reaching over to gently grasp her hand. "If something's bothering you, you can tell me. No matter what it is."

She meets my gaze, searching it as if trying to decide how much to trust me. "I know. And I will. Just not yet."

I nod, respecting her need for space. "Fair enough."

We drive in comfortable silence, the city lights flashing outside the window. Jenna's hand is warm in mine, grounding me in a way nothing else ever has. Even if she's not ready to talk tonight, I'll make sure she knows one thing without a doubt: I'm not going anywhere.

Tonight, I'm going to show Jenna exactly how much she means to me. After that, maybe she'll finally trust me with whatever secrets she's keeping.

Either way, I'm in deeper than I ever thought possible. And for the first time in my life, I'm not looking for a way out.

CHAPTER 28

JENNA

A bram pulls the car up to the valet stand outside Joël Robuchon. We step out, and I have to give myself a second to wrap my head around the sight. I can't believe I'm here. Just the thought of stepping inside has my heart doing back flips. The restaurant is Michelin-starred, dazzlingly elegant, and way, *way* outside my usual league.

"Are you sure about this?" I ask. "I feel a little out of place."

He wraps a protective arm around my waist, his warm hand settling possessively at my hip. "Don't worry about that. I fully intend to show you off."

The low growl of his voice sends a shiver down my spine. God, this man knows exactly how to make me melt. I glance up at him, my breath catching as I take in those piercing blue eyes.

Inside, the restaurant is stunning. There's a soft glow from ornate chandeliers, black and gold accents, plush velvet chairs. The maître d' greets Abram by name, his manner impeccable, leading us to a quiet table near a floor-to-ceiling window with a gorgeous view of the Vegas skyline.

"Abram, this place is insane," I whisper, laughing nervously as I take in the sheer luxury around us. "I'd have to save for a year just to eat an appetizer here."

He chuckles, leaning in so only I can hear him. "If you like it, we can eat here every day."

I roll my eyes affectionately, my cheeks warming. "You're sweet."

He arches a brow, amusement lighting his handsome features. "Sweet isn't something I'm used to being called. But coming from you, I'll take it."

As soon as we sit, a waiter in a tailored suit appears, brandishing a bottle of wine like he's presenting us with a sacred artifact. "A 2012 Château Lafite Rothschild," he announces with pride. "An exquisite Bordeaux with notes of ripe currant, cedar, and just a hint of spice. Perfect for tonight's first course."

I glance at Abram, surprised. "Did you order ahead?"

He shakes his head and leans back in his seat, completely at ease. "Every Saturday, the chef prepares a special five-course tasting menu. No ordering. You simply trust the chef's judgment and enjoy."

"Wow," I breathe. I'm genuinely impressed.

My eyes drift to the deep red wine being poured into the crystal glasses, a wave of anxiety rising within. I can't drink wine, obviously, and refusing such a delectable vintage will immediately raise suspicion. My heart pounds faster, nerves twisting into a tight knot in my stomach. Is now the moment? Should I tell him here, at this beautiful table, that I'm pregnant?

I swallow hard, my fingers nervously tracing the edge of my napkin. Abram must sense the shift in me because he places his hand over mine. The warmth of his touch grounds me instantly.

"Everything alright?" he asks.

I lift my gaze to meet his. Those eyes—so intense—always seeing more than I want to reveal.

I force a small, reassuring smile. "Yeah. Just overwhelmed by all of this." I wave a hand around us, gesturing to the elegant surroundings, the perfectly poised waiter, the wine shimmering invitingly. "It's a lot."

He studies me carefully for a long moment, and I swear he sees right through me. But instead of pushing, he simply gives my hand a gentle squeeze, settling back again. "Relax. You deserve a night like this."

His words ease the tension just enough for me to breathe again, even though I know the truth still lingers between us, unspoken.

Abram chuckles softly, a deep, warm sound that rolls over me like velvet. "Trust me, you'll like everything."

Before he can say another word, the waiter moves in with ninja-like silence, slipping a plate onto the table between us.

I eye the delicate hors d'oeuvre in front of me skeptically. "And this is...?"

"Balsamic bruschetta," the waiter says.

Abram gestures for me to take a bite. "Go ahead."

I lift the small piece of bread topped with diced tomatoes, basil, and glossy dark balsamic glaze, feeling a little unsure. Abram watches, his gaze intent and confident. The moment the flavors hit my tongue, my eyes widen.

"Oh my God, that's delicious!" I exclaim before quickly covering my mouth to chew politely. The flavors are incredible, fresh and sweet with a perfect tangy twist.

Abram's eyes gleam. "I told you. And that's just the beginning."

I can't help but smile, a warmth blossoming inside me. He's clearly enjoying my surprise. He sips his wine slowly, his gaze lingering on me as if he's savoring the sight of me enjoying myself. I swirl the wine in my untouched glass, feeling another wave of nerves. Abram doesn't notice. At least, I don't think he does.

He leans forward slightly, his voice soft and encouraging. "So, tell me more about your life. I want to know more about you."

I glance down, hesitating. I've never enjoyed discussing my childhood. But something about Abram, about the gentle intensity in his eyes, encourages honesty.

"It's nothing glamorous," I begin quietly, poking at my plate. "I was pretty much raised by the system. My mom, she was always looking for her next high, never had time for anything else. I was in and out of foster homes until I turned sixteen. Then I got emancipated, tried to build a life for myself."

He watches me carefully, sympathy flickering in his eyes but no pity, which I appreciate. He doesn't interrupt, just silently waits for me to continue.

"It wasn't easy," I say softly, the old ache of loneliness stirring. "But it taught me resilience, how to rely on myself."

Abram reaches across the table and gently touches my hand, his thumb stroking softly. "You're the strongest woman I've ever known, Jenna. Your past doesn't define you —it just makes you all the more impressive."

His words send a wave of warmth through me. My throat tightens, but I smile gratefully. "Thank you. That means a lot." I clear my throat, suddenly feeling self-conscious. "What about you? You rarely talk about yourself."

Abram chuckles softly, leaning back in his chair, one finger tracing the edge of his wine glass. "I prefer to hear you talk."

I arch an eyebrow. "Well, that's not fair. I've spilled plenty of my secrets."

He sighs, looking reluctantly amused. "Very well. I was born in St. Petersburg, Russia. It's a beautiful city. It's cold, with harsh winters, but there's a warmth beneath all that ice." His expression softens with nostalgia. "My sisters and I grew up playing in Palace Square, the snow almost as high as we were sometimes. My father was strict, but he cared for us deeply. Family was—is—everything."

I smile, touched by the image of him as a little boy in the snow. "That sounds kind of magical, actually. But how did you end up here? Vegas isn't exactly the next stop after St. Petersburg."

He nods with a small smirk, then goes on. "My father saw opportunity here. Vegas was still growing. It was lawless and hungry for structure. He founded Vasiliev Holdings from nothing, and when he passed, I took over." He pauses for a breath, eyes flicking to the horizon outside. "He always said the desert was honest. It doesn't hide what it is. You either thrive in it or you don't."

"Do you ever miss Russia?" I ask softly.

"Sometimes," he says, with a shrug. "But Las Vegas is my home now. The past matters, but the future matters more."

His gaze finds mine as he says it, and something in my chest stutters. The future. *Our* future. My fingers curl and uncurl nervously in my lap. I have to tell him. As I take a deep breath, preparing myself, the waiter brings our plates, interrupting the moment.

He gracefully places pan-fried garlic butter steak, golden crispy potatoes, and tender asparagus in front of us. My stomach rumbles at the delicious aroma, and Abram laughs softly.

"I can see someone's hungry," he teases. "Or should I say, *hear*."

I blush as I take a bite, savoring the rich, buttery flavor, an involuntary moan of appreciation escaping my lips.

Abram's gaze darkens instantly, and he leans in close over the small table, whispering, "I can't wait to hear you moan like that again, but for me."

A rush of lustful heat floods through me, momentarily scattering all coherent thoughts. My breath catches as I meet his eyes, my heart hammering. I swallow hard, excitement mingling with anxiety.

He brushes his lips softly against mine before settling back in his chair, and my resolve returns, stronger. Now is definitely the moment. Even if it changes everything, Abram deserves to know.

I set down my fork, taking a slow breath. "Abram, there's something I need to tell you."

Concern instantly takes over his expression. "What is it?"

I hesitate, swallowing the anxiety bubbling up in my throat. "I've been trying to find the right moment—"

He gently takes my hand again, his voice calm and steady as he says, "Whatever it is, you can tell me."

My gaze searches his face, needing reassurance, finding it instantly in his expression.

"Tell me, *Malyshka*."

CHAPTER 29

ABRAM

"Tell me."

Jenna looks like she's bracing for something seismic. Her fingers twitch slightly on the tablecloth, the smile she wore a moment ago gone.

I can see it in her eyes. Whatever she's about to say is no small thing. It's not a whim or a flirty aside. It's serious. Life-altering.

She opens her mouth then closes it. A flicker of nerves crosses her face as she looks down at her untouched wineglass.

My focus narrows. The restaurant disappears. The scent of the food, the din of the other diners, the gentle clink of cutlery... it's all gone. There's only her.

"Jenna, you can tell me anything, really." I reach across the table and take her hand, curling mine around it.

She looks up at me, those big eyes filled with what appears to be fear, but a different type. Not survival fear. Not the kind I grew up knowing. It's much different, more like the kind of fear you feel when everything you care about hangs in the balance.

I draw a breath, steadying myself. I have something to say, too. I've been circling it for days, maybe longer. It's not a decision, it's a truth.

I'm in love with her.

And I'm going to tell her.

But not now. Not yet. Whatever she needs to say comes first.

She squeezes my hand and draws a deep breath. "I'm—"

A crash interrupts her, loud and sudden. A chair scrapes hard against the floor. A scream, high-pitched and panicked. The front of the restaurant erupts in chaos, movement and shouting colliding in an instant. Diners are standing, some ducking. Others are grabbing their phones. Someone yells, "Get down!"

The air shifts. The mood fractures.

I turn sharply, every sense on high alert. The maître d' is standing near the entrance, gesturing wildly at someone just out of view. The tension in the room isn't random. It's focused. Directed toward me.

I feel it, like the shift in pressure before a storm.

I slowly push my chair back and stand. Jenna remains seated, frozen in confusion. Our hands are still clasped.

I look down at her, voice low but firm. "We need to go. Now."

She blinks up at me, her expression shifting from confusion to alarm. "What's happening?"

"I don't know yet. But I know it's not safe."

That's all she needs to hear. She stands up quickly, grabs her bag, and slides instinctively into my shadow. She trusts me. And right now, that terrifies me. Because I have a sinking feeling that all this chaos, this threat, followed me here.

No matter where I find myself, I always know where the exits are. Part of the lifestyle. Every restaurant, every club, every venue, I clock the layout within minutes of walking in. And tonight, that observation just might save our lives.

I slide the Glock from under my jacket with my free hand and keep it low, angled against my thigh, half-shielded by the drape of my coat. I spot two men near the entrance. Black tactical gear, semi-autos in hand. They're yelling but not firing. Not hurting anyone.

Not yet.

They're not here for the patrons.

They're here for me.

"Where the fuck is he?" one of them shouts.

I curse under my breath.

Two tables away, a family sits frozen in fear. Young couple, maybe mid-thirties, a little girl hugging her mother's arm like it's the only thing keeping her grounded. Jenna sees them too. Her body tenses beside me.

I meet the father's eyes. "Come with us."

He hesitates, eyes wide. I don't repeat myself. I just give him a firm nod. He gets the message. We move quickly, quietly. Others begin to join us. The more people around, the better. A crowd makes us harder to isolate. Easier to disappear.

We reach the kitchen door just as it swings open. More armed men, shouting at the staff. "Get out! Now! Go!"

They're clearing the kitchen, not executing it, which tells me what I need to know.

This isn't a hit. Not yet at least.

Still, I don't like the way they're spread out, front and back, herding. Someone planned this with military efficiency.

I gesture to the small group of civilians toward the rear exit. "Go. Move."

They quickly get out along with the kitchen staff. They're safe.

The actions of these men tell me they're under orders to avoid casualties. They're here to frighten, to apply pressure for leverage. They're not here for blood.

I reach for her hand again and press my mouth close to her ear. "Come with me."

I take Jenna's hand and guide her quickly from the kitchen back into the main dining room. The elegance we entered mere moments ago is shattered now—fine linens scattered, crystal stemware toppled, frightened patrons scrambling toward the doors in desperation. Five men are methodically clearing the place, weapons drawn, eyes cold and professional.

Agosti men.

My jaw tightens as I watch one of them roughly shove an elderly man toward the exit.

Nico, you reckless prick.

Instinct takes over, a sharp urgency twisting in my gut. I tighten my grip on Jenna's hand and pull her close, speaking low and direct. "You need to hide. Now."

Her eyes widen, confusion flashing behind their emerald depths. "What? Abram, no—"

I shake my head once, cutting her off before her protest can take shape. "Don't argue. Not this time."

I quickly lead her toward the side hall, eyes scanning for the safest place to tuck her away. My gaze lands on the restroom signs, and I move decisively, pulling her to the men's room.

"Wait," Jenna whispers, digging her heels in slightly, confusion furrowing her brow. "Why the men's?"

"They might not think to check there," I explain. She hesitates again, but I press a palm gently to her cheek. "Get into a stall and crouch on the toilet. Stay absolutely silent no matter what you hear, understand?"

Her eyes flicker, understanding sinking in alongside fear. My gut twists. I never wanted her to see this part of my world. The darkness. The violence. She opens her mouth to protest again, but before a sound can escape—

"ABRAM VASILIEV!"

The roar splits the tense silence, and Jenna freezes at my side, her eyes darting over my shoulder. I turn slowly, already aware of who's calling my name, dread coiling inside me like a serpent.

Nico saunters in, gun held loosely, arrogantly at his side. His dark eyes glitter with malice beneath perfectly groomed dark hair, his expensive suit precisely tailored, flashy. The heir apparent of the Agosti empire, acting like he's already the don when he's little more than a spoiled boy playing dress-up. He sees Jenna immediately, and a slow, predatory grin spreads across his smug face. His gaze drips over Jenna's curves, pausing in a way that makes my blood seethe with barely restrained violence.

"Is this the flavor of the month?" Nico drawls. He flicks his eyes up and down her body in sleazy way. "Can't say I blame you."

Rage boils beneath my skin, every muscle tensing. I fight the urge to snap his neck, maintaining control. I smirk instead, letting sarcasm sharpen my tone. "I don't think daddy would be very happy with baby boy's decision here."

The taunt lands exactly as intended. Nico's confidence falters, the carefully constructed bravado giving way to anger. The spoiled, insecure little boy lurking beneath the surface emerges for an instant, his eyes narrowing in childish fury. He lifts the gun abruptly, aiming it straight at Jenna.

In one fluid movement, I step directly in front of her, shielding her completely from Nico's line of sight. She stiffens behind me, her breaths coming quicker in fear and anxiety. I despise myself for bringing her here, for allowing my world to spill into hers.

It's too late. Nico sees everything, the smug satisfaction in his expression intensifying into a twisted smile of triumph.

He's figured it out. He knows she matters to me, that she's not just any woman. I can practically hear the calculations churning behind those cruel eyes.

The room is quiet now, eerily so, emptied of patrons and staff. Nico's men watch us carefully, awaiting their orders, but Nico seems content to savor his advantage, to drink in my discomfort.

He finally lowers the gun, still smiling coldly. "Well this is an interesting discovery," he quips, taking a leisurely step toward us. "I never imagined you as the one-woman type, Abram."

I glare at him evenly, fist clenched at my side, the other hand gripping my Glock. "Careful, Nico. This is a dangerous game you're playing."

He chuckles dryly, raising a brow. "Dangerous? For me or for her?"

His tone sends ice rushing through my veins, but I hold steady, refusing to show weakness. "If anything happens to her," I say, "I promise you, it will be the end of you and your entire family."

He stares at me, weighing the threat, trying to gauge how far he can push. Nico might be reckless, but he's not entirely stupid. He knows I mean every word.

He shrugs dismissively, holstering his pistol with deliberate ease. "Relax, Abram. No need for theatrics." His eyes flicker toward Jenna once more, then back to me.

He leans in. "Now. Let's talk."

CHAPTER 30

JENNA

"**D**o you actually have feelings for this one?" Nico asks. The insult slides under my skin, hot and sharp.

Abram stiffens beside me. I can practically feel his blood pressure spiking.

I keep my voice low. "Don't let him get to you," I mutter, though it's hard to keep a tough girl façade when a 9mm is waving in your direction.

Abram is in kingpin mode, devoid of emotion. "No, Nico. Flavor of the month, like you said. Send her out with the riffraff, and we'll talk like gentlemen."

Translation: I'm expendable. His words sting even though I know it's pure strategy.

Nico sneers, pure shark. "You lie well, Vasiliev, but not well enough." He switches his gaze to me. "How long have you been fucking your boss, sweetheart? Three weeks? Four? Bet the benefits are great. A bit cliché, isn't it?"

I offer him my best homicidal glare and say nothing. He laughs like it's the funniest thing in the world.

Abram counters. "Almost as cliché as the loser son who can't wait to succeed his father."

Abram is baiting him. Why? My nerves teeter at the edge of panic. I want to trust he's got a plan, but the plan looks a lot like lighting a fuse and daring the bomb to blow.

Nico's grin fractures. He raises the pistol straight at me. I stop breathing. One misstep and we're both done for.

The man's eyes glitter. He chuckles as he lowers the gun, then snaps his fingers. Two of his gorillas close ranks and grab my arms.

"Hey!" I jerk hard, digging my heel into his ankle. He growls. He's as solid as a brick wall.

Abram pivots, driving his fist into the nearest thug's jaw. I hear a crunch. The guy folds like wet newspaper. The second bodyguard whips a pistol out so fast the muzzle almost hits my temple.

Abram's voice is lethal. "We don't involve women or children. You know that. Let her go."

Nico strolls forward, inspecting me like I'm property. He strokes a knuckle down my cheek. I snap my teeth at him, almost landing it. His laughter is pure malice. Then he slaps me—open-handed and sharp enough to sting my eardrum. Bright stars speckle my vision.

Abram erupts, lunging. Three more men tackle him, pinning his arms. He's all muscle and fury, but he's also outnumbered. They hammer their fists into his ribs while Nico watches, delighted.

I scream, my voice cracking, "Stop! Leave him alone!"

Nico lifts a hand. The pummeling ceases, but the look he gives Abram is pure evil. "See," Nico says, smug. "Negotiation requires leverage, and she," he flicks the gun barrel my way, "is leverage. You behave, she remains breathing. Simple."

Abram's chest heaves. "Touch her again and I'll carve your heart out."

Nico beams. "Romantic." Then he jerks his chin to his men. "Get her out of here."

The men drag me backward. My heels scramble against the floor, trying to find traction. My mind spins. Abram shouts something in Russian, raw and desperate. I'm able to twist just enough to catch his eyes. Dark blue ice, wide with worry.

"I'll find you!" he promises. "I swear it."

I nod as tears blur my view. The love in his stare guts me.

I pass by Nico, his eyes narrowed in my direction as the goons drag me away. He grins. "I'm going to have a lot of fun with you, bella."

Something about his tone, the way he looks at me causes me to snap. I wrench my arm free and pull it back, slapping him hard across the face. The air is still for a long moment as he faces away from me, his hand on his mouth. Then, he turns slowly. Blood trickles down his chin from where my slap split his lip.

Another grin. He's amused by it.

I catch a smirk forming on Abram's face. He's proud of me.

"You'll pay for that one," Nico says, wiping the blood away with his knuckle. "But later. Later." He nods to his men. "Get her out of here."

The men comply, grabbing me tighter, making sure I can't get free this time. I scream bloody hell as they drag me out.

We clear the doorway to the foyer, the marble floor littered with abandoned purses, smashed wineglasses, and shiny silverware. Suddenly, a gunshot pierces the air. Deafening. My stomach drops to the floor.

I have no idea who fired.

"Abram!" My scream is ragged as I fall apart inside.

Pain explodes across the back of my skull. Darkness swallows the glitter of the chandelier, the gleam of the marble floor. I fall, out cold, Abram's name echoing against the blackness.

CHAPTER 31

ABRAM

Blood dots the white tablecloth like red confetti. The stench of gunpowder hangs over the dining room—sweet, bold, metallic—impossible to ignore. Nico's shot punched a hole in his own soldier's leg. I watch steam curl off the barrel, disgusted.

The man hadn't even regained consciousness after I flattened him. That's Nico's idea of loyalty management.

"Trash takes itself out," he says, waving the muzzle in lazy circles as if he's bored.

I stay calm, my movements calculated. Rage is a blade you hide until the perfect moment. "A *pakhan* who mistreats subordinates and hides behind a woman is no *pakhan* at all. You're an immature fool. And that's why you'll never be in charge."

The words cut through him cleanly. I see it in the twitch beneath his left eye. He recovers with a shrug. "Tomorrow. Noon. I'll text the location. Just you and your brothers-in-law are to attend. Bring anyone else and your curvy toy dies on live stream." He pumps a finger as if pressing a button. "Boop."

I lunge for him, but three of his lapdogs shoulder into me. I could drop them and I almost do. But I know if I waste a second fighting these idiots, Jenna's gone. Nico backs toward the door, humming some Sinatra tune, before vanishing into the foyer. Only then do the goons release me, keeping their guns trained on my chest until they're out the door.

I sprint after them, hitting the sidewalk just in time to see taillights fishtailing off into the Vegas night. Two SUVs, black glass. A third idles at the curb. One look and I know Jenna isn't inside. I'm sure they have her tucked in the middle vehicle like precious cargo.

I pull my Glock and finger the trigger, considering a hopeless parting shot before lowering the weapon. I won't risk Jenna's life or innocent bystanders on an ego spasm.

Instead, I memorize plate digits and find the valet, expressing my urgency. He brings my car seconds later. I jump in and slam the accelerator.

Ten blocks. Twelve. The Strip's neon blurs past, alive with tourists oblivious to the mob war boiling underneath it all. I slow at every intersection, scanning for blacked out Escalades, but it's useless. I'm at least five minutes behind, an eternity where Jenna's concerned.

I use the voice command on my dash-mounted phone. "Denis. Mikail. Conference."

I hear two clicks as they come on the line.

"He ambushed us," I say. No greeting, no preamble. "Parking-garage stunt was kindergarten. Tonight was the real play."

Denis hisses. "She's alive?"

"Alive—for now."

Mikail curses in Russian before slipping back to English. "Cameras?"

"Restaurant system probably loops locally—no live relay. But there's street CCTV at Flamingo and Koval. Get Detective Johnson into the feed." Detective Simone Johnson is one of many LVPD cops we have on payroll.

"I'm on with her already," Mikail says. I can hear keys jingling in the background. "She'll pull everything northbound."

"Good." I carve a tight left, tires screeching. City lights strobe across the windshield. "Send a crew to the bistro. One Agosti soldier down, bullet in the leg. I knocked him out before Nico shot him. Pick him up before the cops do."

"Fucking hell. We'll do a sweep. And the staff?" Denis says.

"No casualties, staff and patrons got out safely. Nico wanted a show, not a body count." Except for his own man. Fucking idiot.

I hit a red light and punch the steering wheel, feeling the leather give beneath my knuckles. Regret gnaws at me. I should've accepted protection detail tonight instead of waiting until tomorrow, should've clocked blind spots. Jenna's scent lingers on my shirt, vanilla now mixed with a tangy trace of gunpowder. I grit my teeth until my jaw hurts.

Mikail breaks in. "Traffic camera at Paradise Road picked up two black SUVs headed east toward Henderson. Johnson's tagging plate fragments."

"Push it," I snarl. "Offer the detective a charitable contribution. I want a live trace."

"Understood."

Denis sounds a lot calmer than I feel. "What's your plan?"

"Nico's plan is to have our long-awaited meeting tomorrow at noon. *My* plan is to end this before sunrise." I accelerate through a yellow, cussing at a cabbie. "We pull every asset. Street sweepers, club security, drone eyes. Nico thinks he's top dog; clearly he's forgotten who owns half this desert."

"Abram," Denis says quietly, "you sure you can stay focused? Nico's using Jenna as leverage."

"You think I don't know that? I'm still in control. I'll be precise. I'll also be ruthless."

They accept it. We are all built from old Bratva rules: family, honor, vengeance measured in blood.

I end the call just as the asphalt shifts into suburbia. Henderson's sleepy cul-de-sacs sprawl beneath dimly lit streetlamps. Too many turns, too many places to hide. The Escalades could've vanished into any driveway.

My phone buzzes with a text from Nico.

Remember. Tomorrow, noon. Don't be late. Bring the brothers-in-law only—no extras. She'll be the guest of honor.

My knuckles turn white as I grip the steering wheel harder.

Another buzz, this time a photo attachment. It's Jenna, wrists zip-tied, seated in the back of a car. Her cheek is still red from where he slapped her.

Fury consumes me.

I toss the phone to the passenger seat before I pulverize it. I need to think. Nico's weakness is vanity. He wants a spectacle, wants me to feel cornered.

I'll give him what he wants.

Everybody knows what happens when you corner an animal that feels threatened.

Back at my penthouse, I pour two fingers of vodka but don't drink it. I stare out at the glitter of the Strip, my mind racing.

Jenna. My bright, blazing woman. I caged my emotions, telling myself distance would keep her safe. Fool's logic—wolves smell love like fresh blood.

I grab a burner phone and dial a number I haven't used in years.

A gravelly voice answers in Russian. *"Pakhan."*

"Sergei. I need a favor. Tonight."

"Name it."

"Need eyes on a convoy. Black Escalades. License digits

inbound. Find it. I want location, security headcount, guard rotations." I pause. "No civilians harmed."

"Understood." He doesn't ask questions.

Next, I send a text to Denis.

Pull warehouse 17C—toy shipment. Load crates marked "vodka." Deliver to my storehouse by 4 a.m. The crates contain ballistic plates, suppressed rifles, and GPS scramblers. If Nico wants a meeting, we're showing up prepared.

The night stretches thin. I pace the floors, replaying every moment of Jenna's abduction in my head. She remained strong even when terror swam in her eyes. The way she tried to bite Nico. The way she broke free and slapped him. Pride mixed with fear knot my chest.

I imagine her locked up in some gaudy room at the Agosti estate, Nico's ego dripping off the walls. She'll be scared, but she won't fold. My lioness.

I vow right then and there that she will never again attend a public dinner without half a platoon watching. She will never doubt her worth, never fear the shadows I walk in. She will carry my name and my protection.

Sergei texts at midnight.

Convoy spotted an hour ago stopped near Lake Las Vegas. Two SUVs, nine men, one bound female, one medic. Visual lost, but we'll track them down.

I breathe a sigh of relief. Jenna's alive.

I fire back a reply.

Eyes on. Radio silence until dawn.

Then I force myself to sit. To plan. Rage is like a candle—it burns bright, burns fast, then leaves you blind. Jenna deserves better than blind vengeance; she deserves me at my sharpest.

My phone pings again, another photo from Nico. Jenna is still tied, now with a mocking caption: Sleep tight, lover boy.

Wrong move, ass clown.

I polish off the vodka, ice shards crunching between my teeth, and stride to the elevator. The night hasn't ended, it's simply reached intermission.

Time for act two.

CHAPTER 32

JENNA

"**O**h... shit."

I groan, pain being the first thing I register lancing from my jaw to the base of my skull. The second is movement, a low-grade vibration humming through padded leather, the sound of asphalt beneath tires. I blink, vision swimming, until overhead lights sharpen into focus. The scent of new-car leather mixes with the copper tang of blood in my mouth.

I shift, testing my limbs. My wrists are zip-tied behind me, ankles cinched with more plastic. They left my dress on, thankfully, but the belt has ridden up, pinning fabric beneath my ribs. Breathing hurts. Everything hurts.

A man the size of a vending machine sits to my right. He's the one who cold-cocked me; the bruise blooming across his knuckles confirms it. Another enforcer, tall, hawk-nosed, sits to my left, pressing a .45 into his thigh, grinning at me like he's ready to use it at any moment.

In the passenger seat is Nico Agosti.

The sight of him yanks me into complete consciousness. Dead, dark eyes, slicked-back hair, impeccable suit in a shade that might as well be called "blood-money burgundy." He's half-turned, forearm draped over the seatback, watching me like a trophy horse he hasn't mounted yet.

"Sleeping Beauty opens her eyes," he says. "Welcome back."

My heartbeat spikes, but I grind it down. Panic never saves anyone. Staying calm and gaining information does. I lick my split lip, grimacing as I taste copper. "Where are we going?"

"Someplace scenic," he replies, gaze dipping to my neckline before flicking to the streetlights flashing past. "You're gonna love the view."

The gorilla on my right snorts. "Boss, she's a feisty one. Split your lip good."

I allow myself a fractional smile. That at least feels like a small victory. His smug face now sports a partial red hand-print and a split lip. I hope it stings.

"I went easy on him," I mutter.

Hawk-nose elbows me hard in the ribs. My mouth opens as my breath explodes out of me, but I refuse to make a sound. Not a chance I'm going to give Nico the satisfaction of making my suffering obvious.

Nico studies me. "You still have bark, even muzzled. Interesting."

I lean forward as far as the restraints allow. "You should worry less about my bark and more about Abram's bite.

Release me now and maybe he won't remove your spine through your throat."

His grin widens, humorless. "Who's to say your lover even survived our little dinner interruption?"

My stomach twists. "He's alive. You have no reason not to kill me if he wasn't."

Saying it makes it true. It has to be true.

"Is he?" Nico shrugs with theatrical indifference. "I fired, the bullet flew. Maybe I missed. Maybe I didn't."

Anger explodes within. I kick sideways, raking my bound wrists across Hawk-nose's lap, catching soft tissue. He yelps, the pistol clattering to the floor mat.

Hands clamp my shoulders, slamming me backward. The vending machine drives a fist into my sternum. All the air abandons me in one whoosh, my vision going tunnel-dark. Tears sting my eyes, hot and humiliating.

"That's enough," Nico says, voice flat, lifeless. "We don't damage the merchandise—yet."

Merchandise. I want to vomit.

The SUV banks off the highway onto a narrower road. No more neon, just desert darkness swallowing the windows. My brain catalogs landmarks through the tinted glass—rare street signs, the silhouette of a faux-Tuscan gate. It looks like the Lake Las Vegas community.

Minutes pass. My ribs ache, and my wrists and ankles burn from the ties. Nico scrolls through his phone, casual as a commuter. Then he peers over the seat again, licking dried blood from his lip.

"So, my pet," he drawls, "how long have you been servicing Abram?"

"None of your goddamn business, sleazeball."

He doesn't react. "I bet you're very good at it. It's easy to imagine how you could make a man very, very happy with those lips of yours. Hell, I'm imagining it right now."

"You fucking—"

Hawk-nose raises his gun, but Nico waves him down, eyes bright with cruel delight. "Such spirit. I respect that. But spirit doesn't change facts. Your Bratva prince walked straight into a trap. That makes you leverage. If he obeys, perhaps you'll live. Perhaps."

My throat constricts. *Protect the baby.* "What do you want?"

"Recognition. Respect." Nico's smile is boyish, chilling. "First meeting tomorrow, he treats me as an equal. Second meeting, he treats me as an heir, signing over all rights to everything he has upon his death. Third, well, we'll see if there even is a third."

I let out a brittle laugh. "You think killing Abram will get you Vegas? His sisters alone will feed you your liver."

He shrugs. "Women have their place. Especially widows needing comfort."

Disgust curdles my stomach. "Your father's still alive."

"For now," he says breezily, "but cancer doesn't respect hierarchy."

I swallow hard, willing my voice not to shake. "You really think this ends with you on a throne?"

Nico turns, his face faintly lit by the glow of the dash. "Everything ends, my dear. Even the reign of kings."

The SUV rolls to a stop. A tall iron gate creaks open ahead, darkness yawning like a mouth ready to swallow me whole.

He glances back again. "Be grateful. Most never get to witness history being rewritten."

I lift my chin in defiance. "You're the only history I see."

He laughs humorlessly. "Save your strength, bella. The night is just beginning."

The SUV rumbles on. And for the first time since this insanity started, I find myself wondering if I'm going to get out of this alive.

CHAPTER 33

ABRAM

"Fourth time," I say quietly. "Where did Nico take her?"

I flex my fingers, testing the sting in my knuckles as crimson trickles down the drain in the floor. One deep breath. Another. Control settles over me like ice.

The room is nothing but poured concrete, a single naked bulb, a steel worktable, and the wet rasp of a man who should have kept better company. The goon from the restaurant who I'd knocked out cold, the one Nico shot, breathes heavily, loudly. Now he's tied to a steel chair, wrists and ankles bound tightly with zip-ties.

His face is pulp: one eye a swollen to the size of a plum, lips split, teeth spotted red. Every time he tries to inhale through the wreck of his nose, it whistles.

I step closer. The bulb hums overhead, throwing a hard circle of light across his wrecked features.

His good eye rolls up, unfocused. A pink froth swells at the corners of his mouth. "I t–told you, don't—" A cough shakes him. The stench of copper sits thick in the air.

Mikail stands against the far wall, phone in hand. Denis is beside him, keeping a steady, emotionless watch. His phone chimes every few minutes, another source, another dead end.

Two hours. One hour and sixty-three minutes, to be exact. That's how long Jenna's been gone, every tick of the second hand driving a splinter deeper beneath my ribs.

I kneel, forearms braced on my thighs so we're eye to swollen eye. "Listen carefully," I say, voice low enough he has to strain to hear. "This is the last time I'll ask nicely. Where. Is. She?"

His head wobbles, blood spilling from a fresh split in his brow. "I swear... don't know... just security... no one tells us..."

"Lie."

I tilt my head, studying the fear twitching under his bruised and bloody face. He'll break eventually, they always do. The only question is how messy I'm willing to get before he does.

I extend a hand without looking away. Mikail presses a bottle of water into my palm. I twist the cap off with a crack. I tip it and take a slow swallow, letting him imagine, for a heartbeat, that humanity might still live inside me.

Then I upend the bottle over his head. Water and blood sluice down his cheeks, jolting him. He blinks, sputters, blinks again. When his focus locks onto me, it's laced with panic.

"Last chance," I repeat calmly. "If you know anything, tell me now."

He huffs a broken laugh that ends in a wet gurgle. "What else... can you... do to me?"

"Wrong answer."

I stand and casually walk to the stainless worktable. On it sits a rubber mallet, a welding torch, pliers, and a sharp set of gardening shears I brought for this special occasion. I choose the shears first and turn back.

"We'll start small," I say. "Pinkie toes first. Then fingers. We'll work inward until there's nothing left to prune."

Terror shreds what's left of his composure. "Wait, *wait*! I–I—"

"Shoes," I order.

Denis and Mikail tug them free, peeling off filthy socks. The man tries to kick, but the chair barely rocks—the bindings are too tight. I crouch slowly, laying the cool steel across his smallest toe. He jerks as the sharp blade nips flesh, drawing a bright bead of blood. His scream ricochets off the concrete.

I don't lift the shears. "Where did Nico take Jenna?"

"I–I don't know—" His voice trembles.

I raise my eyes, meeting Mikail's and Denis's. "Toes always work."

Panic crosses his features. "Please! Stop! I'll talk!" He sucks in a breath. I wait for him to speak before removing the shears. "He's got two ghost houses," the thug gasps. "They don't show up on paper as belonging to the family. One of them he lives in, the other is for parties. Girls, coke, no witnesses."

"Address. Now."

"I only know the party drop. North of Lake Las Vegas. Corner of Sloan and Hadley. Brown stucco, busted fence."

Denis is already hammering away on his phone. "It's a shell corp out of Reno, eighteen month old deed. Satellite matches the description." He shows me the screen. It looks like a squat eyesore drowning in weeds.

I stand, shears in hand. "He'd keep her where screams could get swallowed up by loud music," I mutter. The thug nods too fast, eyes glued to the blades.

"Shut him up," I say, turning away.

Denis cracks him across the temple with a pistol butt. The chair lurches as dead weight slumps, then topples over. I don't bother to watch him hit the floor.

CHAPTER 34

JENNA

The lights of Vegas fade the further we drive, every mile uglier than the last. By the time the SUV jerks to a stop, the horizon is nothing but busted streetlamps and desert dust.

We're in front of a sprawling, Spanish-style house that was probably gorgeous at one time, if someone hadn't let it rot. Boarded-up windows. Spray-painted graffiti everywhere. The pool glows an unholy swamp-green under a single security bulb. Broken beer bottles crunch beneath the guards' boots as they yank me out.

It's even worse inside. A mix of weed, bleach, and stale perfume stings my nostrils as we enter. Confetti sticks to my heel where the marble's tacky with something that spilled. I open my mouth and offer a cocky insult before I remember I'm supposed to be terrified.

"Throw all your parties in dumpsters or is this place special?"

The guard beside me twitches. Nico stops mid-stride, turning like a bad Disney villain—slow, dramatic, and slightly amused.

Right. Rule one, Jenna: Don't poke the psycho.

Too late.

His hand flashes out before I can react. *CRACK*. I refuse to give him the satisfaction of a response but damn, my head rings.

He grabs my chin, fingers digging hard enough to bruise. "You've got twelve hours, sweetheart. If your Bratva prince doesn't hand over every asset, I start trimming pieces. Starting with that sharp tongue of yours."

I glare at him, blood coating my teeth. My gut tells me to keep quiet.

"Bedroom one," he snaps, shoving me toward two of his grunts.

I force my brain to stay focused. Ten guards plus Nico. Two pistols, one shotgun, one knife on a belt. Exits: front door, kitchen, broken window by the staircase though too high to reach cuffed.

The hall reeks of stale beer and cheap body spray. One of the guards—big, young, and nervous—leans in close, voice barely above a whisper. "No one touches you unless the boss says."

I angle my head as I walk quickly to keep up with the large men. "He planning to stay?"

"Not supposed to," he mutters.

I'm guessing bedroom one used to be cute. Rose wallpaper, wrought-iron bed, but now the wallpaper's curling, ashtrays overflow, and there's a crusty handprint on the headboard I do *not* want to know about. They cut the zip ties around my wrists, cuffing my left wrist to the bed frame. My right arm stays free.

Nervous guard checks the cuff. Too tight. I hiss. He loosens it a notch, meeting my stare before backing out of the room.

The door slams, and I hear a heavy bolt being turned before quiet drops like a blanket. I yank—nothing. The frame's welded to the floor. Screwheads rusted solid. I dig at one until my nail cracks.

"Dammit."

I lay my palm over the flat of my belly. *Hold tight, little one. Mom's working on an exit plan.*

Boots stomp down the hallway and fade. A bassline pulses, men laugh. I hear Nico bark an order. He sounds paranoid.

I breathe deep, cataloging every sound, timing the rhythm of patrols. Fear trembles in my spine, but fury burns hotter. Abram will come. I know it. And when he does I intend to be very much alive, and I intend to watch Nico learn exactly how bad his bad decision was.

The room smells awful. I take inventory because that's what a girl does when she's cuffed to a bed and trying not to lose her mind.

First, the furniture. One busted dresser with a drawer hanging by a single rail. A nightstand scarred with cigarette burns. Mirror over the dresser spider-cracked straight through the middle—handy, if I decide to turn a shard into a shiv.

There's a tiny window nailed shut and painted over a hundred renovations ago. A splintered chair sits in the corner, one leg snapped half off. If I ever get free, that leg is mine.

I flex my left wrist—cuffed so tight my pulse throbs against the steel. I twist sideways, digging my toes into the floor, stretching my free arm as far as it'll go. Fingertips brush the nearest bolt but I can't get the leverage.

Okay. Next idea.

I don't have my purse. Nico's guys took it when they frisked me, making sure I didn't have anything useful. But the mattress has springs. I wedge my free hand into the seam, yanking until one breaks loose. It's thin and a little rusty, but the end is sharp. I tuck it under my thigh. If someone gets handsy, they'll get a surprise.

Voices filter down the hallway. Nico barks, "I've got leverage. Vasiliev will crawl."

Crawl? Please.

Another man's voice, warning him that he's crossing family lines, breaking code. Nico tells him to fuck off.

The door creaks open. I tense and move the spring to settle within my fist. It's the guard from before, the one who loosened my restraint. He balances a tarnished tray of bottled water, two aspirin, and a sad-looking banana. He steps in and shuts the door. He places the tray on the nightstand without looking at me.

"Sorry," he whispers, avoiding my eyes. Up close he looks barely twenty-five, freckles poking out beneath the stubble.

"You got a name?"

He hesitates. "Luka."

"Luka," I echo, tasting every syllable like a warning and a plea. "Luka, I'm pregnant. If Nico goes through with whatever psycho plan he's nursing, that makes you an accessory to a double homicide. One of the victims being a helpless baby. Think you can sleep with that on your conscience?"

His throat bobs. "My sister's expecting," he murmurs. Guilt slides across his face.

I press. "Don Agosti would nail Nico's hide to the wall for this if he knew what was going on. You help me now, you walk away when Abram bulldozes this dump. You don't, you're collateral damage."

Luka glances toward the closed door then back at me. He says nothing, but his hands move to the cuff. He makes it another notch looser. Circulation floods back in a pins-and-needles wave, and I nearly sag with relief.

He tips the water bottle toward me. I take it, our fingers brushing in a silent agreement that this conversation never happened. Then he slips out, leaving the door unlocked.

Small victory. Huge possibilities.

I sip the water. The aspirin goes down without argument. The mattress spring remains in my palm, flimsy but hopeful. I test the loosened cuff. Still snug, but I can rotate my wrist now.

Outside, the sky is solid black. No streetlights shining through that painted window, just the faraway glare of the city I love in the distant horizon.

Abram is out there somewhere, his ice-blue gaze burning holes in the world.

I stroke my belly. "Hang tight, little bean. Daddy's coming. And he's pissed."

CHAPTER 35

ABRAM

I floor the Maybach, the V-12 roaring like a bear.

Vegas streaks past me in a neon blur, but the only color I care about is the red blood Nico will spill when I find him.

Denis rides shotgun, barking coordinates into a secure headset. "Alpha unit posts on Gibson in eight minutes. Bring full rigs, suppressors only. Copy?" After a brief pause, he says, "Two trucks inbound."

Mikail sits behind me, the screen from his laptop glowing ghost-green across his face. "Party house confirmed. Utility records show a spike in power a few hours ago. AC is blasting. Lights are on. They're in there."

A few minutes later I'm punching a code at an anonymous roll-up gate. Steel yawns open, and I nose the car inside the concrete bunker. No signage, nothing but the smell of old brake fluid and CLP gun oil. A freight elevator the size of a studio apartment waits at the far wall. Thirty seconds later we emerge into a subterranean armory lit by a single row of fluorescents.

I walk the steel racks, fingers brushing against cold barrels. The ritual centers me. SR9 pistols—check. MPX-K subguns—check. Four Kevlar soft vests in matte black—check. I sling a shotgun over my shoulder and claim a KA-BAR longer than my hand. Rage should have a blade.

Denis loads magazines methodically, brass clicking like a metronome. "Rules?" he asks without looking up.

"Jenna unharmed is objective one," I say. "Anyone so much as bruises her, you shoot him in the throat. No hesitation."

Mikail zips up his plate carrier vest and raises an eyebrow. "City limits. Metro will crawl up our ass if we light up the place."

"Then we finish before they arrive," I answer. "If she bleeds, Vegas can burn."

They don't argue.

While the men gear up, I step into a side office the size of a closet. I pull Jenna's phone from my pocket, recovered from the restaurant floor after the chaos. The screen comes alive with a picture of Jenna and Claire, shoulders pressed together, sunlight turning her hair to copper fire. She's laughing, open-mouthed, eyes squinting in pure joy.

My chest tightens. It's an unwelcome sensation because it feels like fear, and I don't do fear.

If Nico touches her again, I'll mail his father the pieces in unmarked boxes.

I slide the phone back into my pocket, sealing the softness away, and return to the men.

A minute later, three black Yukons glide out of the garage. We run south on Main, cutting east into the warehouse district. Night vision goggles drop into place, turning the world phosphor green. I breathe deep and slow.

Ten minutes, baby. Hold on.

The convoy ghosts through back streets at a crawl—no headlights, engines idling low. I ride point; my right hand on the wheel, the left brushing the spare mag on my thigh, a nervous tell I forgot I even had.

I picture Jenna's face when I storm that room, her eyes flashing relief and fury in equal measure. When I cut the cuff from her wrist, I'm going to tell her what I should have said over dinner.

I love you, kisa. Let me keep you safe.

Not exactly a polished speech. Just the truth, raw and ugly, the way Bratva men reveal their hearts.

Denis's voice crackles over the comm. "Alpha, thirty seconds to the mark. Heat index unchanged. No patrol outside."

"Copy," I respond. "Bravo, stay tight. No hero shit."

Georg answers with a double click.

We roll past a busted streetlamp. The house is situated at the end of the cul-de-sac, moonlight painting its stucco the color of bone. The Jeep we tagged on FLIR still sits out front, windows fogged from bodies breathing inside.

In the back seat, Mikail closes the laptop and racks his pistol. "You sure you want point?"

I flash a grin he can't see. "The first person Jenna lays eyes on will be me."

He huffs. "Figured."

As we coast the last half-block, I kill the engine, letting momentum carry us to the curb. Silence fills the space, only the sound of my pulse in my ears, steady and certain.

Denis scans the perimeter through his scope. "One guard on the porch smoking. Rifle slung over his shoulder. Eyes on his phone. Amateur hour."

"Take him quietly. We breach in two."

I lean back against the headrest, thumb the slide of the SR9, and allow one more thought of Jenna. She's humming under her breath while typing at my desk, a tune I never recognized. Funny how you can miss something so small until it's threatened.

Almost there, my love.

The Yukon doors pop open in silent choreography. The night breathes around us, hot and dusty. My boots hit the gravel and I ghost forward, every move a laser sight on the bedroom where she waits.

Showtime.

CHAPTER 36

ABRAM

I lead the approach, Denis at my side.

As the house looms closer, I get a better look at the peeling stucco, shuttered windows, and trash-strewn front steps. Parties here must get pretty messy; chaotic affairs no decent woman would ever choose to attend. The image of Jenna trapped inside that filth sends fire coursing through my veins.

I fight the impulse to storm straight through the front door. *Discipline*, I remind myself. Rage can wait.

"Mikail, take Georg and sweep the south side," I order quietly, my voice barely audible even in the stillness. "Check windows, watch for movement." They vanish silently into the darkness, their training evident in every carefully placed step.

Denis and I move toward the north side. Adrenaline sharpens my senses. I smell the faint scent of garbage, hear the distant traffic noise. My own breathing is silent, steady, and deliberate.

It takes only a minute before I hear Jenna's voice.

"Let me use the damn bathroom, you asshole!" she shouts, frustration and fury clear in her tone. She remains strong and defiant. That's my girl.

Denis looks at me. "She's alive."

I nod, motioning for him to follow me toward the source. We slip beneath the window ledge, crouching low, muscles tense. Another burst of Jenna's voice punches through the night.

"I'm serious! Take me to the bathroom or I'll scream until your ears bleed!"

The sound of a door creaking open makes my pulse skyrocket. A male voice answers, arrogant and cruel. "Piss your pants, sweetheart. I don't give a fuck."

Nico.

My jaw clenches, teeth grinding so hard I can hear the scrape of bone. I gesture to Denis, and he signals Mikail and Georg to circle back. They arrive quickly, moving like ghosts, their eyes narrowed and alert.

Another yell from Jenna, this time louder, angrier. My hands curl into fists. Does she not realize her defiance puts her at greater risk? But how can I fault her courage, her stubborn spirit? It's exactly what I love most about her.

"Why did Nico respond instead of one of his men?" I wonder out loud.

Denis shakes his head, skeptical. "We know he's not alone. Cowards never are."

I lean upward cautiously, peering through the corner of the window. My heart stops for a single, sickening moment. Nico is standing over Jenna, who's cuffed to a rusted metal bed frame. Even from here, I can see the dark bruises blooming on her face, her lip swollen and bleeding.

Jenna is glaring up at him, her fierce expression unwavering despite the pain I see etched in her features. I've never been prouder or angrier in my entire life.

Nico leans down and says in a mocking voice, "You scream again, bitch, and I'll beat you unconscious. Understand?"

Jenna stares back in furious silence. Nico laughs, a hollow, hateful sound, and runs a finger down her jawline, slow and sickening. Before I can even register my own reaction, Jenna smacks his hand away with a ferocity that stuns him.

Fury flashes across Nico's face, and in a swift movement, he slaps her hard. The sound echoes, and blood roars in my ears. The thin veneer of control I've maintained thus far shatters completely. Something primal, violent, and unstoppable surges through me.

"Shit," Denis mutters as he realizes my intention. "Abram, wait—"

It's too late. I'm already moving, weapon drawn, storming around to the front entrance with a speed I didn't know I was capable of. I hear my men scrambling to follow, but my entire world narrows down to one objective: Nico's death.

I hit the front door full force, my boot connecting solidly, splintering wood and metal hinges giving way. As the door crashes inward, two men in the living room leap up, startled, hands scrambling for their weapons.

I don't hesitate. My pistol snaps up, muzzle flashing twice in quick succession. Both men collapse without a sound, blood pooling beneath their bodies.

Mikail falls into step behind me, weapon trained forward as we sprint toward the hallway. Another guard steps out, eyes wide with panic, gun half-raised. Mikail drops him without hesitation.

We reach the bedroom door. My vision tunnels, all thoughts consumed by the need to get to Jenna, to protect her from any further harm.

I kick the door open so hard it slams into the wall, plaster cracking.

Inside, Jenna lies on the bed, cuffed, bruised, her eyes wide with shock and relief. Nico spins toward me, his face contorting with panic, his hand halfway to his waistband.

I raise my gun, eyes locked on the bastard who dared to touch my woman, fury roaring out of me in a single, unstoppable bellow.

"NICO!"

CHAPTER 37

JENNA

My wrists are raw and aching from being cuffed to the goddamn bed for what feels like hours.

My lip's still bleeding from Nico's hits, the taste sharp and metallic at the corner of my mouth. My whole body hurts, from the tension, from the blasting air conditioning, from the fear I'm trying to pretend isn't crawling up my spine like frostbite. I'm exhausted. Furious. Terrified. But mostly, I'm ready for Abram.

And then I hear gunfire. Two sharp pops, then boots pounding across the hardwood. Not Nico's boys. He told them not to fire unless ordered. That means it has to be Abram.

My heart slams into my ribs. I want to scream. I want to call out and tell him to run, that Nico's right behind the door, armed and waiting. But I never get the chance.

The door crashes open in a blur of black force and fury. Splinters fly, plaster cracks. Abram barrels in, wild-eyed and savage, his pistol raised, a rabid storm carved into his features. Mikail follows a beat behind, gun sweeping the hallway behind him, clearing the space.

My heart floods with unbearable feelings. Relief. Rage. Love.

"Nico!" Abram shouts.

Nico spins behind me, pressing the cold, hard mouth of a pistol against my temple. "Drop your fucking weapon!" he shrieks, dragging me upright like a shield.

Abram freezes mid-step. Everything stops. The air thickens as the world narrows to two points: the barrel pressed to my skull and Abram's eyes burning hate into Nico from across the room.

My breath catches. Nico's arm is around my chest now, jerking me against him, and I can feel his body trembling. He's sweating. Scared. But his grip is tight and the gun is real, pressed against my skull.

I don't cry but my voice shakes when I speak one word. "Abram."

He doesn't look at me. He doesn't look at Nico either. He looks through him. Like he already knows how this ends. His jaw tightens as he lowers the gun, slow and deliberate.

"I've got you, Jenna," he says. "I swear it."

His voice is calm. *Too* calm. The kind of calm that means someone's about to die.

Nico tightens his grip on me, yanking the chain of the cuff so hard I stumble with a cry. My wrist wrenches, fiery pain lancing up my arm. He jerks me in front of him like a shield again, his forearm pressed against my throat this time, the gun never leaving my temple.

He's panting now, erratic. Not the smooth-talking manipulator from before. This man is unraveling.

"You came for her," Nico spits, his voice high and cracked. "That's cute, Abram. Real fucking noble. But you're going to leave here with nothing unless you give me what's mine."

His arm drops from around my neck for a brief moment while his hand dips into the back waistband of his pants, pulling out a creased manila envelope. "Your empire. Your hotel. Your fucking birthright. All of it." He waves the envelope like a magician revealing a final card.

"Signed on my end. Just needs your signature." He thrusts it toward Abram, tossing it on the bed before wrapping his arm around my throat again. "Sign it, or I blow her brains out, right here in front of you."

I flinch, my eyes glued to Abram. There's a stillness in him, a terrifying calm like the eye of a hurricane. But I can see beneath the surface, and he's starting to break.

Mikail and Denis slide into view behind him, weapons drawn. Their stances are taut, precise. Ready to end this. But Abram gives the slightest shake of his head, and both men freeze like statues.

He's thinking. Calculating. Not just about escape routes or kill shots, but about legacy, territory, and all the blood that was spilled in order to gain what he now owns.

He's also thinking about me.

I see it the moment it happens. The split-second when he decides.

"I'll sign," he says. "Just let her go."

"No," I rasp, fighting against Nico's iron grip. My wrist is raw, the cuff biting deeper with every movement, but that pain is nothing compared to the agony of watching Abram yield to this monster. "Don't you dare, Abram. Don't you dare give him what he wants!"

"Shut the fuck up," Nico growls, his gun jamming harder into my temple, forcing my head sideways.

My vision pulses black and white, stars dancing from the pressure. But I won't shut up. I won't be his pawn, and I sure as hell won't let Abram lose everything he's worked so hard for because of me.

Abram's eyes meet mine, cold blue fire blazing within. He watches me, his jaw clenched so tight I can practically hear his teeth grinding. Anguish, rage, and determination flash across his face. Beneath it all lies an unspoken promise. He won't let this stand. Neither will I.

"You're bluffing, Nico," I spit out, voice rough from screaming, throat aching from fear and anger. "You don't have the balls to pull the trigger."

"Oh, you want to test that theory?" Nico sneers, pressing the gun even harder. "Keep talking, bitch. See what happens."

A wild, desperate fire roars through my veins. If it was any other situation, Abram would never give up, would never surrender. He's doing this for me. But I refuse to be the reason he falls.

Without another second's hesitation, I snap my head back with every ounce of strength I have left. My skull collides with Nico's face. The crunch is sickeningly satisfying—his nose breaking, bone giving way beneath the impact. Pain explodes through my head, stars flashing brighter, but his gun jerks away instantly as he staggers back, blood spraying across my neck.

"You bitch!" he roars, gripping his shattered nose, eyes wide with shock and fury.

I stumble forward as far as the cuff will allow, barely managing to keep my balance. My head spins, my vision blurred, but the barrel isn't pointed at me anymore.

And that's all Abram needs.

He surges forward, fury incarnate, slamming into Nico like a freight train. They crash into the crumbling wall, plaster shattering beneath the impact. Nico's gun skids across the grimy floor, lost in the chaos.

I slump to the side, barely catching myself against the bed frame. My wrist screams in agony as the cuff cuts deeper, but I can't tear my eyes away from the brutal spectacle unfolding in front of me.

Abram's fists rain down on Nico with a precise, punishing rhythm, every blow driven by rage and vengeance. Nico thrashes beneath him, wiry strength born of desperation. His bloody hands scrabble across the filthy floor, finding a shard of glass from the mirror. He swings it upward, slicing a deep gash across Abram's forearm.

Blood spills hot and red, but Abram doesn't flinch. He grabs Nico's wrist, twisting until the glass shard drops from his fingers. Nico screams in pain, a guttural, animal sound.

"You're fucking dead," Nico spits, bucking wildly beneath Abram. "I'll kill you, I'll kill her—"

Abram silences him with an elbow to the throat. Nico gags, choking, eyes bulging. Abram's control is terrifying to witness, calculated violence radiating from him like heat waves. Nico fights dirty, driving a knee into Abram's ribs, momentarily throwing him off balance.

They roll, a mess of tangled limbs and desperate strikes, careening into the shattered dresser. Wood splinters. Glass rains across the floor. Abram regains the upper hand, knees pinning Nico's chest, powerful hands closing around his throat.

"I should let you die slowly," Abram snarls, voice cold and deadly. "But I don't have that luxury."

Nico squirms beneath him, teeth bared in desperation. His fingers slip beneath his jacket, grasping at something.

"Abram!" I scream, but he's already moving.

Nico drives a concealed knife upward, aimed straight for Abram's throat.

Everything happens in the blink of an eye.

Abram shifts, trapping Nico's arm. He rips the knife away, driving a vicious fist into Nico's temple. Nico's head snaps back, stunned, and Abram's hand goes to the pistol at his hip, smoothly drawing it in a single, fluid motion.

My breath catches, heart slamming violently in my chest.

One clean, deafening shot echoes throughout the room.

Nico goes limp instantly, eyes wide and empty. A hole blooms darkly in the center of his forehead, blood spilling slowly onto the filthy carpet beneath him.

Silence settles, broken only by my ragged breathing and Abram's harsh, controlled panting. My ears ring, my vision pulses, and my whole body shakes uncontrollably.

Abram gets up slowly, blood dripping steadily from the wound on his arm, his eyes still locked on Nico's corpse as if daring it to rise again. The gun hangs limply at his side, fingers twitching slightly with residual fury.

With a visible effort, he turns toward me. His fierce blue eyes soften instantly, rage melting away into tenderness so intense it nearly breaks me.

He takes a slow, careful step closer. "Jenna..."

"I'm okay," I rasp, the lie coming easy despite my battered body and racing heart. "Abram—"

"I've got you," he whispers, closing the distance in one more stride. His uninjured hand comes up, fingers brushing gently against my bruised jaw, eyes blazing.

"I've got you."

CHAPTER 38

JENNA

I float somewhere between pain and numbness while the room tilts and sways around me.

Nico's body lies crumpled on the floor, eyes glassy, blood spreading in a dark halo around his head. It should horrify me. Maybe later it will. But right now, all I can process is the way Abram's arm is wrapped tightly around my body, anchoring me.

My split lip keeps reopening and I taste copper. My cuffed wrist throbs in a dull, ugly rhythm. But when Abram shifts me against his chest, the pain seems to fade into the background.

Denis and Mikail have rounded up the remaining Agosti soldiers, now disarmed, hands laced behind their heads. Wrists are zip-tied, weapons kicked out of reach. No one resists. Nico's corpse has drained every drop of bravado from them.

Luka is among the living, the poor kid likely wondering what the hell he got himself into. But at least he's alive.

"Area secure," Denis calls out. He gives me a quick visual once-over and frowns at the blood on my jaw. "She needs to get to the ER, boss. Concussion for sure, maybe worse."

"I'm fine," I mumble, but the words slur. The ceiling slides sideways.

Abram tightens his hold. "We're done here." He orders Denis to arrange medical transport quietly—no sirens, no questions. Denis nods and steps into the hall, already dialing.

Mikail scoops a set of keys from Nico's pocket, tossing Abram a small handcuff key. The metal is cold against my skin as Abram frees my wrist. He rubs circulation back in with gentle fingers, his mouth a hard line.

"Stay awake for me, *malyshka*," he says, guiding me through the doorway. Stale hallway air rushes over us and I stumble. He catches me before my knees fold.

Outside, the desert night presses on, hot wind kissing our skin. Three Yukons sit at the curb. An unmarked ambulance waits half a block away, parked dark between street lamps. The paramedics wait beside a gurney, an example of exactly the kind of discretion Abram's money can buy.

I open my mouth—*now, Jenna, tell him about the baby*—but Abram presses a finger lightly to my bruised lips.

"Conserve your strength," he says. "We'll talk later."

The paramedics rush toward me with the gurney. They speak calmly as they help me on it, gently placing a C-collar around my neck and checking my blood pressure. I hear mention of possible head trauma.

They wheel me back to the ambulance. I clutch Abram's sleeve when they try to separate us.

"I'm right here," he says, climbing in beside me. His hand swallows mine—steady, warm, and grounding.

I wet my lips, summoning every ounce of consciousness as I tug him closer. "Tell them..." The words sound like sandpaper. "Tell them I'm pregnant."

Raw shock flashes in his eyes, but before he can reply, darkness swoops in. The last thing I feel is his palm against my cheek and the ambulance lurching forward, the siren still mercifully silent.

∾

White sheets. Soft beeping. Sunlight beams slanting through the blinds.

For a second, I think I'm in Abram's penthouse when I first come out of the fog, but then I register the scent of antiseptic instead of espresso and realize the skyline is framed by reinforced hospital glass.

A shadow looms by the door. A mountain of a man in a dark suit, earpiece coiled at his neck. A bodyguard. Of course.

My throat screams when I try to swallow. "Water," I croak, though the word barely escapes my lips.

Across the room, Abram jumps to his feet, chair screeching back. He crosses the space in three strides and presses the call-button for a nurse, while his other hand finds mine, thumb brushing the inside of my wrist.

"*Malyshka,* thank God." The relief in his voice guts me. He turns to the guard. "Get the doctor. Now." The big man slips out, door whispering shut behind him.

I blink, trying to piece timelines together. Outside the window the sky is bright. "How long?"

"Night passed," he says softly, smoothing a strand of hair off my forehead. "Concussion had you under. They kept you sedated so your brain could rest and recover."

Concussion. Right. Nico. My stomach flips, my hand flying instinctively to it. "The baby—"

Abram's grip tightens. "Easy. Breathe."

The door opens and a woman in pale green scrubs enters. She's in her mid-thirties, sharp but kind eyes behind rimless glasses.

"Dr. Reyes," she introduces herself while checking the monitor. "Good to see you awake, Ms. Ridley."

I'm barely able to manage a nod. "My baby?"

She smiles genuinely. "We ran a full maternal trauma panel, repeated scans six hours apart. No placental abruption, amniotic fluid levels are normal. You and baby are both stable."

A sob claws up my throat, relief so fierce it hurts. Abram exhales a breath.

Dr. Reyes palpates gently around the bruise blooming across my jaw. "You'll have headaches for a few days. No sudden movements, plenty of fluids, a light diet." She glances at Abram's bandaged forearm and the dried blood on his knuckles. "Both of you could use plenty of rest, frankly."

He gives a curt nod. "She gets whatever she needs."

The doctor's lips twitch. "Already noted, Mr. Vasiliev." She hands him a folder of discharge instructions before leaving the room, though I get the feeling we won't be going anywhere until an entire security battalion signs off.

Silence settles over us. Abram brings my fingers to his lips, eyes shimmering with raw emotion.

"I was terrified he killed the baby," I whisper.

"So was I," he answers. Then quieter, almost like a vow, he adds, "Never again."

I tug him closer, needing the solidity of his chest against my cheek, the steady drum of a heart that just went to war for me. Sunlight spills over us, and for the first time since the restaurant I let myself believe we're safe.

Abram settles on the mattress beside my hip, his big body somehow fitting there like a disciplined guard dog. His thumb sweeps tiny circles across my knuckles—sweet torture when every other part of him radiates lethal energy.

He clears his throat. "So." The single word is deep, cautious, and weirdly hopeful. "Why didn't you tell me?"

I huff a soft laugh. "You mean why didn't I blurt it out between spreadsheets and threat assessments?"

"That would've worked," he deadpans.

I tug the sheet higher over my lap. "At first I needed to

process it. Surprise pregnancies aren't exactly something you announce on Slack."

His brow arches. "Slack?"

"Figure of speech, Mr. Antiquated Communication." A grin tugs at my swollen lip. He chuckles, but lets me continue. "Then Claire convinced me I should make it special. I thought the Michelin-star place you booked would be perfect—candles, an incredible view, a fancy soup I couldn't pronounce. The perfect setting, right?"

Recognition flashes in his ice-blue eyes and he nods ruefully. "Ideal, before the armed-idiot intermission."

"Exactly." I squeeze his fingers. "Not really the vibe for baby confessions."

He winces, but there's humor behind it. "Point taken."

My smile wavers. The hospital hum fades as all the unspoken fears crowd in. "Honestly, Abram, I didn't know if you'd want any of this." I gesture to my stomach. "We've known each other, what, almost two months? Six weeks since The 13th Floor. That's whirlwind territory."

His thumb stills, the quiet stretching between us until I think I might float away on it. Then he leans in, forehead almost touching mine.

"Listen to me, Jenna Ridley. You are not alone in this. Not for one heartbeat. I am in—blood, bone, and soul. You and our child are mine to protect." Each word is deliberate, intentional.

My chest caves with relief, but old defenses kick in once

more. "You say that now, but what if the Bratva world gets uglier? We survived last night, but what if..." I trail off.

He exhales like a volcano venting steam. "I hated every second of last night, other than our peaceful moments at the restaurant before all hell broke loose. But I promise, I will carve out a safer reality for us, for our family. You'll never be used against me again." His gaze slides to my belly, softening in a way that makes my heart ache. "This baby... it's a gift I never expected."

A ridiculous hiccup-sob escapes me. "So you're not mad?"

"Mad?" His lips brush my bruised knuckles. "I'm furious. I'm furious at Nico, at myself for not preventing this. But about the baby?" He shakes his head, a small smile finally breaking through. "I'm over the moon. I'm just sorry you carried that fear and uncertainty alone."

I dab at my eyes. "Thank you."

"What do you need from me, *malyshka?*"

"Food. I'm starving."

He laughs and stands, planting a gentle kiss to my forehead. "I'll call the kitchen, have them make whatever you're craving."

"Steak and ice cream?"

Another laugh. "Anything. And after that, you rest. Tomorrow, we'll talk names."

Names. The word flutters through me like a sunrise. I watch him stride to the door and issue an order to the guard, letting my head sink back into the pillows.

He's happy about the baby.

He comes back, wrapping his hand around mine. I notice a shift in his gaze—a flicker of storm-cloud gray passing through the icy-blue.

"What?" I ask, heart tripping. "Tell me."

He draws a breath so deep his ribs lift beneath the hospital scrubs someone scrounged for him. "I have a confession. Something I'm not proud of."

Instant panic. "Is this about last night? Are we in trouble with the police?"

"No." He squeezes my hand, cutting off the spiral. "Not legal trouble. Personal." His voice drops to a gravelly hush. "I was going to tell you something at the restaurant. Before Nico ruined everything."

The memory flashes—candlelight, fabulous wine I couldn't drink, my own secret burning my tongue. "Okay," I whisper. "Tell me now."

He inhales again before those eyes lock onto mine, fierce and unblinking. "I love you, Jenna Ridley."

Time stands still.

He keeps going, words rushing out as though the dam finally burst. "I've loved you since the first day you marched into my office. I knew it was reckless, so I buried it under rules and distance. But last night, seeing a gun to your head, and now knowing that our child could have been gone before I even met them..."

He can't finish the sentence. He looks away, shame written in the tight line of his shoulders. "I was a coward. Too scared of how hard my feelings for you hit me." A humorless laugh. "Abram Vasiliev, afraid. Pathetic."

My heart aches and I scoot closer, wincing at the pull of IV lines, and cup his face in my hands. "There's nothing pathetic about protecting yourself. Or about protecting me."

"I failed at both."

"You didn't." I tip his face back so he has no choice but to see the truth in mine. "I'm alive. Baby's healthy. And you took down an entire army for me. So, apology accepted, if you insist on giving one. But there's nothing to forgive."

His eyes flare, hope and disbelief colliding. "You forgive me?"

"I love you, Abram." Saying it aloud fills me with molten warmth. "I've been terrified to admit it because... well, look at you. Crime-lord-slash-sex-god is a bit intimidating on a résumé."

A true smile cracks his serious mask, small but genuine. He bends, brushing his lips against mine—soft, reverent, loving. My hand slips to his neck, feeling the steady hammer of his pulse.

When he pulls back, determination replaces doubt. "Live with me. Full-time, no more overnight bags." His hand slides to my stomach. "Raise our child in a place I can keep you safe."

"Penthouse view and unlimited steak-and-ice-cream room service?" I tease, happy tears threatening to spill.

He huffs a laugh. "Terms negotiable, except for the safety part. That's non-negotiable."

"Then yes," I breathe. "A thousand times yes."

His arms come around me carefully, tenderly, mindful of bruises. I bury my face in his shoulder, inhaling his scent. Right here, in this fortress of muscle and tenderness, is where I'm meant to be, where our baby will be loved and protected.

An unspoken promise is made in that moment, one neither of us has any intention of breaking.

CHAPTER 39

ABRAM

Rain claws at the windshield in silvery sheets, a sight rarely seen in Vegas.

Inside the Yukon the wipers thud a slow, relaxing rhythm. None of us speak. Mikail drives, shoulders hunched, muscle in his jaw jumping every few seconds as he grinds his teeth. Denis sits shotgun, elbows braced on his knees, thumbs flicking the safety on his pistol on and off.

"Feels like we're on our way to our own execution," Denis mutters, gaze fixed on the streaming glass.

"Don't think about it," Mikail answers, voice flat. "We'll walk out. We always walk out."

I roll the tension from my neck and keep my tone even. "One way or another, we're getting our audience with Don Agosti. If he's reasonable, we leave as businessmen. If not, we do things the old way."

Neither argues. The tension grows heavier.

I picture Jenna the way I left her at home—in bed, dwarfed by my hoodie, still banged up but sporting a warm smile. She appeared confident, yet her eyes tracked every move I made, as if memorizing me in case the universe decided not to return me.

I kissed her forehead, promising I'd be back for dinner. I also promised to bring dessert. She nodded like she believed me, but I could read the terror she was trying to hide.

I tighten my grip on the armrest. I'm bringing her that dessert.

We exit the freeway, slipping into a pocket of old-money suburbia—broad oaks, edged lawns, manicured shrubs, and perfectly hedged flower beds. Not the ostentatious palazzo most expect from a Mafia patriarch. Don Agosti prefers camouflage. He resides in a long, two-story Spanish colonial set back behind an iron gate. White stucco, red-tile roof, shrubs trimmed with military precision. Cozy enough to lull fools, defensible enough to deny SWAT a clean shot. Clever old bastard.

Mikail slows at the gate. Cameras blink behind rain-spattered glass blocks. A second later, the iron lattice rattles aside. We roll onto a circular driveway paved with dark cobblestone. The house itself is quiet, windows dark, only a single porch sconce burning like a watching eye.

We step out into the drizzle. Rain needles my scalp, sliding beneath the collar of my jacket, the cool bite steadying me. Denis checks the rear while Mikail scans the roofline. No obvious overwatch. For now.

The front door opens, and two guards stride onto the covered portico. One carries an umbrella large enough to shade a small car; the other flashes a thin smile that never reaches his eyes.

Showtime.

The guard with the umbrella shepherds us across a terracotta foyer that smells of lemon polish and old incense. Mosaic tiles gleam under the recessed lights, Denis's muttered warning from earlier still echoing in my skull.

"Remember *Goodfellas*," he'd said. "Any plastic tarps on the floor, we bolt."

We keep our eyes forward, breath steady. The second guard gestures to an antique console table. We surrender all pistols, backup blades, spare mags. Everything disappears into a mahogany drawer that locks with a soft *click*. They pat us down—professional, quick—then one man stays to bolt the front door while the other beckons us deeper into the mansion.

The hallway is colored in dark walnut, a color so dark it swallows the light. Somewhere a scratchy gramophone croons *"O Sole Mio,"* violin warbling under the thunder rolling outside. Crystal sconces tremble with each boom, as if the house itself is nervous.

We pause outside tall, double doors carved from oak. The guard raps twice, listens, then pushes them open.

Inside, firelight casts a golden glow over a well-kept study. Bookcases line the walls, a large desk with a high-backed leather chair sits near the window, and a large portrait of a long-ago don watches over everything from above the mantel.

And there—centered before the hearth—sits Don Mariano Agosti.

He looks ancient—almost spectral—skin parchment-thin, robe loosely fitting over a body that's run out of muscle but not elegance. A clear nasal cannula loops over his ears to an oxygen cylinder parked at his side, its regulator hissing a faint heartbeat. Yet his eyes—black olives under hooded lids—remain sharp as a stiletto. The flames from the fire cast an eerie backdrop.

We halt three paces from his wingback chair. The guard retreats to a corner after closing the doors. Mikail's shoulders tense. Denis scans the room top to bottom.

The don lifts two translucent fingers in greeting. His voice is a husky rasp. "Signor Vasiliev, forgive me for remaining seated. Even small gestures cost me more air than I can spare."

I incline my head. "Your home, your rules, Don Agosti. I appreciate the time."

He nods slowly, eyes settling on the empty space beneath my jacket where a shoulder holster should be. "You killed my son."

The words hang in the air. How can I respond to that?

"Nico abducted my woman," I reply. "Put a gun to her head. Assaulted her. She's the mother of my child. I did what any man would do."

The old man exhales, a shaky, ominous sound, and for a brief second grief washes over his face. The kind of grief only a father knows. Nico was a piece of shit, but he was still his son.

The flicker of grief fades as quickly as it came, buried beneath decades of practiced composure. He straightens in his chair as best he can, chin lifting.

"So be it," he says. "Let us not waste time pretending our blood cannot be spilled." A brittle smile tugs at his lips. "My son dies, your child lives. Such is the way of things, I suppose. A new life is always a blessing." He taps the oxygen line and the canister hisses louder, matching the storm raging outside.

Thunder rattles the windowpanes. Mikail relaxes his stance slightly but Denis's hand still hovers over the phantom of a weapon locked away. Muscle memory and instinct.

The don's gaze returns to me. "I blame myself. Illness chains me to hospitals, and while I rot, Nico chased shadows of power he never earned. I was not aware."

A ragged cough tears through him, and he muffles it with a monogrammed handkerchief, spots of red blooming like poppies on the expensive white material. When the spasm eases, he sinks back in his chair. "You must believe, Signore Vasiliev, had I known what Nico was up to, this insult to your family would never have happened."

His sincerity feels real, but sincerity can be weaponized. My expression remains neutral, voice level. "Your ignorance is no excuse for what happened. There's a score to settle here, Don."

He studies the reflection of the flames against the window for a moment, as if searching for an answer in the dance of the sparks. Another wheeze then, "Which is why we must cut away the rot before the city burns. Why we must, together, choose to end the violence before it can continue, regardless of who wronged whom." The old man lifts a trembling hand toward the doors. "There is someone I'd like you to meet."

Thunder cracks again as the study doors open. Every muscle in my body tenses, expecting the flash of a muzzle.

Instead, a woman enters. Early forties I'd guess, though the poise makes age irrelevant. Long black hair swept into a low twist, strong cheekbones, mouth set in a line that suggests she's issued orders men had no choice but to obey. Tailored navy suit, pearls around her neck and in her ears, a silk shawl the color of old wine draped over one shoulder. Southern-Italian royalty on a funeral errand.

She crosses the room with unhurried confidence and offers me her hand. Her grip is firm, certain. "Isabella Agosti," she introduces herself. "It's a pleasure, Signore Vasiliev." She repeats the ritual with Denis and Mikail, nodding politely to each, assessing us quietly.

The don's eyes soften. "My daughter," he tells us. "And soon, my voice."

Isabella settles into the armchair beside him. Only after confirming his comfort does she turn her attention to the three men invading her father's study.

The don exhales a shaky breath. "I wish to die under my own roof, not among sterile hospital walls." A rueful smile. "But I refuse to leave bloodshed as my epitaph."

Isabella takes over, her tone measured. "You have our deepest regret for Nico's excesses, Signore Vasiliev. My brother coveted power he did not earn. He believed violence equaled strength." A brief pause, pain flickering in her gaze, but there's steel underneath it. "His death ends one problem, yet it presents another."

I incline my head, unsure if she's a diplomat or a velvet-gloved threat. "Succession."

"Precisely." She folds her hands. "In Sicily, my life is my children, vineyards, art foundations. But I am the last direct Agosti heir." She glances at her father, who nods. "I return to America to assume stewardship of our holdings—cleanly, respectfully—without a war."

Denis arches a brow. "Territory lines have already been crossed, Ms. Agosti."

Isabella accepts the point with a graceful nod. "Lines can be redrawn rationally. Murders invite federal spotlights. Accountants make far better allies than coroners." She allows herself a small smile. "Besides, America adores brilliant women. Your country will accommodate me."

The don chuckles, a rattling sound. "She has claws, Signore Vasiliev. Sharper than mine ever were."

Jenna's face flashes in my mind, still fierce even with a gun at her head. "Our city does appreciate brilliance," I concede, my voice cool, "but trust has to be built, not forced."

"Then let's begin building." Isabella leans forward. "Over the next months, you and I will meet often. We'll settle the border disputes, repair damaged businesses, bury the dead with dignity. And we will both make a great deal of money." Her gaze hardens. "My brother was a fool. No more kidnappings. No threats to women or children. Agosti honor demands it."

I study her for a long moment. She doesn't blink.

The storm outside fades to a dull rainfall. The fire pops in the grate, scattering sparks that glow briefly before dying—exactly what this war could become—if we so choose.

I give a single nod. "Then we have the beginning of an understanding."

Isabella smiles. "That's all I came to secure tonight. We'll write the fine print tomorrow."

Denis exhales. Mikail lowers his shoulders a fraction. The guard in the corner even visibly relaxes, just enough to prove this meeting really was a negotiation, not an execution.

The don's breathing grows more shallow, each inhale dragging like gravel through a pipe. He lifts one trembling hand, palm open in farewell. "There is nothing more to discuss," he rasps. "The fate of the family sits in Isabella's hands now. The next time we meet, Mr. Vasiliev, will be at my funeral, if you'd honor an old rival with your presence."

I nod once. "I will stand to pay my respects, Don. But I expect that day is still a long road off."

He wheezes out a laugh that turns into a cough. "Ah, that famous Russian sense of humor."

Isabella rises, gently touching her father's shoulder, then gestures for us to follow. The guards open the study doors, and she walks us back through the silent, dark corridor.

"At dawn, I'll arrange a preliminary agenda," she says. "My advisors will reach out to yours. Let's give Las Vegas a quarter without gunfire, shall we?"

"We'll see what we can manage," I answer.

At the foyer she stops, extending her hand once more. "I look forward to a very profitable relationship, Signore Vasiliev."

"Likewise, Ms. Agosti."

The front door swings open. Rain sheets off the portico roof, silvering the drive. Two guards return our weapons—magazines separate, chambers empty. Professional courtesy. Denis slides in behind the wheel of the Yukon while Mikail takes shotgun. I climb into the back and rest my head against the cool leather.

The moment the gate shuts behind us, Denis expels a long breath. "*Bozhe moi*, I thought we were headed for a mass grave."

Mikail rubs a hand over his face. "If Isabella's half as reasonable as she sounds, we might actually get a cease-fire."

"Reasonable people can play unreasonable games," I mutter, watching the slow strobe of streetlamps pass over wet pavement. Is this truly peace, or just the calm before a new storm? Hard to tell where Isabella's ambition ends and her pragmatism begins.

What I do know is Nico's dead, Jenna is alive, and the city isn't burning tonight. That's enough for now.

My phone vibrates.

Everything okay?

A second bubble pops up before I can reply.

Don't forget—first ultrasound at 9 a.m., Daddy.

A grin breaks before I can help it, the first real smile in a long while.

Meeting wrapped. Still in one piece. Can't wait to see our little troublemaker on the screen.

Three dots pulse then disappear. She's probably fallen asleep again; the concussion really zapped her. I picture her curled in our bed, hand resting unconsciously over the slight curve sheltering our child—my family.

Lightning forks over the valley as rain drums the roof. Denis takes a sharp corner slow, tires hissing.

Peace may be temporary, but I'll fight like hell to make it last long enough for Jenna to bring our baby into a city that's quiet. Long enough to teach a son—or daughter—how to load a magazine and quote Pushkin in the same breath.

The storm finally begins to break, clouds thinning into gray tatters. Tomorrow morning I'll be staring at a black-and-white screen while a tiny heart beats, filling the room with its hopeful sound, proof that even men like me can make something better than war.

And if Isabella Agosti or anyone else decides to test that hope, they'll learn exactly how much blood I'm willing to spill to protect it.

CHAPTER 40

JENNA

The alarm on my nightstand chirps its gentle, melodic trill, worlds away from the busted cell-phone timer I used in my old apartment. I blink up at a twelve-foot ceiling, crown molding catching the early sunlight, silky sheets sliding down my shoulders. Vegas glitters beyond the glass wall, but what dazzles me more is the quiet realization that this is my home now.

Our home.

I push upright, yawning, still not used to the California-king acreage of our bed. My hand skims the still-warm indentation where Abram's body should be. I frown, swing my legs over the edge, and pad across heated hardwood into the walk-in.

A quick toss of yoga pants, a soft tee, and a messy ponytail before following the scent of dark roast and something fruity, the distant whir of a blender guiding me to the kitchen.

Abram leans over the island looking sexy as ever in navy chinos that hug his thighs, a charcoal henley stretched just right across broad shoulders, sleeves pushed up exposing corded forearms and that intriguing bit of wrist ink I love tracing with my tongue. Navy loafers—Italian, of course—finish the look that says billionaire crime lord meets Saturday-morning dad.

My ovaries practically throw a parade.

He notices me, icy blue eyes lighting up. *"Dobroye utro, malen'kaya."* Good morning, little one. A kiss lands on my forehead before he steals another from my mouth.

"Morning," I murmur. "Why does your smoothie smell like a tropical vacation?"

"Doctor said folate, calcium, and antioxidants," he answers, sliding a tall glass toward me. "Spinach, pineapple, Greek yogurt, flaxseed, and a pinch of ginger for nausea."

I take a sip. The thing is obnoxiously delicious—sweet and tangy with absolutely illegal-levels of creaminess. "You realize you're setting an impossible standard, right?"

He smiles. "Good. I intend to be impossible." He glances at his watch. "Ultrasound is in forty-five minutes. We leave in ten."

"You already ate?"

"Protein bar. I'm wired enough." His gaze sweeps over me from head to toe—loving, assessing, a little naughty. "You, however, look like you're contemplating skipping medical science in favor of something more recreational."

Heat crawls up my neck because, yes, I absolutely thought about dragging him back to bed. "Behave, Vasiliev. The baby's ready to strike a pose."

He chuckles, cupping my cheek. "I still can't believe we're going to see our child today." Wonder dances behind that brutal exterior, and for a heartbeat, I forget he's the same man who kicked in doors to rescue me just a few days ago.

I jog back to our room, swapping my tee and yoga pants for a loose sundress. I return to find Abram loading a small gift bag into his briefcase. I raise a brow.

"A little something for Claire after the appointment. She kept your secret, kept you sane."

He thought of everything. My heart swells almost painfully. "You're unbelievable."

He locks eyes with me, seriousness edging the grin. "I'm just getting started."

The elevator ding echoes from the hall—our driver paging up. Abram snags my hand, pressing a kiss to the inside of my wrist where the cuff bruises have faded. "Ready?"

I squeeze his hand in response. "Let's go meet our mini troublemaker."

We step into the corridor, fingers threaded, the door clicking shut behind us.

The valet already has Abram's Maybach idling at the curb, glossy black reflecting a sky rinsed clean by last night's rain. He guides me in, hand at the small of my back, then slides behind the wheel.

As we ease onto Las Vegas Boulevard, somehow the city feels softer, quieter. Maybe that's what happens when you have a gorgeous, terrifyingly devoted boyfriend who will kill for you and a tiny life fluttering beneath your heart.

Still, anxiety prickles just under my skin. What if the baby took some hidden hit during Nico's abuse? The doctor at the hospital said we were both fine, but what if there's damage the ER scans missed? I chew the inside of my cheek, staring at the passing palm trees.

Abram reaches over and laces our fingers without taking his eyes off traffic. "You're worrying," he mutters.

I swallow. "Just a little."

His thumb strokes my knuckles. "The doctor cleared you. The sonographer will confirm it. And if anything's wrong, we'll fix it. No matter what it costs."

The certainty in his voice warms me like the sun. "Thank you," I whisper. And I mean it—for the words and for the impossible resources behind them, for the man himself.

My phone buzzes with a message from Claire.

Ultrasound day! I want gummy-bear pics ASAP. And we're still on for girls' night, right?

I grin.

100%. Will inundate you with tiny baby images the second I get them. Bring those Nutella Crumbls. The spawn demands sugar.

She responds with a laughing emoji. *The spawn has good taste. Good luck! And tell Mr. Bratva I said hi!*

I tuck the phone away. "Claire sends her love."

"She can have as many pictures as she wants," Abram replies, a smirk tugging at his mouth. "In a sterling-silver frame if she wants."

"You spoil her."

"She kept you alive. Spoil is the bare minimum."

The Maybach glides into the medical district, past plain brick clinics and beige insurance buildings, before turning through wrought-iron gates into something that looks more like a boutique hotel than a doctor's office. Sculpted hedges, glass façades, muted fountains—money has clearly been poured here in buckets.

"Welcome to Desert Serenity Prenatal Center," Abram says, pulling into a spot reserved for expectant mothers. "Best imaging center in Nevada."

Of course it is.

Inside, the lobby smells of vanilla and lavender. Soft jazz filters down from hidden speakers. A receptionist in dove-gray scrubs greets Abram by name. He prepaid, preregistered, and probably bought the damn ultrasound machine while he was at it. Within minutes, a nurse ushers us down a hallway lined with abstract art to a private suite that's nicer than some spas I've visited.

"Ms. Ridley," she says, "Dr. Rhee will be in shortly. You can change behind the screen, gown opens in the front." She hands me a whisper-soft wrap and disappears.

I slip out of the sundress and awkwardly tie the gown. The paper-covered table looks less terrifying with Abram parked beside it. I settle in, appreciating the comforting warmth of his hand on my knee.

A few minutes later we hear a gentle knock and the doctor enters. "Good morning, Jenna. Mr. Vasiliev." A warm nod to Abram; clearly they've spoken already.

Clipboard in hand, she runs through preliminary questions regarding dizziness, spotting, diet, and stress levels. I manage to downplay the whole kidnapping ordeal with a straight face. Abram's jaw ticks, but he stays silent.

Satisfied, Dr. Rhee smiles. "Ok then. Let's meet your baby."

I turn my head toward the monitor, pulse throbbing. The screen blooms gray and grainy, searching for the tiniest flicker of life.

I hold my breath.

The room is dim except for the bluish glow of the ultrasound monitor. Cool gel coats my belly, the wand sweeping side-to-side before Dr. Rhee finally murmurs a quiet, "There we go."

A grainy shape flickers onto the screen—tiny, curled, unmistakably alive. The doctor taps a key, and the room fills with a thwump, thwump, thwump sound, rapid and fierce. My breath catches. Tears haze my vision until the gummy-bear silhouette blurs into silver fog.

Beside me, Abram's fingers tighten around mine. For once, the man who stares down mobsters without blinking is trembling—just a little—but I feel it. He leans closer, as if the slightest distance is suddenly unbearable.

"That," Dr. Rhee says, smiling, "is a textbook heartbeat. You're about six weeks, five days along, give or take. Everything looks perfect so far."

I swallow hard, relief flooding through me so deeply it almost hurts. "Perfect," I echo, the word tasting like expensive chocolate on my tongue.

The doctor scrolls through a few more views, explaining what we're looking at, then switches to a color overlay so we can watch blood course through microscopic chambers. The embryo's heart glows red-blue, pumping hard.

When the scan is done, Dr. Rhee wipes away the gel and hands me a towel. "No fluid issues, no sub-chorionic bleed. The bruising on your abdomen remained superficial, nothing went near the uterus. Magnesium for the concussion headaches, plenty of hydration and light activity only—which I suspect your bodyguard here will enforce." She nods at Abram with a wink.

"I intend to," he replies.

The doctor leaves the room and I start to get up. Before I can, Abram presses a gentle kiss to the slight swell of my belly, then another to my lips.

"That's our child," he whispers, awe threading through every syllable.

"Our unstoppable, heartbeat-like-a-drum child," I respond, laughing through happy tears.

He laughs as well—a genuine, unguarded sound—but I catch the shadow behind his eyes. Guilt. Always the guilt. I reach for him, thumb tracing the faint scar Nico's mirror shard left on his forearm. "I'm okay, Abram. We're okay."

He swallows hard. "Based on the strength of that heartbeat, I'd say you're right."

A nurse returns with a thumb drive, a 4×6 photo, and a small strip of glossy prints. Abram slips the smaller photos into his wallet beside a faded shot of his mother. It's as if he's filing us under 'family,' 'permanent.' My heart somersaults.

Outside, sunlight glints off puddles, turning cracked pavement into scattered mirrors. Abram guides me to the curb, his hand hovering protectively at the small of my back. The Maybach glides up and the valet steps out. He opens the passenger door like I'm royalty, and maybe today I am.

I text Claire a photo of the sonogram.

Baby Vasiliev debut!

Her reply pings back in seconds. *Aww!* Several heart emojis. *Cookies ordered.*

Abram settles behind the wheel but doesn't pull away. Instead, he reaches over and covers my hand—still clutching the ultrasound printout and thumb drive. Two heartbeats pulse beneath his touch: the swift flutter of new life, and the slower, iron vow thrumming in my veins.

"I told Nico once," he says softly, eyes fixed straight ahead, "that I would burn this city down if you bled. I think he believed me."

"He should've," I answer, turning the photo so the sunlight illuminates the tiny, stubborn spark of our future. "But let's hope Vegas behaves. I kind of like our view." He smiles and shifts into drive.

The city may never know how close it came to fire, but I do. As Abram's fingers lace with mine, I also know that whatever else the universe throws our way, we're already stronger than anything it can bring.

EPILOGUE I

ABRAM

Isabella's face fills the monitor—olive-gold skin, glossy black hair pinned into a severe twist, a single strand of pearls that looks disarmingly domestic for a woman who commands half of Las Vegas's underworld.

The rain outside her mansion slants across the camera in gray streaks, but her eyes are sharp, amused.

"Your Albanian problem," she says in Italian, lips quirking, "has officially become *our* Albanian problem. They set up another stash house off Charleston Boulevard last night."

I lean back in my office chair, steepling my fingers. "We've warned them twice. Third time, we draw blood."

She nods. "Scare them first. A burned warehouse. No fatalities unless absolutely necessary. My people will handle the accelerant—no fingerprints."

"Fine. But I want eyes on their lieutenant. If he tries to relocate, I want him stopped at the county line."

Isabella tips her head, studying me. "Always efficient, Abram. I like it."

"Efficiency works."

Her smile turns gentler. "How is Jenna? I believe your child is overdue?"

"Three days," I reply. Saying it aloud makes my chest tighten with anticipation. "The doctor says it's normal."

"Some babies are like Sicilian judges," she laughs. "Stubborn until bribed." I return the laugh and she goes on. "Enjoy these quiet hours, Abram. Parenthood shifts the weight of every trigger. I thought myself ruthless—until I held my first son. I'm still ruthless, but now there are nightmares to match."

I remember Jenna's ultrasound image taped above my desk, the tiny silhouette, the pulse that sounded like a hummingbird. "We don't always have the luxury of softness," I say. "Not in our line of work."

"True. But softness will find you anyway. Embrace it or drown in bitterness." She glances off-screen, someone calling for her. "I must go. We'll coordinate the warehouse job through the usual channels."

We exchange a nod—professionals, partners, occasionally reluctant friends—and end the call.

A new message pings from Denis. *Got intel on the Albanian importer. Sending dossier.*

I've barely skimmed the attachment when I hear a startled gasp echo down the hallway.

"Abram!"

Jenna's voice—breathless, excited, and afraid all at once.

I'm out of my chair in half a second. She's in the living room, standing beside the sofa, leggings soaked, one hand braced on the small of her back. Her eyes are wide but shining.

"It's time," she says, half laughing, half crying.

For a heartbeat I just stare—at her wet leggings, at her flushed cheeks, at the way she bites her lip the moment another contraction grips her. All the planning evaporates. There is only her.

"Okay," I breathe, crossing the room and cupping her face. "Okay, *malen'kaya,* we've got this."

She nods, squeezing my wrist when the pain hits. "Hospital bag's by the door. Contraction timer's on the counter."

I move automatically, sending a text to the driver, grabbing the overnight bag, barking a quick order to the security guard outside the elevator. "Car downstairs in two minutes." My pulse hammers harder than it ever did facing a gun.

Jenna exhales shakily. "Abram?"

"Yes?"

"Don't forget the car seat."

"Right." I almost laugh as I snatch the infant carrier from the hallway bench and return to her side, sliding an arm around her waist. Another contraction steals her breath, and she clutches my shoulder, forehead pressed to my chest.

Six minutes since the last one. The number ricochets around my skull as if it's lit in neon. Too close. Too damned close.

"Six minutes isn't bad," Jenna says. I help her ease into the passenger seat before slamming her bag into the trunk on my way around the car.

"It's too close for my liking," I say, sliding behind the wheel.

She laughs, bright and breathy, then curls a hand behind my neck. When I lean in, my intention to buckle her belt, she tugs me the extra inch and kisses me—slow and confident— as if we've got all the time in the world.

"I love you," she murmurs against my mouth.

"I love you more if you don't deliver in my Maybach." I try for stern though it comes out teasing.

Another contraction claws through her. She squeezes my wrist, teeth sinking into her bottom lip, but the sound that escapes is controlled. Counted breathing from the class we took, every exhale a practiced hiss. I wait until the tremor leaves her shoulders then gun the car down the ramp.

The Strip glitters in the rearview, every red light magically turning green as we approach. My foot hovers on the edge of illegality, but Jenna keeps steadying me with small facts from the birthing class. "Average first-stage labor lasts eight hours; airway flexes under adrenaline; my dilation at the appointment Tuesday was barely two centimeters."

She's being brave for both of us.

"Average isn't you," I say. "You're an overachiever."

"Flattery will get you everywhere." She touches the dashboard timer. "Three minutes, forty-five seconds now. See? We're textbook."

"Textbooks don't factor in Vegas traffic if a tour bus breaks down in the middle of the road."

She snorts. "You own half this town; if a bus flipped, someone would clear your lane."

That earns a reluctant smile. I weave past a delivery truck, pulling under the porte-cochère of Centennial Women's Medical Center in record time. A nurse is already rolling a wheelchair toward us.

"Forty-three weeks," I bark, scooping Jenna out before she can object.

She swats my shoulder. "I can walk."

"I can't breathe," I counter. "Humor me."

Triage whips us through vitals and paperwork, but Jenna's text had apparently set off its own alarm—Claire barrels into the waiting area in mismatched sweats.

"You couldn't hold it until the weekend?" she teases. "Abram, how are you?"

"I'm fine," I deadpan. "Focus on the mother."

"Focused." Claire grips Jenna's free hand as the nurse scans her wristband. "Do you need ice chips? Memes? Sarcastic commentary?"

"Breathing," Jenna pants through a new contraction wave. Claire shifts into coach mode while I sign consent forms no one actually reads.

Elevator doors open onto the birthing wing. We have a private suite and the best view in the building because, of course, I made sure to sort that out. I glance out the window, a commander's instinct mapping streets, imagining what kingdom my child might inherit—if they want it.

Jenna's gasp snaps my attention back.

One nurse calibrates monitors while another tags an IV. I station myself at Jenna's left, hand enveloping hers, counting breaths with her. Her grip is crushing, but I don't flinch. Pain shared is pain stolen.

"You're five centimeters," the midwife announces. "Moving fast, Mama. Let's get you settled."

Five centimeters already. My pulse slows. My job is simple now—protect, support, breathe.

Jenna meets my eyes, sweat dampening her temples. "Told you we had plenty of time."

I press a kiss to her knuckles. "Indeed you did. But I'm still glad we didn't test the upholstery."

The double doors of Labor & Delivery sigh shut behind me, and for the first time in twelve hours, my shoulders loosen.

The corridor is quiet and dimly lit, smelling faintly of antiseptic and lemon floor polish. A janitor pushes a mop past the vending machines, earbuds in, oblivious to what just occurred behind those doors.

I pause halfway to the elevators and lean against the wall for a second.

Vanya.

The name floats up from my chest like steam. I say it aloud, barely above a whisper.

"Vanya."

My daughter.

The sound tastes sacred. Like a word I've been waiting my whole life to speak.

My hand moves reflexively to my shirtfront, where traces of her first feeding left a faint circle over my heart. I didn't care. I didn't even think to wipe it away. There was only the blur of her entrance, the sudden silence after Jenna's final push, then the wet squall of life. A sound that split me wide open.

I remember the crown of dark hair, slick and impossibly small. The way the doctor lifted her—red, furious, and beautiful. My knees nearly gave out. I've seen death up close—hell, I've dealt it out more than once—but this was different. This was life at its rawest.

And Jenna. My girl. Glowing with sweat and tears. When they placed Vanya on her chest, the whole world narrowed to that one frame, mother and daughter, skin to skin, heartbeats colliding.

I didn't know it was possible to love that hard. To feel joy that deep.

I close my eyes, remembering the moment. Nothing else existed. Not the empire. Not the threats. Only them.

My angels.

Tatiana spots me first, unleashing a banshee shriek as she hurries towards me. Anya barrels past Denis to clamp both arms around my neck. Little Charles tugs at my pant-leg, round eyes searching.

"Uncle Abram, where's the baby?"

I crouch, ruffling his hair. "With her mama right now. You'll see her soon, *malysh*." Everyone's talking at once, and I raise my hands like a conductor. "Seven pounds even," I announce. "Full head of dark hair and the longest fingers I've ever seen. She latched like a champion. Your niece is an absolute warrior."

Mikail smirks. "Kid already has the Vasiliev grip. Good luck, *pakhan*." Laughter breaks the tension.

Tatiana presses a tiny ivory and blue crocheted blanket into my palm. Denis slips me a slim envelope—college fund, first deposit, written in his precise block letters. I tuck both gifts close to my chest, struck speechless.

"Family dinner when Jenna's home," Anya says firmly, wiping mascara streaks. "Non-negotiable."

Tatiana teases, "Try to get some sleep while you're here, big brother."

After my family leaves, I signal two plain-clothes Bratva sentries to plant themselves at the ward entrance. They nod, palms on concealed weapons.

It's quiet inside Jenna's room other than the soft beep of her monitor and Vanya's ribbon-thin breaths. A bedside lamp washes everything in amber light. I sink into the chair beside the bassinet.

Jenna lies on her side, hair a dark red spill across the pillow. I brush one knuckle down her cheek. She doesn't wake, but her lips curve, instinctively knowing I'm here. Vanya stirs, and I slide a fingertip into her miniature fist. She squeezes, soft but relentless. My pulse stutters at the fragile nails, the little wrinkles on her knuckles, the tininess of her hands.

My kingdom used to be red lines on a map and envelopes of tribute. But now it begins and ends in this room with one sleeping queen and one newborn heir.

Two angels.

I'll bleed dry before I let the world bruise either one of them.

EPILOGUE II

JENNA

Two years later...

S unlight pours down, warming my shoulders as I lean back against the lounger, letting my gaze drift lazily over the party.

The rooftop is a dream, our own private oasis perched high above the city. The sun glints off the sparkling blue pool, and the garden planters lining the edge are in full bloom, spilling over with bougainvillea and lavender.

The breeze carries a hint of jasmine, mixed with the faint smell of sunscreen and frosted cake. Beyond the high glass railing, Vegas stretches out in every direction—hazy mountains off in the distance, glittering hotels and casinos below. It still takes my breath away, even after all this time.

But today, our oasis has been transformed. Balloons sway gently, tied to the railings in soft rainbow hues, enough pastel frosting around to give a dentist nightmares for weeks. Abram went overboard as usual, turning this already-stunning rooftop into a storybook party scene—unicorn decor everywhere, from the bounce house to the glittering cake topper. It's outrageous. It's adorable. And it's perfect.

I catch sight of Vanya, her silky black curls bouncing as she races past, giggling wildly with her cousins. Those ice-blue eyes—the exact same shade as Abram's—light up with pure, unfiltered joy as she blows past, her little feet moving with the confidence of someone who knows just how adored she is.

Watching her now, I'm struck again by the disbelief that this perfect little human came from us.

Beside me, Claire laughs, taking a sip of her mojito. "She gets prettier every time I see her. I'd say she takes after her mother, but damn, those eyes of hers are all Abram."

I grin, warmth blossoming in my chest. "She's got his personality too—fearless, bossy, always thinks she's in charge."

"Sounds like someone else I know," Claire says, shooting me a pointed look.

I roll my eyes, but I can't exactly deny it. "We can't help it. It's in our blood."

Claire leans in close, nudging me conspiratorially. "Speaking of things in your blood, when are you and your Russian billionaire going back to that sex club? It's been ages."

"Oh my God, Claire," I sputter, playfully scandalized, swatting at her arm. "It's our daughter's birthday. I refuse to discuss kinky billionaire sex clubs right now."

She shrugs casually, eyes sparkling with mischief. "Fine. Maybe I'll go by myself. Who knows? Maybe I'll find my own Abram. I'm thinking a tall, dark, morally ambiguous billionaire. Sound familiar?"

I shake my head, laughing softly. "Sorry to burst your bubble, but I'm pretty sure Abram's one-of-a-kind."

Claire sighs dramatically. "That's my cue to check on the kids before your perfect romance completely ruins my day."

I wave her off, my heart light as I watch her cross the rooftop toward the chaos of shrieking children. Vanya is orchestrating a game involving at least ten kids, directing them with miniature Abram-like intensity. I smile softly, pride swelling inside me.

Abram stands near the edge of the rooftop, flanked by Denis and Mikail. I narrow my eyes suspiciously—if those three think they're allowed to talk business at our daughter's birthday, they have another think coming.

I rise from my seat, grabbing Abram a cold beer from the cooler. His eyes light up when he sees me approaching, and I feel a warm blush spread over my cheeks. Even after all this time, that look still does things to me.

He excuses himself from the guys and pulls me in close, his lips brushing mine. "Enjoying yourself, *printsessa?*"

I hum contentedly against his lips. "Yes. I'm watching our daughter boss around half the kids in Vegas while sipping sparkling water at a party you clearly had too much fun organizing. I believe I'm in heaven."

Abram laughs, fingers brushing along my jaw. "She gets that from you, you know. The bossiness."

"Funny," I tease back. "Claire was just saying the same about you."

He smiles, a soft, tender look he reserves just for Vanya and me. "She's perfect, Jenna. Just like her mother."

A flutter rises in my stomach—there's a secret nestled there, one I'm desperate to share—but now isn't quite the right time. Instead, I rest my head against his chest, breathing him in. "So, Mr. Vasiliev, think our little family is big enough yet?"

Abram pauses, considering, before his voice rumbles gently against my ear. "Our family will always be perfect, no matter the size."

His fingers lace gently through mine, and I squeeze his hand softly, smiling to myself. Soon enough, I'll tell him, but right now, in the golden sunlight, with my daughter's laughter echoing across the rooftop and Abram's heartbeat steady beneath my cheek, I allow myself to simply savor the moment.

Because this right here is everything I never knew I needed.

The rest of the afternoon passes in a whirlwind of laughter, squealing kids, and Abram's sisters hugging me goodbye so tightly I'm almost breathless. Claire pulls me into a bear hug, promising to text me later to nail down lunch plans. By the time the rooftop empties and the gentle twilight settles in, I'm blissfully exhausted.

I start to gather plates and abandoned cups scattered around the tables when Abram intercepts me, catching my wrist gently. "Don't even think about it," he says, his voice low and warm. "You've done enough. Leave the mess for someone else."

I open my mouth to argue—old habits die hard—but he silences me with a slow, soft kiss that melts my protests.

"Vanya needs her bath," I murmur against his lips, trying to regain some semblance of self-control.

Abram grins, eyes glinting mischievously. "It would be my pleasure."

Before I can object, he sweeps Vanya up into his arms, making airplane noises as he carries her inside. Her delighted giggles trail down the hallway, and my heart swells until I'm sure it's going to burst.

I pour myself another sparkling water and sip slowly, savoring the rare quiet as I move through our home. Everything feels peaceful, beautiful, my secret news humming softly beneath it all. Exciting, but nerve-wracking, too.

Curiosity and love draw me toward the sound of splashing from upstairs. I follow the laughter and peek discreetly around the corner of the bathroom. Abram, sleeves rolled up and kneeling beside the large tub, is creating elaborate bubble-beards on Vanya's cheeks. She giggles helplessly, splashing him gently as he laughs, murmuring silly rhymes to her in Russian. He's completely captivated by her, and she adores him just as fiercely.

I linger quietly, my heart aching sweetly at the sight of the man I love more than life itself being the father our daughter deserves. But anxiety nudges at me. Will he be just as thrilled this time around? Will another baby be welcomed news, or will he feel overwhelmed?

Shaking away my worries, I slip into our bedroom and change into soft pajamas, feeling nerves and anticipation twist gently in my stomach. Soon, I hear Abram's voice whispering softly to Vanya down the hall, singing the same lullaby his mother once sang to him.

I crawl into our bed, heart racing a little faster when Abram finally appears, eyes full of warmth as he closes the door gently behind him. His gaze turns molten as he catches sight of me, and heat pools low in my belly at his blatant appreciation. He wastes no time stripping away his clothes, revealing his perfect, muscled body—hard and ready.

He slides into bed next to me, a low growl rumbling from his chest as he draws me close, his fingertips skimming the small of my back. I lick my lips, my body responding instantly, but then I remember the news I need to share.

"I have to tell you something."

He pauses, his lips against my neck, breathing softly. "Can it wait? Because the way you looked at me when I walked in—"

I smile teasingly, pulling back just enough to meet his hungry gaze. Slowly, I slip from the bed and stand in front of him, my fingers inching beneath the edge of my pajama top. Abram watches, utterly mesmerized, as I shed my clothes piece by piece, baring myself to him until nothing remains but my panties.

"Do you want to hear my secret?" I ask softly, hooking my thumbs beneath the waistband and sliding them down.

He nods distractedly, eyes trailing over my body, filled with heat and barely restrained desire.

"I'm pregnant."

The words hang in the air between us. Abram's eyes snap upward, locking onto mine, shock swiftly melting into overwhelming happiness. His grin widens, radiant and boyish, and then he's leaping from the bed, laughing with a joy that fills every corner of the room.

He sweeps me up into his strong arms, spinning me around until I laugh breathlessly. His hands cup my face tenderly, his lips brushing softly across my forehead, my cheeks, my lips.

Abram sinks gently to one knee, his eyes filled with awe as he presses soft kisses to my belly. His arms wrap around me, holding me close, warm and protective. I thread my fingers through his hair, my heart so full it almost hurts.

Abram gazes up at me, his voice thick with emotion. "You're amazing, Jenna. I didn't think my life could get any better, but every day with you and Vanya proves me wrong."

My heart squeezes and I bend, capturing his lips in a tender, lingering kiss. "I love you," I whisper against his mouth.

"I love you too. Always."

He stays kneeling, broad shoulders framed by dim lamplight, lips brushing a slow, reverent path across my abdomen.

"You're sure?" he asks.

I laugh. "Positive." My fingers cup his face. "Doctor confirmed. You, sir, are absurdly potent."

"Let me show you just how potent."

"I'd love nothing more."

A deep, primal growl rumbles from Abram's chest, raw and hungry, vibrating through me and setting my skin ablaze. He stands and crashes his mouth against mine, the kiss starting soft but erupting into a desperate clash of lips, tongues, and teeth.

We settle onto the mattress, his body heat a searing wave that consumes me. I sink back into the silken sheets, my nerves sparking as liquid fire surges through my veins, pooling hot and heavy in my pussy, my skin flushed and tingling.

He pulls back and looks at me. His eyes, dark as a storm at midnight, bore into mine with raw, animalistic need. "Tell me if I'm too much."

"Too much? Never," I purr, my voice thick with want.

My fingers seize his wrist, guiding his rough hand to my cheek, his calloused fingertips grazing my jaw. Slowly, I drag his touch down my throat, over the swell of my breasts, and along the curve of my hips, my body arching to meet his touch, a blatant invitation for him to take me apart.

Abram moves like a man possessed, each caress branding me with heat. His lips blaze a trail of wet, open-mouthed kisses, nipping the sharp edge of my collarbone, sucking lightly at the tender underside of my breast. My nipple tightens under his hot breath, his teeth grazing just enough to make me gasp. His stubble scrapes my flesh, a rough contrast to the slick heat of his tongue, leaving my body humming with electric need.

A moan tears from my throat as his hand cups my breast, his thumb circling my hardened nipple with slow, deliberate strokes, each pass sending bolts of pleasure straight to my clit. My back bows, pressing my chest into his grip, my thighs clenching as my pussy throbs, slick and aching.

My breaths come in shaky pants, my pulse hammering as he tunes every touch to my body's rhythm, knowing exactly when my craving tips into raw, desperate need.

"Still with me, baby?" His voice is a low, sultry sound, his lips brushing the shell of my ear, his breath hot and teasing.

"Always," I gasp, the word fracturing as his fingers slide lower to find my pussy, dripping and ready. His touch is relentless, fingers circling my clit with agonizing precision before dipping inside, curling against the spot that makes my hips buck wildly.

Pleasure crashes through me, a blinding, pulsing wave that shatters me. I clench around his fingers as I cry out, my body trembling through the white-hot aftershocks. Abram holds me through it, his thumb brushing my parted lips as I shudder, the heat ebbing slow and molten. Then, with a possessive grip, he rolls me onto his lap, my body still pulsing with need.

I revel in the shift, straddling his hips, my thighs spreading wide as his hands clamp onto my ass, fingers digging into the soft flesh. Moonlight spills across his bare chest, glinting off the hard lines of muscle, the faint scars etched into his skin, and the inked eagle spread over his heart, fierce and proud.

His cock, thick and hard, presses against my inner thigh, and his eyes, molten with lust, track every move as I guide him to my entrance, my pussy slick and aching for him. I sink down slowly, savoring the stretch as he fills me inch by torturous inch, until he's buried deep, a low groan tearing from his throat.

The world narrows to two racing heartbeats, two bodies locked together, one shadowed room. Our breaths tangle, hot and ragged, his growls vibrating against my skin as I ride him, my hips rolling in a slow, deliberate grind. My hands brace on his shoulders, nails biting into his flesh, his cock hitting every sensitive spot inside me with each thrust.

His fingers grip my hips, guiding my rhythm, his jaw tight as he fights to hold back. His gaze burns into mine, dark and feral, but soon softened by a flicker of devotion that makes my chest ache.

When the release hits, it's a tidal wave, raw and all-consuming, my walls clenching tight around his cock as pleasure soars through me, my moans echoing throughout the room. He follows, my name on his lips as he spills inside me, hot and pulsing.

We collapse together, laughter spilling between us as we tangle in the sweat-damp sheets, trading slow kisses, our bodies pressed close as our heartbeats slow.

He draws me against his chest, palm protective over my belly. "You make me better," he murmurs into my hair. "Stronger and gentler all at once."

"I was thinking the same about you," I manage through lingering bliss.

A comfortable silence follows. Then Abram shifts, clearing his throat in that the nervous way I've learned means he's plotting something. He slips from the bed and crosses to his dresser. I prop myself on an elbow, admiring the view.

He returns holding a small, midnight-blue box. My heartbeat trips.

"Abram..."

He sits on the edge of the bed, suddenly solemn. "I wanted to do this at Vanya's party, but toddlers and cake aren't conducive to speeches." A wry smile tugs at his mouth. He opens the box. Inside sits a cushion-cut diamond, glittering like captured starlight.

My breath catches.

"I have my empire," he says quietly, "but none of it matters without you. Marry me, Jenna Ridley. Build a family, a life with me, another empire of our own."

The answer bursts out before I even register it. "Yes! Of course, yes!" My voice cracks on the last word.

He exhales and slides the ring onto my finger. It settles as if it's always belonged there. Tears blur the look of the gem until it's a rainbow.

We kiss—slow, grateful, lovingly. When we part, I rest my forehead against his. "Claire joked I'd snag a billionaire at a sex club," I whisper, half laughing, half awed. "She might have been onto something."

Abram chuckles. "That reminds me... how do you feel about revisiting The 13th Floor? Masks, private room, a little nostalgia before pregnancy cravings hijack our nights?"

A wicked thrill sparks. "One condition: you wear the same black mask. Then afterward, we get a hotel room and order every dessert on room service."

"Done." He brushes a strand of hair from my cheek. "Anything my fiancée desires."

Fiancée. The word hums through me like newfound electricity. I glance toward the window where Vegas shimmers. A familiar skyline, but tonight it looks different. Brighter.

He follows my gaze, threading his fingers with mine. "City of sin and secrets," he says softly. "But it gave me you. I'll never curse it again."

"And it gave us Vanya." I squeeze his hand. "And now..." I rest my palm over the pulse of new life. "There's so much more coming."

Thunder rolls faintly beyond the glass, a summer storm sweeping the valley. Inside our penthouse, everything is calm—warm lamplight, joined hands, the distant sound of our daughter's soft breathing through the baby monitor.

"I promise," Abram whispers, voice fierce yet tender, "no one will ever threaten this family again."

I believe him completely. Because the man who was once a storm has become my shelter. And together we'll face whatever rises, armed with love stronger than fear, and a future bright enough to outshine the Strip itself.

I lean into him, the ring catching the light in tiny starbursts. A fitting reminder that every ending can blaze like a new beginning.

And this is only page one of the life ahead.

The End

Still swooning over Jenna and Abram?
Same, babe. 😎

Good news—your silver-fox obsession doesn't have to end here.
If one taste of that forbidden, melt-your-Kindle heat wasn't enough (and let's be real, it never is), dive into the **Silver Fox Daddies** series and meet the men who redefine *off-limits*.

🔥 **His Son's Ex** — Amazon Top 12 Bestseller
🔥 **Sinful Union** — Amazon Top 10 Smash Hit
These daddies don't play fair... but who says we want them to?

Here's what readers had to say about His Son's Ex:

★★★★★ **"Wow! This book was a wild ride!"** - *Michele, Goodreads Review*

★★★★★ **"Eva and Dante--HOT HOT HOT. I love how Dante just stuck up for Eva even**

though he had no idea who she was at first." -
Christina M., Goodreads Review

★★★★★ **"I normally do not like mafia books
but this one's preview intrigued me and i'm so
glad i read it. it was outstandingly written,
richly detailed, gut wrenchingly real, gritty,
exploding with plot twists, action, emotion and
more."** *-Shelley G., Goodreads Review*

Printed in Dunstable, United Kingdom